Matters of the Heart

A Shumard Oak Bend Novel - Book 3

Heidi Gray McGill

Heidi Gray McGill Books LLC

FUSING FAITH
AND FICTION™

eBook ASIN: B0B2V6R58L
Paperback ASIN: B0B6XJBGB7
ISBN-13: 9798833115565

Imprint: Independently published
Publisher: Heidi Gray McGill Books LLC

Cover design by: Erin Dameron-Hill
Library of Congress Control Number:
Printed in the United States of America
Publisher: Heidi Gray McGill Books LLC

Dedication

In memory of
Mary Cole Parks Nibarger
August 4, 1930 to August 14, 2021

Mrs. Nibarger loved God, her family, education, being outside, and staying active. She enjoyed cross stitching, knitting, and tatting crosses in her quiet moments. She always wore a smile, and it was beautiful.

Epigraph

"When we encounter the word of God, we encounter God… His word, indeed, is his personal presence. Whenever God's Word is spoken, read, or heard, God himself is there."

JOHN FRAME

Chapter 1

Late May 1866

Shumard Oak Bend, Missouri

A flush of adrenaline tingled through Katie's body. She'd made it into the kitchen without the floor squeaking or the door scraping. Right hand on the latch, she applied pressure to the wood with her hip, hoping that the door would be just as silent as it settled into the warped frame.

"Katie, me girl. Where've you been?"

Katie yelped and flung herself around, her hand at her throat to hide the pulsing vein in her neck. The empty plate and fork she'd tucked under her arm slipped from their hold. She grabbed for the plate, but the fork clattered to the floor.

"Oh, my! Aunt Aideen, you gave me a fright. Where have I been?" Katie's voice rose in pitch. "The barn." She felt a flush cover her cheeks and bent down to retrieve her utensil, hiding her face, hoping Aideen would think the redness in her cheeks was from the exertion of the movement. When Katie peeked up, she spotted Aideen's familiar, reddish-brown eyebrow lift, letting her know Aunt Aideen expected the rest of the story. Katie set the items down, then busied her hands with making tea.

"Care for a cup of tea?" Katie's heart raced, and she could not quell the fluttery feeling in her belly.

"That and an answer." Aideen sat and folded her hands in anticipation.

Katie's posture stiffened. With her back to her aunt, she forced a smile before turning with two cups of tea. "Fine." Katie hesitated as she took her time placing the cups on the table. "Would you care for a cookie?" She reached for the tin.

"I wish for the truth."

Katie arranged her skirts as she sat, delaying the inevitable. "I was in the barn feeding . . ." Nerves frayed, her leg bounced as if the pumping motion would help get the words out.

"Kathleen Orla Murphy."

Katie's heart thudded in her chest, and she was sure her aunt could see her tatted collar move up and down. Why was she nervous? She'd done no wrong. She crossed one leg over the other, her knee hitting the underside of the table. Ignoring the pain, she used her napkin to wipe up the tea that had breached the rim of her cup.

"Care to explain the plate?"

Katie lifted her chin. She did not want to burden Aideen, nor would she be dissuaded from her mission. She carefully uncrossed her legs and willed herself not to choke, stalling as her small sip of tea went down wrong.

"I see," Aideen said. "If you'll not tell me, perhaps I'll simply guess. We've no animals but a stray cat. Are you to tell me, or not as it seems, that you have someone holed up out there?" Her Irish accent increased along with her volume.

"Now, before you get your dander up, I took nothing that didn't already belong to me." Katie's indignant tone did not help the situation.

"Serving yourself a double portion and only eating half?" Hands flat on the table, Aideen's eyebrow raised higher than Katie thought possible.

"Aunt Aideen." Katie's bouncing legs slowed, as did her speech. "I can't let them go hungry," she argued.

"But Katie girl."

"No!" Katie shot to her feet and began pacing with a purposeful stride, picking up speed around the table and increasing in volume as she spoke. "The women and children did not ask to be left widows and orphans from the war. Even the Good Book says we're to care for them. Aunt Aideen, you of all people, widowed now less than a year, should know the devastation, the loss they are feeling. You have a home. They've lost theirs. They have nothing." Her voice cracked with emotion.

"Oh, me girl. I know you be right, and I don't mind you giving to the needy. But the magistrate were most clear on the matter. If he catches you, you'll be in a heap of trouble."

"I won't get caught." Katie straightened her posture even

more, her chin jutting forward, which was difficult with the tightness in her neck and jaw.

"Ach. I pray you don't. For your sake, and theirs. And mine." Aideen's last words came out in a whisper.

Katie had not fully considered the implications of her actions on her aunt and her boarding house business. "Aunt Aideen, please." Katie's voice mellowed but the fervor in her spirit flamed brighter. "I have to help them. I want to help them. No, I *need* to help them. It isn't just that God commanded it, or that my heart aches for them, but I need a purpose. This town . . ." Her arm swept out, then dropped to her side. "It has nothing for me. I want to make something of my life, not just clean rooms until my dying day."

Aideen straightened in her chair. Katie returned to hers. She reached over and placed a hand on her aunt's freckled forearm before lowering her voice.

"Oh, Aunt Aideen, I don't mean to be ungrateful or give offense. I love living here with you in this beautiful home. You have been so good to me, taking me in these last six months." She took deep breaths, trying to quell her racing heart. "Mama gave me your letter on her deathbed." Katie fingered her dress pocket as if the letter her mother had received from her only living sister were still there. "Her last words to me were, 'Go, Kathleen, me golden princess. Bury me and go. Nuttin' here fer ye. Go, and dté Dia leat."

"God will go with you. She said the same to me once." Aideen wiped away a tear.

Katie had not considered Aideen may understand. She had

felt abandoned when her mother had died, forcing her to leave Ireland, but God had gone with her on the journey, and He was with her still. She lifted her hand to her cheek as her mother had done—a distant memory of those final moments. Katie understood the loss of a parent and the devastation of losing everything else as well.

"Aunt Aideen, I know what they are going through." Katie stood and gathered the empty cups. She leaned on the counter for support and spoke to the wall. "In Ireland, I had no funds to pay the landlord what was due, no job to earn enough to keep a roof over my head. No family to take me in. No one to call 'friend.' So, I packed all I needed into a small bag before looking at the four sparse walls I'd called home, and then I left the remaining items for the priest to give to those in need." Katie touched her throat again and turned as if to show Aideen the treasure no longer around her neck. "Only Mother's locket remained, a gift from the man who called himself my father. The man who abandoned us."

Aideen stood and embraced the girl before holding her at arm's length. "You did the right thing by selling it for your passage, me Katie girl."

Katie wiped at the moisture on her cheeks. Her heart pined for the locket but ached more for the widows and orphans, casualties of war. Their dull eyes, thin frames, worn clothes, and defeated demeanors reminded her of the plight she'd been in less than a year ago.

"I have to help them, Aunt Aideen. These women have lost their husbands, homes, and hopes. They came to Shumard Oak Bend, praying it would be a place of refuge. And the children . . ." A sob escaped. "They've lost more than I ever endured." Katie's deep intake of air cleared her focus. "If I had the resources, I'd open an orphanage. I've been thinking and praying about it for quite some time. You were the cook at one when you first came to America. Please, Aunt Aideen. I know I can do it. Give the women jobs. Raise the children. Provide schooling. I won't be discouraged. I won't back down. I know you think it's too much for me to handle, but I must. Don't you see? I must."

She would not allow a lack of support in any form to keep her from doing what she knew was her calling. She'd continue helping those in need, one at a time and in secret, if need be. One side of her mouth lifted. Her father had been closer to the truth than he'd realized.

"Ye'll not be anythin' more t'an a wench, girl. Wit' ye looks, ye'll have plenty of youngins' to care fer and not a moment fer yerself nor a home ta call yer own."

Her father's voice was as clear as the day he'd hurled the slurred insult. She would have lots of children to raise. It just would not be like he'd thought.

Or I'd desired.

Brushing her hair out of her face, she felt warmth. With such a flush, her freckles would be more pronounced, but it couldn't be helped. A lack of concern for the plight of those considered undeserving lit a fire in her belly.

Aideen rose and placed the dishes in the basin. "Seems to me you need to think this through and get rid of some nervous energy. I've the answer to both. Laundry." Aideen winked.

Katie sighed but followed her aunt outside.

They boiled, soaked, scrubbed, rinsed, wrung, and hung more sheets and towels than Katie believed one family could own. They'd not yet started on their clothing, yet she was exhausted. Even so, her temperament matched that of the boiling water. If she didn't get this off her mind, she'd burst and pop like the air coming from the bottom of the large caldron they were using.

"Help me hang these, so I don't drop them in this dusty yard." Aideen looked at the cloudless sky. "This weather will dry our laundry in no time, but it's not doing our kitchen garden any favors."

Katie bristled. She'd had enough time to formulate all manner of responses to any question Aideen might ask and was waiting for the opportunity to get those words out of her mouth. Her aunt only wanted to talk about the weather. Would they never finish their earlier discussion?

Aideen handed her one end of the large sheet. "Now, let's finish what we were talking about earlier. So far, you've told me how you feel but not how God feels."

The wind blew the end of the sheet out of Katie's hand as quickly as Aideen's words blew all the answers from her mind. She grabbed at the sheet and caught it before the fabric hit the dirt, but she wasn't as successful with the tirade she'd worked out in her mind.

"How God feels?"

"Haven't you taken this to Him?" Aideen asked.

"Well, of course. . . ." No. She hadn't. She'd told Him the details, but she hadn't asked Him what He thought. Her exhale came out like a bull giving a final warning. Come to think of it, she had talked to God. The Good Book said to help the widows and orphans, and that's what she was trying to do. Trying. But everyone around her thwarted her efforts. She shoved a pin over the next sheet, attaching it to the line as if securing her resolve.

"If I'd been born a man, I'd give the Magistrate a good wallop about the head," she added. "Knock some sense into him. He's a typical male, placating me with words while never intending to fulfill his promises." Renewed anger and energy filled her.

Aideen peeked around the bath towel flapping in the breeze, eyes wide. Katie ignored the stare.

"Do you know what he said?" Katie arched her back to mimic the magistrate's rotund form. "Little missy, you have a heart of gold, but you don't need to be worrying your pretty little head with the likes of those who should have made provision for such circumstances."

Katie's exaggerated imitation of the magistrate worked on her aunt, who bit her lower lip to suppress a laugh.

"Can you believe he said that? I nearly choked, trying to hold back. How thoughtless. How unfeeling. How unchristian. And he didn't stop there, oh, no." Katie bobbled her head and resumed her mocking.

"'You seem to be the type of person these people can trust. I'd be much obliged if you'd use your influence to encourage them to be on their way.'" She waved her hand flippantly, as he had done. "We don't need them settling down here and asking for handouts. If we build an orphanage . . ." Katie jammed another clothespin on the line and took deep gulps of air before continuing.

"By the time he'd finished, my jaw hurt and my skirt needed a good pressing. Even my toes ached from curling up inside my shoes. I did some serious praying right then and there. Can you believe the gall of that man? It took every ounce of willpower to hold my tongue, but my body language had a mind of its own. I didn't need words to silence the Magistrate. He understood my meaning quite clearly."

Joyous laughter filled the air as Aideen wiped at her eyes.

"A chuisle mo chroí. Oh, my heart's beloved."

Aideen's endearment did not slow Katie's words.

"The Magistrate might be well-loved by this town's people, but he's met his match with me. That man's wife must be namby-pamby if she puts up with his thoughts that a woman is not capable of more than cooking, cleaning, or . . ." Katie blushed, stomped her foot, and stood ramrod straight, skirts clenched in her tight fists. "I will not allow a man to dictate what I can and cannot do. I will stand up for 'the least of these,' as it says in Scripture even if I have to do it on my own!" Arms akimbo, chin jutted forward, she stood resolute.

"You've got your mother's stubborn streak and your father's reckless nature. You'll need to be choosing which path you plan to follow."

Katie felt rage continue to surface. She bit her tongue, desperately working to keep from lashing out at her aunt's insensitive remark.

Aideen lifted her palms as if in surrender. "Ah, that got your attention. Truth is, I hope you choose neither path. You've shared your thoughts, desires, and plans, but you need to listen to what God would have you do. It's His path that matters. No matter what I, the Magistrate, your father's words floating around in that head of yours, or anyone else says, your heart should only yearn for what God has to say."

Katie's shoulders slumped, and she sighed, releasing the pent-up emotion like the release valve on the new-fangled pressure cooker she'd seen advertised. All the steam of earlier evaporated, and she inhaled the dry air around her. Aideen was right about wanting to hear from God, but He'd been silent.

Even with all her planning, she felt directionless.

Chapter 2

Late May 1866

Missouri Prairie, Korhonen Farm

"**A**re my hands as cold to you as they are to me?" Hans received no answer from Gerta beyond a smack and slurp as she chewed her cud.

"Used to be I could carve intricate designs into wood. Now I'm struggling to milk you." Hans appreciated the warmth of the cow's teats, which helped soothe the incessant ache as he milked. If only it would calm his troubled mind. He rested his head on the animal's flank, willing the warmth to fill the empty places in his mind so other thoughts could not. He would never be the same. The war had made sure of that.

He had joined the Union Army thinking he could make a difference in the war against slavery. The only change had been in his heart—toward mankind in general and toward God specifically. Rhythmic sounds and memorized motions pulled his mind to memories he wished he could forget.

"Soldier, pick up your feet! There's a wagon full of men just

arrived."

Training compelled Hans to straighten and move his weary body with precision, but internally, he slumped, his blue wool hanging loosely on his frame. As one of the lowest-ranking soldiers, he followed orders from sunup to sundown—moving bodies, digging mass graves—he shivered.

"This one might make it." There was no inflection in the wagon driver's voice.

Hans picked up the other end of the gurney from the ambulance wagon, not making eye contact. The medic wore the traditional band around his arm, his only indication to Confederate and Union soldiers that he was assisting the wounded. This man put his life at risk to help these dying men get care in the closest field hospital. The only risks to Hans's life were cold, disease, and the boredom of monotony that allowed his mind to fill with the voices of demons.

"All full, soldier. Put that one in the overflow." An orderly pointed to the makeshift holding area. The man's once-white apron, now stiff with dried blood, moved with the action.

"A full church. Wouldn't that surprise the parson?" the medic said.

At the comment, Hans looked at the medic and saw a glimmer in the man's eyes. Hans did not see the humor.

"That looks as good a place as any." The medic pointed.

Hans followed the man's armband. He did not recall the soldier's name, but he recognized the purplish tinge of the man's waxy, rough hands. The medic likely suffered from pain and tightness, much like his own frostbitten fingers. Stumbling and working to maintain a firm grasp on the handles, they lowered the cloth-covered poles to the ground. Working in tandem, Hans allowed his companion to decide each soldier's fate, listening to the pronouncements over the men they carried: "Goner." "Might survive." "He's got the will to live." "God rest his soul." Simple words said much. Hans knew which direction to head by the man's declarations.

Hans walked the path from the wagon to each soldier's next resting place until there was only one body remaining. There had been no rush to get this one inside. He made eye contact with the orderly in charge, who shook his head. This boy now in his arms would need none of the man's services. Thin arms and legs slapped against his own. He'd not considered blood to be the same, no matter the color of someone's skin. Even dried, it caked to the same glossy reddish-brown, the only thing with any gleam of light in the body he carried. Behind the church, blue and gray blurred as he carefully placed the boy on top, his brown skin blending in with the last of the fall leaves around him. Hans grimly attempted a sardonic smile. In death, they all ended up in one heap.

His work done, he scrubbed his hands in the frigid stream. Only the moon's reflection on the water hinted he'd removed the layer of other men's blood—blood worn like guilt. He had not eaten since breakfast, but the smell of death permeated the air, diminishing any appetite he might have had. He trudged back toward the row of tents where men surrounded a campfire as if guarding its heat. He shivered as he continued past, ignoring their drunken calls to join them.

A bright ring surrounded the moon, drawing his attention to the stars twinkling in the clear night sky. A shiver ran up his spine.

He lifted his worn collar against the wind, and his hands found little warmth in his pockets. With a moon like that, it would not be hard to find his way back home to the farm he'd left so long ago. He had probably walked that far already on his nightly treks within the camp's boundaries. If he walked in a straight line toward his family land in Missouri, he could be there in a matter of weeks. Not twenty paces away, thick woods met with the edge of camp. He could run and leave this all behind. Hans stopped walking, closed his eyes, and inhaled the crisp night air. The stench of his unwashed body and clothing seemed stronger than usual.

He hated this life. He wanted out. He was tired of doing the bidding of others. All he wanted now was to be his own man. He opened his eyes and spied the tree line. Was it worth the risk? Would he forever be on the run? Would he become a casualty of war? How long was this nightmare going to last? When he'd signed up, he had been told the war would not linger. But still, they battled. Still, they died.

Leaves crunched, and the smell of squalid flesh became overwhelming, and he recognized it was not his own stench. Something connected with the back of his head, snapping it forward, then back as someone pulled his hair, causing him to lose his balance.

Hans jumped to his feet, nearly toppling the pail of milk. He wiped his eyes of the memory. He dealt with enough nightmares every time he attempted to sleep. He didn't need his mind reminding him of his shortcomings and failures during the day as well.

"Sorry, old girl."

Gerta stomped and grunted, letting Hans know she was not

pleased with his abruptness. He rubbed the back of his head, still feeling the pain even though it had been over a year ago.

"Hans?"

"Coming, Johann." Hans put the stool away and lifted the pail.

"Wondered where you'd gotten lost. Edna's ready for the eggs."

"It took a little longer than usual to milk Gerta today." Hans lowered his gaze and used his free hand to wipe the sweat from his brow.

"I see." Johann pulled in the fresh air, making his already-broad chest swell. "You know, if you ever want to talk about it, I'm a decent listener."

Hans could not look at his brother. Would it make a difference if he shared the horrors war had inflicted on him? Would some of the weight be lifted? His brother had seen far worse than he. No. He would work through this on his own.

Chapter 3

Shumard Oak Bend

"Good day, Mrs. Gray." Katie wasn't sure which of the elderly sisters she was addressing.

"Shh," the woman answered.

Katie watched her gnarled hand motion her into the alleyway. Katie turned to her left and right, then pointed to herself. "Me?"

"Shh," the woman repeated before turning and moving more swiftly than Katie would have thought possible.

With one last glance around her, Katie dashed after the stooped form. The second row of houses behind Main Street was small, but the Gray sisters' home stood out. Whitewashed with blue shutters and a front door the color of the mercantile sign, their small dwelling was flanked on all sides by bursts of color. Wildflowers greeted her, their smiles shining forth through their blooms.

"Hurry, dear."

Katie followed the woman up the front steps and into a time before she'd been born. Katie tried to take in the room but was drawn to a stark, black-draped figure on the rose-colored settee. A woman, whose expressionless face was likely caused by the strict bun holding her gray locks in place, sat like a statue. Her trim, buffed nails shone in the lamplight, only to be bested by the dazzling stones surrounding her wrist and two fingers. Her bearing screamed culture and strength, but Katie did not miss the movement under the woman's black skirts where she switched and recrossed her ankles.

Uneasiness gripped Katie, and she fought the urge to look down. Feeling like a bug under a magnifying glass, Katie felt heat rise in her cheeks at the woman's scrutiny.

"I am Mrs. Olivia Branch."

One of the woman's porcelain hands with blue veins lifted, palm down, but the woman did not stand. Katie wasn't sure what to do. Was she supposed to kiss the back of the woman's hand? She would not allow this woman to make her cower, nor would she bow down to another. Katie cocked her head and remained rooted.

"Please sit. I would like to discuss a matter of importance with you." The woman did not appear phased by Katie's rudeness. The hand flipped over in a graceful motion, indicating the chair across from her.

Katie paused only long enough to establish she was sitting of her own volition. She fluffed her skirts, mimicking the woman's stance. As she sat on the edge of the chair, her back ached to lean into the cushion. She crossed her ankles, releasing the strain in her lower back.

"I understand you are a businesswoman much like the Gray sisters," Mrs. Branch said.

Pleasure filled her, but Katie schooled her features and willed her hands to remain relaxed in her lap.

"Tea is served." One of the sisters interrupted the staring match, which Mrs. Olivia Branch won.

"Thank you, Elizabeth," the stranger said. "I'll serve."

Katie had never seen someone dismissed so fully in so few words. Mrs. Branch poured and offered a cup to Katie. Vines trailed up the side of the fine china, and an image of this woman offering an olive branch made it difficult for Katie to hold in her mirth. This did not feel like a peace offering.

"Let me be direct, Miss Murphy. I have a proposition for you. I am the benefactor of the Missouri Children's Home for Little Wanderers in Masons Corner. We are seeking a new matron, and I heard you may be available and suitable for the position."

Matron? Available? Suitable? Katie sipped her tea, her mind whirling with questions. Who was this woman? She had not come on the last stage. How had she found out about her?

"Perhaps I should give some background information before we continue. Our orphanage has been in existence for a mere ten years. Our previous matron married, much past her prime, and left for Oregon a few weeks ago."

Katie did not miss the slight nor the implication there was an immediate need.

"The home cares for twelve children at present with room for fifty if distributed evenly between sexes. The wards, or wanderers as we call them, are schooled in the basics of reading, writing, and arithmetic. The boys are hired out during the day as hands, and the girls stay busy working in our kitchen and laundry, learning skills necessary for life should they be fortunate enough to marry or secure employment. If not, well . . ." The woman sipped her tea.

Katie felt her hackles rise as did the heat on her cheeks, which meant the freckles on her face would soon join. The parlor door was to her back, but she heard the rustling of skirts. Were the Gray sisters in on this scheme?

"You would be responsible for overseeing the care and upbringing of the children. There is a staff consisting of one worthless colored woman who barely manages to clean, let alone work her night shift, the schoolteacher whom we are looking to replace, and a cook whose food is barely edible. You would be responsible for keeping them in line."

Katie was appalled at the way the woman spoke of the employees of the school.

"Have you nothing to say?" Mrs. Branch asked.

Oh, she had plenty to say but knew it wasn't something the woman cared to hear. She settled her cup on the tray and took in a steadying breath, blowing it out with a prayer. *God, help me, or forgive me, whichever is more appropriate.*

"Mrs. Branch."

"Olivia, please."

The woman surprised her with a new expression, one with a forced smile.

"Olivia. Might I inquire as to how you learned of my availability and suitability for this position?" She would need to control her tone better.

"I do not see why that is important."

"It is to me, Mrs. Branch. In fact, it's very important." Katie held her ground and noticed a slight flicker in the woman's eyes. Whether doubt or deception, she wasn't sure, but Katie did not budge and placed a smile she did not feel on her lips.

The woman glanced down for a moment, her skirts rustling. "Are you not interested?"

"Are you going to answer my question?" When the woman did not answer, Katie stood. "Good day, Mrs. Branch. I apologize on behalf of whoever caused you to think being a workhouse prison warden would be of interest to me."

The woman's eyes widened before narrowing. "Miss Murphy, I do not believe you understand who I am and what I represent for your future."

"Oh, there you are mistaken. I understand perfectly. You are a bully who believes her money, title, and community standing give her permission to order around those beneath her, all while making those poor individuals feel they have been done a favor." Katie took a step forward, causing the woman to lean back slightly.

"Let me explain who I am. I am Kathleen Orla Murphy, a penniless orphan living under the roof of a gracious aunt who has given me a home and reputable work." Something inside her blossomed like the flowers she saw through the window. "But more importantly, I am a child of God who desires to care for widows and orphans as instructed in His word. Any orphanage I am associated with will need to measure up to His standards and not those of an ungenerous, overbearing benefactor who believes her own will is greater than His."

Katie's chest rose and fell in a great motion. Her throat ached with the restraint of her words.

"Ungenerous?" Indignation rang in the single word.

"Is that the only thing you heard from all I said?" Katie's laughter filled the room, and she huffed out a breath, her tone gentling as she spoke. "I do hope you find someone suitable for the position, but I am not that person."

Katie's smile moved from her mouth to her toes, which turned toward the door. Behind her, the woman sputtered something Katie did not care to hear.

"Did you need me for anything else, ladies?" Katie asked as she passed the wide-eyed sisters in the hall. The taller of the two shook her head, while the other lifted dainty fingers to her open mouth. "Thank you for the tea," Katie added with all the sweetness she could muster as she let herself out the door.

How could one feel so light and so heavy at the same time? Katie trudged back toward town, crossed Main Street, and continued up the hill to the shade of the Shumard oak tree near the church. From this vantage point, she could see the comings and goings of Shumard Oak Bend. The sun glinted on a black horse pulling an equally black buggy. On it sat Mrs. Olivia Branch. The snap of the reins caused the horse and Katie to jump. She was too far away to hear the sound, but she still felt the sting.

Chapter 4

Korhonen Farm

"**M**ichael, it's important to clean the shank and break up the clumps." Hans crushed the hardened dirt in his hand.

"If they made a better plow . . ." the boy said.

"We couldn't afford it if they did." Exasperation filled Hans's voice.

"Maybe not, but new plows use steel. Cast iron is rough and causes the soil to stick. Now, when you use well-polished steel . . ."

Hans tuned out the boy's rambling as Michael repeated words from an old copy of *The Farmer's Magazine*. He'd even memorized the advertisements and was convinced John Deere's plows were the best.

Hours at the plow meant exhausting, mundane work. Michael droned on like a pesky fly at a summer church social. Sweat dripped into Hans's eyes, and he lifted his shirt to wipe away the dampness. The smell of sweat and grime was overpowering, and he gagged at the all-too-familiar smell. He rubbed the back of his neck. The steady rhythm of horse hooves pulled at his mind like the plow digging deep into the earth. He felt the familiar pinch in his side and willed his mind to stay in the present, but the power over him dragged him into the past.

"You'd be smart to keep your mouth shut." The man's nasal tone held a hint of threat.

Hans felt the tip of an icy blade poke through his thin jacket and touch flesh.

"You'll take us to that hospital and get my brother the care he needs. You understand me, you worthless . . ."

"Ahh, Joe," moaned the injured man.

Hans knew that sound. The other man was in pain. Severe pain if the increase in moaning was any sign.

Joe pressed the knife deeper, causing Hans to gasp, then gag at the stench of the arm under his neck, causing his chin to remain pointing upward. In his peripheral vision, he saw the brother. A stained rag encircled one thigh while his gaunt form leaned heavily on a makeshift crutch. No distinguishing colors showed the man's loyalty, but it did not matter. The injured man needed help and would receive care, no matter his views.

Hans pulled in air through his mouth before speaking, his voice steady, his words measured, even in his predicament. "Are you in need of care?"

"Of course, you bluebelly! Bunch of imbeciles. Can't you see the blood pouring out of my brother's wound?"

Warmth trickled down his side as the man somewhat released his neck hold. Hans turned enough to see his abductor and attempted to take a step, but the sneer he received was like that of a rabid dog guarding his meal.

Hans's voice remained calm, hoping to placate the man. "Follow me, and I'll get you the help your brother needs."

"Federals. Bunch of yellow-bellied sapsuckers with no more sense than a cockroach. 'Follow me.' Ha! I'm the one with the knife, you idiot."

Hans bit his tongue at the man's words. The bluster held no weight as both men followed Hans to the front of the tent. Slowly lifting his hands, he opened the flaps to enter. No one acknowledged their presence. His captor removed his arm, moving the knife to Hans's back.

"Make a move, and you're a dead man."

Hans kept his hands visible and stepped inside.

"What kind of outfit are you running here?" Unlike the stranger's previous whisper, these words were loud and harsh.

Hans flinched as the man adjusted the knife's position before moving to support his brother. A bedraggled man looked up from a stack of papers in his hands at the disturbing sound and moved toward them. Dark circles hung like weights under his drooping eyelids. Like Hans, it appeared he could not sleep either.

"I'm Doctor Haney. How may I be of assistance?"

The doctor may not look like much, but he spoke with an air of aristocracy and authority. He didn't seem to notice the severity of the situation.

"Some doctor you are if I must explain the blood running out of my brother's leg. Took us three days to walk here. Think you could find my brother a bed?" Disrespect dripped from the captor's mouth like venom.

"We may have room in the lean-to just outside. Soldier?"

Hans realized the doctor was addressing him and now recognized the man before him as one of the chief surgeons. Perhaps he walked these rows of beds like Hans did the path he had created outside.

"Sir. Yes, sir. I'll see to it right away, sir." Hans's voice demonstrated his respect, but his body remained as relaxed as possible, and he did not salute.

"Lean-to? It's nigh to freezing out there. You'll make a place for us right here, or, better yet, in that church I saw up the hill." The spit left dripping on Joe's cracked lips emphasized his words.

Hans had the fleeting thought that this rabid dog needed to be put down. The idea, as well as the smell of rotting flesh, unwashed bodies, and death inside the tent, made his stomach churn.

"Well, get to it, man," the man continued. "Find my brother a bed and not one in that lean-to."

Hans blinked at the order given by the filthy man. Perhaps he and his brother didn't notice the smell in the tent because of their own disgusting odor.

"Hurry up, you moron. Do you expect me to hold my brother up all night?"

At his words, Joe's injured brother faltered, reminding Hans of a woman swooning for effect, though the man remained conscious, *even if in obvious pain.*

"Back right, soldier," the surgeon said. "You can take the former occupant as you go."

Hans followed the surgeon's hand to the prone form covered by a woolen blanket.

"Looks like I'll need to stay to make sure you get the care you deserve, Jack." Joe's words had no soothing effect on the brother he called Jack, and Hans knew his captor meant them for anyone who would listen.

Hans led the way, passing several half-covered soldiers, their gazes following every move. Joe was getting under his skin, and he took controlled steps, hoping they would reign in his emotions.

"Hurry it up, boy," Joe said. "My brother here needs food and care. You think you can handle that, soldier?"

Hans had agreed to care for the injured, but this was still war, and he'd had enough of this man. Without thinking of his own safety, he whirled, his fist hitting Joe in the nose. The contact had a ripple effect, and both men staggered, each trying to support the other.

Hans watched as a prone soldier grabbed the crutch out from under Jack, causing the man to land hard on his back. With similar swiftness, the patient slipped his arm back under the worn blanket as if nothing had happened, but not before snatching up the knife Joe had dropped.

"What's going on here?" The larger of two armed guards filled the tent's opening.

"Both of these men require accommodations this evening,

gentlemen. One of them here, and one with you." Dr. Haney remained poised, his arms behind his back as if at ease.

"Yes, sir."

Hans heard bellowing as the guard hauled Joe away.

"Do you know who I am? Joe Clemons. You may know my father, Magistrate James T. Clemons, Esquire? Unhand me, you filthy swine, or you'll have . . ."

"Well, there you have it, Master Joe Clemons." The laugh that escaped Hans's mouth at his own joke felt good.

"Clemons? I know that name. If it's the family I'm thinking of, they're slave owners. If he keeps spouting off like that, he'll end up in prison," the soldier at his feet said. "You might be wanting this." The mere boy lifted the knife to Hans. "He won't be needing it where he's going."

"He'll be getting what he deserves." Hans flinched at his words and the pain in his side.

"You hurt?"

"I'm fine. It's just a minor scratch."

"More than one, I'm guessing from the looks of the stains on your jacket. They'll be calling you a hero by morning. You throw a mean punch."

Hero. He was no hero. Only moments before, he'd contemplated desertion.

Hero. Hero. Hero, voices mocked, and he covered his ears, attempting to squeeze out the sounds.

"Hans. Hans. Hans!" Michael's voice shattered the memory.

"What?" He knew his tone sounded harsh. His breathing was labored, and not from the hard work.

"Mom's yelling, saying it's time for lunch. You know she doesn't like to be kept waiting. Are you coming?"

"Sure. I'll be right in after I finish here." Defeated, he leaned on the plow. He'd survived the war, even made it back home to his family farm. But he'd traded one militant leader for another, and the torment in his mind would forever keep him from the freedom he craved.

Chapter 5

Korhonen Farm

Hans took slow, controlled steps, willing his feet to cooperate and carry him from the field to the house. His joints and extremities ached, and he doubted if the health of his youth would ever return, but he was alive, unlike his brother Otto.

The wide stone steps supported his weary limbs as he removed dirty shoes and rubbed tired feet. Michael bounded out the door, nearly tripping as he jumped to the side and off the porch, the pail in his hand swinging.

"Mom said I can take my lunch and go fishing." The boy grabbed the pole from inside the barn door and continued on to the pond.

"I guess I'll be finishing up the plowing by myself," Hans murmured.

Inside the house, the unpleasant tone of his sister-in-law's voice forced its way through the open door. He stilled, the words becoming clear.

"I'll not have him influencing my boy." Edna's incessant whining filled the air.

"*Our* boy," Johann interrupted, his words controlled and sharp. "And keep your voice down, Edna."

"I will not have *our* boy learning of laziness from that heathen."

Hans envisioned Edna placing her hands on her hips for emphasis. An exaggerated sigh confirmed his thoughts as she continued her haughty tirade.

"And under our roof, Johann. Motivate him to carry his share of the load or marry someone who can lessen mine. At the very least, encourage him to lodge elsewhere. Franc and Betsie have an extra room, you are aware."

Contentious woman. Johann was so oblivious to Edna's conniving ways he couldn't see the wedge she was driving between the brothers. Johann was a patient man. Too patient. And if Edna thought Hans had sway over her miscreant, good or bad, she was sorely mistaken. Michael did nothing but recite long passages of ridiculous nonsense while Hans gave his all in sweat and labor.

"Edna." Johann drew out the name. "Hans is not lazy. On top of tending the fields and building carts, he rises before dawn to care for the animals and does his best to teach your worthless son to do the same. But *your* son is not interested in learning unless it comes from a book. Besides, when Hans takes a break is not your concern."

"Not my concern?"

"Edna." The name came out like a curse on Johann's lips.

Johann could put Edna in her place, but he seldom did. Hans heard the familiar tap, tap of Johann's boot scraping on the wooden floor and smiled. When a bull pawed at the ground, you had better be a fast runner. Edna had not yet figured out the signal. The slow smile widened. There was no way Hans was going to miss the tongue lashing he anticipated she was about to suffer. He had sparred enough with Johann over the years to remember his brother was just as skilled in verbal assaults as with physical blows.

"We did just fine without you both while *you* served in the war." Dead silence followed Edna's caustic remark.

Hans heard Edna's insult but struggled to believe she had given it voice. Did she think he'd done nothing more in the war than sit in a chair and roll bandages all day? Just because he hadn't served on the front lines did not mean he was free from battle scars. And if the shingle at his feet were a sign, she had not done as well as she let on with no men to help on the farm during the war. The house was falling down around them.

"Edna, you'll do well to control your tongue."

The steel in Johann's voice was sharper than before and made even Hans stand up straighter. Edna often went too far. This was one of those times. The war had changed Johann, changed them all. The eldest brother now walked with a limp —the pain forever etched in his face. His once strikingly blue eyes were now dull and provided a window to gauge all he'd endured.

Hans rubbed his face, feeling the callouses scratching at

his heavy, closed eyelids. Physically, he was thinner, his joints ached constantly, and his hands and feet may never heal from frostbite, but at least his body was whole. He had come home in one piece, but oh, the torment in his mind. Hans heard a slight sniffle.

"Edna. Please don't cry. Let's sit and discuss this."

"There is nothing to discuss. Hans refuses to take part in family prayer and mocks God during Bible time, so do not justify his actions. He sits there, worthless, the same way he works the fields. I am forever looking out and seeing his lazy hide shirking his duty, leaving more work for my, our, son, and he, he . . ." Her voice trailed off into a preposterous sob, covering her empty words.

Air escaped from Hans's nose in loathing. If she did her own work, she should not have time to check on him in the fields. Most likely, she was making sure her precious son wasn't overdoing it.

What a waste. His son, if he ever had one, would understand the value of a good day's work. *My son.* That all depended on if he ever married, which wasn't likely. One thing was for sure, he'd not be getting a mail-order bride like his brothers. They had foolishly thought God had given them the desires of their hearts when all they'd received was a heap of heartache.

And he assuredly would not marry a willful, conniving, manipulative, heartless woman. No, he'd take no attitude from a woman. The last thing he wanted was some busybody telling him what to do or using tears to get her way. He did not need a woman. He did not need this family, and he did not need God. He'd be just fine on his own.

Chapter 6

Shumard Oak Bend

K atie disliked gardening more than any other chore, well, maybe except for laundry. And canning. She detested the hours over the steaming jars. But weeding the garden was a never-ending job. At least with canning and laundry, there was an end, for a while. Weeds shot up overnight, threatening to steal the life out of the plants whose bounty would eventually need to be canned. She sighed, looking at the dirt stains on her apron. Gardening even caused more laundry.

"Dreadful task, I know, but a necessary one." Aideen's shadow offered a moment's reprieve from the sun.

Katie took the presented cup of water. "Thank you."

"I was thinking we may need to focus on a few outdoor chores tomorrow if the weather holds. The barn needs a good sweeping, and we should replace the straw in the stalls before the reverend arrives. Would you mind asking Mr. Finch to deliver a load? We're low." Aideen fidgeted.

"Would you like me to offer a meal or two for payment?" Katie asked.

"If Mr. Finch will do that, I'd be much obliged. The stagecoach hasn't brought more than a few folks who want meals. Planting season isn't a time for travel, so he'll understand. If you'd like to stop by Martha's, you might see what she'd take in exchange for her cheese."

"She did mention your beautiful tatted cross the other day. You know, you really should sell those at the mercantile," Katie said.

"Ach, no one be wanting to buy one."

"I disagree. I think they would be a lovely gift and easy for a man to transport or post with a letter to his sweetheart. How many do you have made?"

"A dozen or so. Do you really think I could sell them?"

"I'm happy to ask. When I've finished here—if I ever finish here—I'll take them to Mr. Taylor and see what he thinks. It's worth a try."

Katie searched the street and alleyways for the Gray sisters as she walked. She had not seen them since the unusual meeting. How had they even known she was considering—not considering, *wanting*—to build an orphanage? Well, not build physically, yet.

"Good day, Miss Murphy." Mr. Finch removed his hat and

turned the edges in his hands.

She'd walked the entire length of town and not realized it. "Good day to you as well. Aideen would like to know if you'd bring fresh straw for our barn?"

"Can do. Need me to clean out as well?"

"Oh, no. Thank you. We can do that."

"All right." He drew out the words.

Katie expected he didn't enjoy discussing the financial side of the interaction, although, as a business owner, he would need to do it frequently. Still, the man seemed flustered, almost nervous.

"Aideen wondered if you might consider a trade for your troubles. Perhaps we could provide a few meals or bread?"

"You bake every morning, don't you?"

"Nearly every day but not on Sunday, of course."

"Sure would be nice if you'd deliver a loaf every now and again. You know, bring it by when you've time."

"I'd be happy to do that, Mr. Finch."

"When do you want the delivery? Is tomorrow morning soon enough?"

"That would be perfect. We'll have it cleaned and ready by the time you arrive and will have fresh bread waiting for you."

The man was acting unusual, and Katie hoped he wasn't regretting the trade. Perhaps he needed funds as well. She turned at the jingle of a harness.

"I've got to get back to work," he said. "I'll see you in the morning."

Katie watched for a moment as he focused his full attention on his new customer. "Lord, thank You for kind folk like Mr. Finch," she whispered as she headed to Martha's.

"Sorry I'm so late." Katie hefted the basket onto the table, removing the cheese Martha had given her and other items she'd picked up at the mercantile. "I have news." Her lyrical tone had the desired effect.

"I'll make tea." Aideen busied herself.

"Are we expecting boarders tonight?"

"Not to my knowledge. If we do, it will be a simple dinner."

"Good. This cheese smells heavenly. Let's make it our main course." Katie lifted the round to her nose.

"That's a poor man's meal and sounds delightful." Aideen fidgeted with her apron strings.

"Here, let me help you." Katie had not realized how nervous Aideen might be about her visit with Mr. Taylor. She hoped that was the only thing bothering her aunt. The woman's hands shook.

"Thank you, dearie," Aideen said.

"Did you know there are four young ladies graduating this

year?" When Aideen shook her head, Katie continued. "Martha is so excited. These are her first students. One is heading to Normal School, one will care for her ailing mother and her siblings, and two are betrothed."

"Ach, so young," Aideen said.

"Anyway, I took up far too much of her time. She'd like to know if she can purchase four of your crosses to give as gifts to the girls."

"Four? You don't say?"

"I do say." Katie blew steam across the top of her cup before taking a sip.

"Oh, for goodness' sake, Katie. I can't stand it. What about Mr. Taylor?"

"Who?" Katie took another sip to cover up the smile fighting to win out over the nonchalant look.

"I'm your elder, and I can still pack a wallop if need be." Aideen winked.

"Mr. Taylor thought they were lovely, but he suggested you vary your thread color. He believes they will sell well before Christmas and asked if you could also make collars."

"He didn't."

"He did." It was Katie's turn to wink. "Truth be told, he took every last one of the crosses you gave me. Mrs. Taylor said she has admired the one in your Bible." Katie pulled a few coins from her pocket and placed them in front of her aunt. "Your first sale."

"Well, I'll be." Aideen fingered the coins.

"What you'll be is busy. The crosses may only take an evening to tat, but the collars will take longer. And we need to get thread. Mr. Taylor said he could order what you need and take the cost out of your sales. What do you think?"

Aideen continued to turn the coins over, moving them across the table. "I think I need to get busy."

Katie wondered how the woman could add one more thing to her extensive daily list but knew her aunt needed the extra income. Katie's fingers and brain didn't work in tandem, so she would not be able to help create the masterpieces. That meant finding other ways to help. How would she ever earn enough money to start an orphanage? Unless God grew it on trees or sent it down from above, Katie would never have enough money to fulfill her dream.

"Trust Me."

Chapter 7

Korhonen Farm

H ans caressed the wooden handle of each tool before he placed it in the handcrafted leather pouch. He felt the birch shaft, smooth from years of use. His father had crafted, then gifted Hans the cherished items before Hans and his brothers had departed Finland, and he would not leave these treasures behind.

The spacious basket, once filled with a scant few articles of clothing, now rested vacant, empty of its former contents. Hans stood and reluctantly picked up his Bible and blew the dust from the cover. He turned the cracking leather over, and a yellowed piece of paper drifted to the floor.

Hans tucked it back into the cover and wrapped the Bible inside his winter trousers. His mother's handwriting was on that paper—and on his heart. He would leave this book behind, but it had been her parting gift. His mother's lilting Finnish filled his mind as he recalled the words.

My dearest Hans,

You are the joy of my heart. You were amenable from the moment you were born, always desiring to please me, your father, and your brothers. Now you are a man. No longer should you seek to please others, but God.

"And whatsoever ye do, do it heartily, as to the LORD, *and not unto men; knowing that of the* LORD *ye shall receive the reward of the inheritance: for ye serve the* LORD CHRIST."

I will pray for you with every breath until I take my last.

Isän käteen,

Mother

Isän käteen. Into the Father's hand.

The bed sagged under his weight, mimicking the droop of his shoulders. His heart ached, knowing he'd disappointed his mother. He no longer desired to please either his brothers or God, and he would never be able to please Edna, never find peace in her home. Perhaps he would find happiness and a new life elsewhere.

In the recesses of his mind, he heard his mother's voice quoting a Finnish proverb. *"Happiness does not lie in happiness, but in the achievement of it."*

"Well, then, a journey it is." Slapping his hands on his knees, he stood tall.

Yet even with this declaration, Hans knew starting over would be challenging. He'd always done everything with his three brothers. But life had changed once the others had married, leaving Hans floundering and his carefree relationships forever altered.

Then the war had happened. Hans felt a bead of perspiration trickle down his temple, but he did not wipe it away. Taming the Missouri wilderness and spending time with his brothers had once been enough to make him happy. The war had not only changed their personal lives but it had also changed the lives of everyone around them.

"How am I going to do this?" It wasn't a prayer. It was a reminder of the reality of leaving family. Cooling weather would be upon him soon enough. Shelter was important, as was finding work. He would travel to the nearest town of Shumard Oak Bend and seek something to sustain him until he figured out what he was going to do and where he wanted to settle. He needed a new life away from Edna, the memory of Otto, the strained relationship with Johann, and the reminders of war.

Hans plopped back onto the bed, still damp with sweat from the demons of war he fought every night, and weaved his fingers into his hair, pulling until it hurt. He'd never get away from the memories.

Hans's nightmares, which had begun only months after enlisting, hadn't lessened. He still heard men crying out, haunting his dreams. The memories mocked him for his ineptness and what the men had perceived as his lack of willingness to help them or offer relief. He had no idea what that help would have been, nor would he have given it. Why should he help others when God had forsaken him, His people, and this land?

The war had been brutal, not only on those who'd served but also on those left behind. Edna and Betsie, his sisters-in-law, had taken care of the plowing, planting, and harvesting, which had allowed them to keep themselves and many a troop fed. How they had accomplished it, he wasn't certain, but a wry smile formed at the thought of General Edna ordering her troops. A snort left his lips, and he moved to stand.

"'Bout ready then?"

Johann filled the space as he leaned against the doorframe, taking the weight off his injured leg. He'd been fortunate to keep it. Hans knew all too well that most injuries from a Minié ball resulted in massive damage to tissue and splintered bone. The ball might prove more accurate in a rifle than gunpowder, but the soldier aiming at Johann had not been an excellent shot. For that, he was grateful. Hans watched as lines furrowed his brother's brow, his lips thin as his square jaw twitched in unspoken agitation.

"Yes. I'm ready." Hans faced his brother and matched his serious tone. "I know you disagree with my decision, but it's time for me to go." Hans equaled his brother's stare and body language, reminding him of the many scrapes they'd gotten into as boys. His pulse increased even as he saw the vein in Johann's forehead pulse.

"You are running from something. Korhonens face their fears." Johann did not retreat.

"I am not running from something. I'm running to something." Hans's voice was sharper than he intended, and he wiped his mouth of the spit that escaped. An image of a man from his past crossed his mind, and he brushed it away.

A slight movement in Johann's right cheek brought back the feelings of doubt Hans had wrestled with for weeks, yet he squared his shoulders even more, keeping his chin lifted in defiance.

Johann sighed in acceptance of the inevitable. "You are always welcome here, brother. I wish I had more funds to give to you, but I'm hoping the sale of the cart you made will be enough to hold you over until you find work. When the crops come in, you'll receive your share."

"I'll miss you, Johann." The breath that started deep in his soul ended in his words. He looked into the tortured face of his brother.

"And I you, little brother."

"You know I can't stay. I . . ." Hans dropped his eyes to his shuffling feet. To remain would drive the wedge Edna had started even further into their relationship. Hans respected his brother too much to let that happen.

"We could build a small house for you on the north side near the creek where Otto had planned to build."

Hans considered Johann's words. Did his brother desire him to stay so badly that he would use their precious resources to build Hans his own home?

"You know I can't cook more than ham and eggs. I'm worse

than Franc."

"You could marry."

"No." The word came out sharp and much louder than he had meant it to be. Hans watched Johann's expression change.

"Is she that bad, little brother?"

The snort that escaped Hans's nose was embarrassing. Words flew through his mind but never left his lips.

"Well, then. If you must go, you have my blessing, though you do not need it. You are a man now, Hans. You will make your own way."

Johann's words were convincing, but Hans noted the slight slump in his brother's frame. They'd all lost Otto. Was Johann feeling his loss as well?

"Johann . . ." Hans moved forward, but words would not come.

"Thank you for staying long enough to help us get the fields planted."

Guilt crept in. How would Johann manage the harvest? The large man stepped into the room and extended his hand, holding a few dollars. Hans placed the bills in his pocket, then grasped the still-extended hand. Johann pulled him into a familiar hug.

"Saattakoon Jumala sinua matkallas."

May God go with you. Hmph. He doubted that, but the whispered words echoed in his mind long after he'd gone.

Chapter 8

Missouri Prairie

Hans relaxed the reins when his horse bobbed his head slightly. The chestnut stud walked with pride as if he were the creator of the masterpiece he pulled behind him. His flaxen mane and tail swished with each step in cocky confidence. He snorted, the white markings on his muzzle twitching with the action. Hans threaded his fingers through the mane, and his friend neighed in response. Although it wasn't the same as having a discussion, the familiar sound comforted him.

Hans almost started a one-way conversation with the beast when he felt the stud swell at his sides, then noticed the ears twitch and swivel, locking on the woods to the right. The hair on the back of Hans's neck rose as he scanned the area. Two birds emerged from the trees, giving him a clue as to the disturber's location.

With his left hand on the reins, Hans's right hand moved in practiced motion to the gun strapped to his right thigh. Although his horse was sturdy, he would not be able to outrun riders with the attached conveyance. And even though Hans was a decent shot, he had no desire to use the weapon still holstered.

"Hello." The unknown man's voice was overly loud, allowing Hans to locate his position without effort.

A horse and rider slipped from between a slight opening in the trees a stone's throw away. The man sat deep in the saddle, one hand flat and loose on the reins, while the other waved a hat that had lost its stiffness. Hans debated moving his hand from the holstered gun. Even as the man approached, he saw no weapon, yet Hans remained wary. With controlled movement, he lifted his hand in greeting but did not speak. The last thing he wanted to do was spook the stranger with quick actions.

"Good to see another traveler. I tire of my own stories."

Hans understood this all too well. The smile offered seemed genuine, but the man swayed a bit more in the saddle than an accomplished rider would. The rider's laugh moved through his body as he approached, and Hans wondered if the fellow had been drinking. The man's horse fell in step beside his own.

"Now, that's some contraption you've got there. Did you build it?"

Hans nodded once.

"Well, you've got some ingenuity. I imagine it would work well for those going short distances or into the mountains. Yes, it would work well. Is that where you're headed, the mountains?"

Hans sucked in air, concentrating on the man's hands, then cutting to the woods for any signs of danger should there be others with him, then back again to the rider, only an arm's-length away. He would take his chances and befriend this stranger.

"No, I'm headed to town."

"Ah, yes. I am as well. A blessing, absolute blessing, to have someone with which to share this glorious day." The man looked up as the wisps of clouds danced across the sky. "I'm Scott Jenkins, the reverend in these parts, and I do mean parts. Too much territory for a man my age. Yes siree, too much territory. But the good Lord hasn't seen fit to let me stop, so I just keep going on my circuit each month."

Parson. Just his luck. He would almost have preferred an outlaw. It wasn't like he'd be able to get rid of a clergyman. The man had already said more words than all his brothers combined did over a meal.

"I used to stay in the schoolhouse, which serves as a church on Sunday, but now I have a room at Grammie's Boarding House. Is that where you'll be staying?" When Hans did not reply, the man kept talking. "Ah, you probably don't even know. Well, Aideen fixes the best food around."

Hans heard the man's stomach growl.

"Apologies." He patted the offending paunch. "I'm low on rations and only ate half of my biscuit for breakfast."

"I'd be happy to share when we stop later, Parson."

"Parson? Well, now, I've yet to be called by that term. Been called a few others I won't mention."

The laugh startled Hans, but the boisterous noise didn't seem to bother the man's mount.

"Where do you hail from, son?" The man removed his hat and wiped his bald head with a handkerchief before replacing the misshapen item.

"A day's ride east. My brothers and I own a farm." His words sounded curt to his own ears, but his traveling companion didn't seem to notice.

"Don't get east much, although my circuit takes me through quite a bit of territory. Too much territory for a man my age. Yes siree, too much territory. But the good Lord has not yet seen fit to let me stop, so I just keep going on my circuit each month."

Hadn't he just said that? Hans looked over as the man once again rubbed his protruding stomach. The parson was short, round, rosy-cheeked, and devoid of hair except where it all seemed to rest in a straight, singular, bushy line above his eyes. He looked weary, with dark circles under his dull gray eyes, which were in stark contrast to his booming voice and jovial tone.

"Only ate half my biscuit this morning, so I'd have some for lunch." He looked over his shoulder toward the sun. "Guess I'll be needing to wait a bit longer. There's a nice creek up ahead where we can water the horses. I'm happy to share what I have with you when we stop."

Hans smiled when their gazes connected, but he replayed the conversation in his mind. He had offered to share his own food, hadn't he? The reverend's eyes held no sparkle, but his smile was genuine, and Hans figured the man might be tired, causing him to be forgetful. Or was it Hans who was forgetful?

Hans surveyed the area one last time, feeling the tightness in his chest and shoulders relax. The man's horse indeed appeared familiar with the path. The parson had not directed the mare once, the reins still limp in his hands. Hans realized he was staring and returned his focus to his own mount.

"Do you like my horse? This here is Dorcas." Reverend Jenkins laughed, and Hans wondered what joke he'd missed. "Familiar with the Bible?"

"Enough, I suppose."

"Ahh, yes, well then, the Bible mentions Dorcas in Acts, chapter nine. God's Word doesn't speak of her physical beauty, but it tells us she spent her life in service toward those who were less fortunate." He gestured to the drab, unmarked coat of his mare.

Dorcas responded with what Hans thought looked like a smile when the mare's rider rubbed his hand along her neck.

"The Dorcas of the Bible committed herself to good works and gave alms to the poor continually." As if letting out a heavy load with his breath, the reverend exhaled. "This girl here, my Dorcas . . ." He said the name lovingly as his hand continued to stroke the smooth hair over her neck. "She has plowed farmers' fields, transported injured men, and carried me more miles than I care to calculate. Never asks for a thing and listens to an old man's rambling. Why, she's listened to more sermons than a preacher's boy." He laughed again before catching Hans's gaze and winking. The snort that came out of the man's nose and mouth made Hans laugh as well.

"Sounds like a fitting name," Hans replied without further addition, not wanting to get into other Bible character discussions. Images of Jonah and the whale crossed his mind.

"Does your mount have a name?"

"Rauti." The Finnish R rolled from his tongue without thought.

Reverend Jenkins seemed to be thinking about the name, then responded, "Ah, yes, Rowdy. Well, I suppose a strapping stud like that would have a good bit of energy. There it is." Reverend Jenkins pointed up ahead. "Good water source. Dorcas here deserves a cool drink, and I do believe I'm a right bit hungry and ready for something myself." He patted his paunch. "I only ate half my biscuit for breakfast, so I'd have some for lunch. Happy to share with you, young man, if you're hungry."

Hans dismounted with haste, offering his companion a hand to the elbow when the man wavered on shaky legs.

"Thank you, son. What did you say your name was? I'm a might forgetful these days."

"Hans, and you didn't forget. I hadn't yet said."

"Hans? That's a new one for me. I know a few Hanks."

The reverend removed his well-worn hat and wiped the perspiration from his bald head. Before the man could replace the covering, Hans realized his name alone would give away his heritage. Concern gripped his chest. He was not sure if that would be an issue in this town. Just because the war against slavery had ended was not a guarantee people didn't have other prejudices. The parson, or reverend, he reminded himself, didn't seem bothered, or perhaps he hadn't noticed.

Hans placed his lunch on a small open cloth. The horses drank the creek's cool water, and Hans watched as the reverend gingerly dropped to one knee to wash his hands and face upstream. Moving quickly, Hans cleaned his own hands before assisting the man from the water's edge to his feet.

"I've laid out food for us right here." He pointed out two logs and assisted the man onto one.

"Why, you didn't have to do that, son. I'd have been more than happy to share my meal. I have a biscuit left, I believe."

Hans noticed the man eyeing the fresh cheese and small bread loaves.

"Mighty fine feast the Lord has blessed us with today. Mighty fine. I've been thanking Him all day for His provisions, but I'd like to say a proper blessing over this meal."

"Of course." Hans took a quick glance around as his companion began, then bowed his head and watched an ant make its way over a rock.

"Thank You, Lord, for this new friend and the food he has provided by Your hand. Amen." The reverend wasted no time reaching for the bread.

Hans never cared much for the religious men he'd met. Pompous and self-righteous fit their descriptions well, but this man had an easy way about him, a non-judgmental air. He talked too much, but Hans had the feeling a friendship was forming. His lips turned up. *Friendship.* That was something he hadn't considered. The thought settled on him, feeling much like it had when his brother's hand had rested on his shoulder.

Hans struggled to understand as the reverend talked, mouth full, through the entire meal, before patting his stomach.

"Yes, I do believe Aideen has met her match with the apple turnover. Just don't let her know I said that." The reverend chuckled and jabbed his elbow toward Hans, who sat too far away for him to reach.

"We should move on, Reverend."

"Right you are. Right you are." With some help, the man stood and moved toward his horse, who remained still as he mounted. "From the location of the sun, I expect we'll make it there just in time for dinner. Have I mentioned Aideen? She's the best cook in town. I stay at her boarding house. My home away from home. I'm sure she'll have plenty of room for you. She makes a breakfast like no other. . . ."

Hans listened once again to the same stories and information he'd already heard, answered the occasional question, and realized how much he enjoyed his new friend's company. He had a good feeling about this fresh change. Excitement coursed through his veins. He yearned to tell the reverend about his plans to start a business but couldn't find an opening in the conversation.

He felt a flutter in his stomach. Leaving his past behind had been the right thing to do, hadn't it? With the reverend's company, he'd not thought of home. At the moment, everything felt right. Johann had been wrong. He wasn't running from anything. Yet even as he pondered this, he wondered if he could ever outrun himself.

Chapter 9

Shumard Oak Bend

K atie lifted the iron from the stove and pressed the hem of the dish towel. Aideen's wild hair notion of cutting up a torn sheet and creating an intricate design around the bottom edge turned out lovely—impractical but beautiful. Katie pressed each one, folding it into thirds, then over in half. She mentally added ironing to her list, just below gardening and canning.

Lamplight flickered in the corner as Aideen's hand-carved tatting shuttles blurred with her fingers. She hummed a joyous tune. The woman was more than happy; she seemed content. Katie wished the same calm assurance would fill her soul, but she felt restless. She was tired of waiting on God and needed to do something.

A knock at the door startled her, and she burned her finger on the hot iron. "Ouch."

"Are you all right?" Aideen glanced up before continuing her handiwork.

"Yes, ma'am. I'll get the door." Katie replaced the iron on the stove, ran a bit of cold water over her finger, and walked to the front entrance.

It was late for a caller, and she looked out the window but didn't see a horse. It was likely someone from town. She opened the door to humidity and heat, but no one was out there. After a quick look, she shut the door and returned to the parlor.

"Who was it, dearie?"

"No one was there. Perhaps a limb fell on the roof, and we only thought it was a knock."

Aideen sighed. "The roof. That's a project for another day. I need to have it looked at before winter, but there are other pressing needs." Aideen never stopped, her fingers a blur of motion.

Tap, tap.

Aideen stilled. "That sounds like it came from the kitchen."

The light in Katie's hand illuminated the kitchen walls. The tapping sounded again, causing Katie's heart to mimic the rhythm.

"Who is it?" She wasn't taking any chances.

"Julian Preston. Might you have a room and meal?"

Katie opened the door to a small-framed man. Behind him was a wheelbarrow filled with what looked like carpet bags.

"Can I help you, sir?"

"I'm traveling through, and I hope you might have a room until the stage arrives."

"Yes, please come in. I apologize for not answering sooner."

"I went to the front, but when you didn't answer, I thought I'd try the door nearest the barn. I figured it was the kitchen, and it looks like I was correct." He stepped inside, leaving his belongings behind.

"Welcome, sir." Aideen joined them. "We do have a room available, and the stagecoach should be in tomorrow. Katie, show the man where he can freshen up and place his belongings while I pull together something for his supper."

"Oh, thank you, ma'am. Miss." He looked at each woman, bending in a polite bow. "It took longer to walk here than I anticipated. Well, the distance wasn't longer, but pushing that wheelbarrow was a might more tiring than I'd bargained for."

"I'm Aideen O'Sullivan, the proprietor. Katie will help you settle, and I'll have food to refresh you when you return."

"Might I store my goods in your barn for the night? There is no reason to bring them all in."

"Of course, Mr. Preston. Let's do that first," Katie answered.

Katie showed the man where he could place his cart and then led him to his room. Of all the beautiful bags in the cart, he carried only a small leather one. She returned to the kitchen.

"Do you need help?" Katie asked Aideen.

"Is he all settled, then?"

"Yes, ma'am. You should see the bags in his cart. Such lovely fabrics with braided handles." Katie poured a cup of hot tea as their guest came through the door.

"Ladies, you have a lovely boarding house. And this feast— you did not have to go to so much trouble."

"Would you like to sit in the dining room, Mr. Preston?" Aideen offered.

"If you ladies have work here, I'll pull up this stool and enjoy my repast and your company."

Katie smiled. There was always something that needed to be done. She set to work soaking raisins for cinnamon raisin bread in the morning.

"What brings you to town, Mr. Preston, if you don't mind my asking?" Aideen sliced cheese and bread and then slid the plate over to the man.

"I'm headed to St. Louis for business."

"How exciting." Aideen added a napkin, spoon, and apple butter to the table.

"Did you make this?" He lifted the jar, examining the dark golden-brown contents.

"That we did. You should have seen our kitchen on that day," Aideen exclaimed, sweeping her arms to encompass the entirety of the room.

"Oh, I well remember. I'm the only boy of eight girls. I was thankful all I had to do was haul the wood and keep the fire consistent."

"There is a trick to that."

Katie finished preparations and turned to her aunt, who nervously moved her hands as if she still held the shuttles. "Aunt Aideen, you go on back to the parlor. I'll stay with Mr. Preston and clean up."

"I believe I'll take you up on your offer." Aideen turned to the guest. "If you'll excuse my lack of courtesy, Mr. Preston."

"Please, I have interrupted your evening past a reasonable hour," he said. "I should be apologizing to you."

"Eight sisters?" Katie turned her focus to the man. Steam rose as she poured more hot water into his mug. "What a unique childhood you must have had."

"I was the baby, so I had nine mothers. It's a wonder I know how to blow my nose since someone was always doing everything for me."

Katie laughed. "So, you're running away, then," she teased.

Now it was Mr. Preston's turn to laugh. "Smart girl." He tapped the side of his nose. "That's what we used to say to my father once a year. We have a family business. My father passed in the war, and the military conscripted our horses, but before Father died, it was he who drove our load to St. Louis. Now I'm both courier and horse." The side of his mouth lifted.

"I'm sorry for your loss."

"We've all suffered in different ways with the war." He placed his napkin down and stood. "Thank you for this fine meal and your company." He took one quick sip of his tea.

"If you'd like a refill and a cookie, I'm sure my aunt would enjoy your company."

"I'd enjoy that immensely. Not having another to talk with all day was as taxing as the walk."

Katie led him to the parlor and was thankful she wasn't carrying a tray. His exclamation scared her witless.

"Exquisite. I see you are a true artisan, Mrs. O'Sullivan."

"I don't know about that, but thank you," Aideen said. "Do you know of tatting?" Her fingers continued their movement.

"I do." He fingered the thread on the table near the lantern. "You are using my thread."

Aideen's fingers stilled. "Your thread? I don't understand."

Katie watched the man straighten and turn to her. "Remember when I told you we have a family business? It is a thread business, and this is one of ours." He held it aloft. "An older color, if memory serves me correctly."

"Aunt Aideen was about to buy thread from the mercantile," Katie said. "I'm guessing he orders it from St. Louis?"

"You guess correctly."

"You made this? It is so fine, not like homespun. I would have thought it machine-made."

"Thank you for that compliment. That is my sisters' doing. Is this the only color you own?"

Katie followed his gaze as he took in the area and the pile of crosses of the same color.

"It is." Aideen resumed her work, shuttles jumping over and skipping under each other.

"We need to remedy that come morning if you are willing to make a trade for my room and board."

"Only God could have orchestrated this. Only God," Aideen said.

Chapter 10

Shumard Oak Bend

"Welcome to Shumard Oak Bend, umm..."

"Hans. Hans Korhonen," Hans filled in the forgotten words for the reverend.

"Right. Hans. So, welcome. This here town is about the nicest you'll find."

Hans took in his surroundings, noticing the impressive livery to his right. The whitewashed, two-story structure boasted large double doors at each end of the substantial building. Off the back, several goats ate and frolicked in an enclosed area.

"Hmm. I wonder where Paul is hiding? He's an ornery old goat and is usually over there on top of that rock, trying to figure out a way out or waiting for his next victim to jump on when they walk by." The reverend leaned in and said in a hushed tone, "Grammie used to say he goes from sinner to saint in a flash of light."

The man's chortle at his own joke caused Hans to laugh as

well while he surveyed the flat land behind the livery, looking for the rock the man had mentioned.

"That would be William Finch's place. He lost his boy, Billy, at Hartsville in January of '63. Word that he'd be coming home on leave within a few weeks arrived a month before the notification of his death. Not two months later, William lost his wife. Broken heart, they say. God rest her soul." The reverend paused for only a moment, as if out of respect, before continuing. "If you require work, he might have something for you at the livery. Seems you know the business end of a horse."

"I am good with animals. If the pay is fair, it's as good a job as any, I suspect, and it might give me opportunities to show my craftsmanship." There might even be a space in the livery for him to sleep. It wasn't his preference, but he would do what he had to until he finalized plans.

As they passed the jail on the left, Hans tilted his face toward a tall, rugged-looking man and lifted two fingers to the brim of his hat. The man stood with his large hands on the shoulders of two boys but glanced Hans's way. He lifted his angular chin in greeting, the motion causing the sun to glint off the star he wore.

"That there would be Sheriff Henry Adkins. Best lawman around, absolutely the best. Those two boys, well, more like young men now, are Thomas Shankel and his best friend— hmmm—can't rightly remember the other boy's name. It'll come to me. It always does. Smiley? No, no. Happy? No, that's not right." He paused a moment, scratching at his graying stubble, before blurting out, "Gabe, yes, Gabe."

"Gabe?" The name didn't come close to Smiley or Happy,

but whatever system the old man used to remember seemed to work.

"Yes, as in Gabriel. That boy has quite the story to tell. Met the Lord's angel face to face." His head bobbed as he spoke.

"Is that so?"

"Is what so?"

Best to avoid that discussion. Hans shielded his eyes as he squinted toward the setting sun and pointed to the stone structure off to the left in the center of town. "What might that be?"

"Ah, yes, that would be our bank. John Sneed is an honest man, and there has never been a robbery in this here town."

Hans chuckled. He didn't have money to put in a bank, no matter how safe.

"And that there is Magistrate Bill Marley."

The man waved and called a greeting from another building attached to the left side of the bank.

"Be prepared," the reverend added. "He'll ask you more questions than you thought you had answers."

A raucous tune came from Hans's right. He couldn't see the structure behind the building on Main Street, but the tinny and out-of-tune piano was loud enough to make his ears hurt. Hans looked to see two men stumbling between dilapidated buildings before being met by garish laughter and coarse language. He knew that sound and didn't need an explanation for what he'd find back there. Most towns had a saloon and women available for a price.

One of the inebriated men pushed the other into the wood siding of the structure. "I always pay, you low down, good-for-nothing. It's your turn to ante up."

Hans tried to ignore the feeling, but something in the small-framed man's voice made him tense. Rauti shook his head, sensing his owner's anxiety. Hans felt the familiar squeeze in his chest and moved his fist to rub at the spot. The surrounding sounds became muffled, and he jutted out his chin to ease the tightness in his neck. Sounds of the tinny piano mingled with words, and his breath caught as he recognized one drunkard. All bluster, the man turned on his comrade and pointed a finger in the man's face.

"Don't be calling me no welcher, you yellow-bellied sapsucker. I'll shoot you down right here. Is that what you're wanting? Hmm?"

The voice and the derogatory term made Hans's skin crawl. Only one man he'd ever known had used that phrase. A man he had thought to never see again.

"Nah, come on, Joe. You know I was just fooling with you." The other man reached his arm over the finger shoved in his chest and wrapped it around his companion, leaning on him when he stumbled.

Joe. How did he end up here? He should still be in prison or on a work farm somewhere.

"Don't push me, or you'll be sorry," Joe threatened the man while snaking his arm across the other one's shoulder.

"I hope you have no interest in . . ." Reverend Jenkins's words broke into Hans's train of thought, then trailed off, as if he didn't want to voice the offending sins that occurred back between those buildings.

"No, sir. I don't abide by drink or, you know." Hans turned and saw a broad smile form on the reverend's face while heat swept over his own. He hoped his traveling companion would interpret the red creeping up his neck and not require him to finish his statement.

Reverend Jenkins pointed to the hill off to the left as they continued down Main Street. "That there is the church. You might hear the same tune on Sunday as you heard back there, but the words will be quite different. Quite different, indeed. And our piano sounds a mite better." He guffawed, having to wipe his eyes with his handkerchief. He used his other hand to wave at and greet a mother and her two daughters. Dorcas seemed to not need guidance. "Good day, Mrs. Kilpatrick. Girls."

Hans didn't have the heart to say he wouldn't likely know the tune no matter where played, as he didn't abide much by church either, but he kept silent. A weathered sign for Gray's Mercantile on the right caught his eye. Through the large window, he could see two elderly men sitting at a table, using the last rays of sunlight to play a game of checkers.

The reverend's horse slowed, and Hans figured they were nearing their destination. He was tired of being in the saddle and expected the older man to be weary as well. Dorcas stopped in front of a large two-story home at the end of town. A sign in the yard read, "Grammie's Boarding House."

"This here is my home away from home," the reverend said.

"Which pretty much means it's my home since I don't have one anywhere else. Mmm . . . something smells good. I bet Aideen's fixed a feast."

They led their horses to the trough, allowing them to drink their fill before tying them to the post out front. Hans helped the wobbly-legged man up the steps.

"Thank you, son. You've been a mighty fine companion on this trip. We can grab our gear later."

Before they could knock, the door swung open. An older woman, the high, full crown of her white mob cap askew, squealed in delight. Reaching up, she brushed her hair away from her face. Hans expected it had once been red but had faded into a rose gold. Using her apron, she wiped her aged hands.

"I be hoping you'd make it for supper, Reverend. Made your favorite. Who be your friend?"

Without waiting for a reply, she turned toward Hans, her ruddy complexion making it impossible to tell if her cheeks were that color from exertion or if her skin was always that red. The robust woman extended a hand that Hans took without thinking.

"Hope you're hungry, young man. We've a fine meal ready, and no one to eat it. Stagecoach didn't come again today."

Without releasing his grip, she pulled him forward and into the house, leaving the reverend to navigate on his own.

"Don't worry about me, Aideen, I'll be right there." The reverend chuckled as if the occurrence were not unusual.

"Katie, me darling girl, we be having guests for dinner," Aideen called.

Hans heard a crash of metal. His eyes widened, but Aideen seemed not to be bothered by the noise.

"Reverend, show this young man where he might wash off the dirt." She turned to Hans with a look he remembered his mother using when she was all business. "You'll be staying here for the night."

It wasn't a question, but he felt compelled to answer. "I'm low on coin at the moment."

Hands on her hips, eyebrows raised, she took in the length, or rather the breadth, of him. "Can you work?"

"Yes, ma'am."

"Then we've a deal. I be needing wood hauled in after dinner and more chopped for tomorrow."

"Yes, ma'am."

How had she done that? He had agreed before he'd even thought. Even at twenty-six years of age, Hans felt resentment at having been told what to do and suffocated under the thumb of another. He didn't have to trade work for room and board. He had money. He just needed to be frugal until he had a plan.

"Come on, boy. Best wash our hands, or she'll have you fixing the roof." The reverend's hand on his arm directed him to the stairs.

"That be another day, Reverend," Aideen called as she headed to the kitchen.

"Something sure smells good, Aideen. Sure does." Reverend Jenkins sat in a chair as if he owned it. Hans remained standing, mouth watering, as their hostess carried in a platter of meat, coated and floating in a rich gravy.

"How did you prepare a meal like this during these tough times?" Reverend Jenkins used his hand like a cup and moved the wafting scent closer to his nose. "I thought flour was still scarce, and this does not smell like wild game."

"Oh, we have our ways, Reverend." Aideen winked at Hans. "Sit, please, young man. Where are my manners? I'm Aideen, and this sweet thing be Kathleen Murphy. She prefers to go by Katie." A young woman carrying a large tureen in her arms pushed the door open with her backside.

The smirk he received from the newcomer before she headed back behind the door made him think of her as anything but sweet.

"She's a handful but a blessing all the same," Aideen said. "My sister should have named her Brigid in honor of Ireland's red-haired saint. Katie isn't what you'd call a patroness of hearth and home—more like giver of smart and sassy."

Hans blinked, and the reverend coughed into his napkin.

"Listen to an old woman blabbering. You know more about us than you'd probably care to." She looked from the table to the sideboard and back, never meeting his gaze. "My, I've not even asked your name."

"Hans. Hans Korhonen."

"Pleasure to make your acquaintance." Aideen moved

butter, salt, pepper, preserves, and honey from the sideboard to the table. "Your travels good?"

"Yes, ma'am."

"Weather cooperate?" Aideen lit the candles, the flame flickering when she jumped at the loud crash in the kitchen.

"Yes, ma'am," Hans answered.

"Ah, yes, the temperamental Missouri weather. You never know what mood it might be in today," Reverend Jenkins added.

"That be so, Reverend. Reminds me of a young woman I know." Aideen wiggled her eyebrows, and the reverend again covered a cough with his napkin. "Well, Hans, it's a pleasure to have you at our table."

"Thank you, ma'am."

"Oh, those sweet manners. I detect an accent. Are you from down south?"

"A small farm east of here," was his only reply.

"That's nice."

He watched as her distracted eyes roamed over the table to ensure nothing was missing, much like his own mother had done at each meal.

"Katie, please bring the bread," Aideen called to the closed door.

"Of course, Aunt Aideen," the young woman replied as she entered.

His gaze followed the golden-crusted bread, sliced thick, to the table. Not a single crumb moved with the gentle placement, not until the girl bumped the table as she plopped into the dining room chair across from him in a most unladylike manner. Back slouched against the chair, arms flopping as if the last bit of escaping air had left them limp, she sighed.

Wisps of fiery red hair stuck out beneath a mob cap not doing its job. A pretty pink tinged her cheeks, causing her freckles to dance across the bridge of her nose. She remained relaxed in her chair, a vivid portrayal of how tired she must be, until her penetrating green eyes met his.

Hans watched as Miss Murphy sat up in her chair, back straight, chin just so. Her slim finger moved the loose tendrils back into her mob cap, setting both her hair and fabric to rights. *Fascinating.* All the women he knew wore their hair in tight buns, but this hair seemed to have a mind of its own. He blinked, realizing he was staring. Her direct eye contact made him squirm in his seat like a schoolboy. She raised her eyebrows and placed her hands primly in her lap before settling back in her chair with an exaggerated casualness.

"Reverend, would you do the honor in the absence of me dearly departed, Paddy?" Aideen asked.

"But of course. Of course. It was a tremendous loss for us but a gain for heaven. Let us pray. Heavenly Father, we thank You for this fine food You've graced us with during this time of lean. May Your hand of mercy remain on these dear ladies. Thank You for this new friend at our table. In Your name, we pray. Amen."

"Áiméan," Aideen echoed.

Those green eyes stared at him the entire prayer, her face a mask. He wouldn't have bowed his head anyway, but he hadn't been able to pull his gaze from hers, mesmerized by her perfect balance of haughtiness and mischief.

The clinking of silver on dishes broke the spell, as did the slight smile that crept onto Katie's face before she turned a full smile on Reverend Jenkins and asked him to pass the potatoes, interrupting him from the beginning of another of his stories.

"Do you have plans to stay, Mr. Korhonen?" Aideen asked.

"Hans, please, ma'am. I don't rightly know." Hans watched the reverend's fork stop just shy of his mouth as his gaze darted Hans's way.

"Well, nothing like a good meal and night's sleep to help make your decision," Aideen said.

The food was excellent. Edna made a decent pot roast, yet, as stingy as she was about most things, she over-salted everything. The thought of home transported Hans back to his brothers. Every meal at Johann's table had been stilted, not full of talking like this meal. He wondered how he could already feel so comfortable at a stranger's table when he'd never once felt this way after Edna had arrived and taken over their household.

"Food to your liking, young man?" Aideen broke the silence.

It took him a moment to realize she was talking to him. "Yes. Thank you, ma'am." He took another bite of the meat. It wasn't gamey, but it wasn't veal. "This is good. I can't quite place the cut." His tone held a question as he lifted his gaze to ask what it was, but he saw the slight shake of his host's head and her eyes flitting over to the reverend, who was slicing his meat.

"Aideen, how do you get your swiss steak so tender?" the reverend asked. "You must have pounded it for hours. And wherever did you get the flour?"

"Buttermilk. It's the secret to most things. We save the flour for our bread. This I made with ground chestnuts." Aideen used her fork to point to the meat on the reverend's plate. "That be the rich, nutty flavor you be tasting."

Hans watched as Katie nearly choked on the bite in her mouth, most likely caused by her exaggerated eye roll. He examined his meat more closely.

"Mighty fine. I can always count on a good meal when I'm here." Reverend Jenkins continued chewing as he slathered creamy butter on a thick slice of bread before using it to sop up the gravy from the meat.

Hans kept his head lowered, his focus on chewing, but chanced a glance at the woman across from him. Katie moved her large amount of food around on her plate, speared a beet, and looked at it before putting it in her mouth as if it were a chore. She cut the meat, turning her fork over and back before wrinkling her nose and putting it in her mouth. He struggled not to laugh as her face contorted before she swallowed with what appeared to be great difficulty.

"Sorry, Paul." Katie wiped her mouth.

Paul? Hans wondered who that might be. Someone vying for her hand, perhaps? She was a pretty sight.

Aideen spoke up, her voice a little louder than necessary since they were seated in such close proximity to each other. "Katie made us a wonderful apple pie with raisins for dessert."

"Wonderful! Marvelous! I always look forward to dessert," was Reverend Jenkins's exuberant reply. "Apple. My, I haven't had an apple pastry in quite some time. Would you pass the butter, please? I believe I'll try a slice of this bread. It looks wonderful, and I haven't had fresh bread in a day or two."

Watching Katie's eyes nearly disappear into her mob cap was entertaining and mesmerizing. The green glinting in the light from above the table was almost hypnotic. He covered his groan with a cough. It would do no good to get under this woman's spell. It bothered him that he'd been taken in by those green eyes so easily when he should be focusing on the fact that Reverend Jenkins hadn't remembered Edna's apple turnover at lunch or that he'd already had a slice of Aideen's bread.

"Are you quite all right, Mr., I mean, Hans?" Aideen asked.

"Oh, yes, ma'am."

"We really must work on increasing your vocabulary." She winked at him before turning toward her neighbor. "Katie here comes from Ireland. I've known her to have quite the vocabulary on occasion."

Hans noted the slight pause and glance shared between the two women. Katie did not try to join the conversation.

"She's me sister's child. Been with me nigh unto six months."

Hans looked between the two women until Aideen made a motion with her head. It took a moment before he realized she was encouraging him to engage in conversation with his tablemate. The meat sat like a rock in his stomach, and he worked his brain to come up with something to say. Something about this girl had him tongue-tied.

"Miss Murphy, do you like it here?" He immediately knew he had asked the wrong question when she huffed before allowing her fork to clatter against the plate.

"No, Mr. Korhonen. I would na say I like it here. Ta be fair, I dunna enjoy most things in life. 'Tis nothing to do in this town but cook, clean, and make idle conversation with people who arna interested in listenin'. Iffen they were, they would have asked a more fascinatin' question."

Her sassy tone would have had his mother pulling her up by the hair and washing her mouth out with lye soap. He remained motionless, the only sound the plop of gravy as it hit his plate from the bite that had not yet made it to his still-open mouth. Her Irish brogue sure came out when she was mad. He'd have to remember that.

"Did I ever tell you the story of when sweet Thomas first came to Shumard Oak Bend?" Reverend Jenkins took over the conversation.

Hans was thankful for the interruption and watched as Katie took a moment to close her eyes, draw in and release a haggard breath, then resume eating. He focused his attention on the head of the table where the older man recalled a story with great detail.

"And the moment Thomas saw her, he ran straight into the arms of his Grammie." Reverend Jenkins turned to Hans. "That was the original owner of this here boarding house. No one called her Widow Brooks after that. When asked how Thomas knew she was his Grammie, the child told them God had shown him a picture of Grammie before they'd ever arrived." The reverend took a sip of coffee, which Aideen had refilled during the telling of the story. "Thank you, Aideen. Grammie loved that boy and his father like they were her own kin. Never saw anything like it. That child can still hear the voice of God nearly as well as Grammie did once upon a time."

"Grammie was a blessing to us all," Aideen replied as she shook her head.

"Dinner was delicious, as always, Aideen." Reverend Jenkins patted his now-bulging stomach. "Miss Katie, the apple pie had just the right number of raisins and amount of molasses. I sure do miss cakes, but with the shortage of sugar, I don't suppose we'll be having any of that in the foreseeable future. Mighty thankful for this cup of coffee, though. Mighty thankful." He sipped the hot brew.

"Thank you for a wonderful dinner, Mrs.—" Hans said before being interrupted.

"Just Aideen, young man." She winked at Hans.

"Yes, ma'am. I appreciate this fine meal." He stood and reached to gather his plates.

"Oh, no, you don't. Me Katie girl will take care of it."

His eyes grew wide when he saw Katie's lips move between her teeth as if she were working hard to refrain from speaking.

It appeared he wasn't the only one tired of taking orders and blindly following someone else's rules.

"Well then, I'd be happy to assist with the wood you mentioned," Hans offered.

"Not on a full stomach," Aideen said. "You head out and get your things, and then I'll show you to your room. The reverend here will show you where to put your horse."

"I'll make sure the barn, I mean the stalls, are clean and ready." Katie bolted from her chair, grabbing only her plate on her way.

Hans noted she'd eaten little even though she'd served herself a substantial portion. Hans reached to help Aideen gather plates and silver from the table.

"No, no. I've got this. When you're finished with the horses, you'll rest a spell in the parlor before starting on that wood." She swatted at his hand then startled as the kitchen door slammed.

"Yes, ma'am." Hans heard Aideen's soft laughter at his reply as she moved into the kitchen. He really needed to work on his responses.

"Come now, boy. Let's get our gear, then see to our friends." The reverend took the last gulp of his coffee before releasing a contented sigh and securing the button he'd undone on his jacket during dinner. "Mighty fine coffee. Mighty fine."

Chapter 11

Shumard Oak Bend

S weat dripped from Hans's brow, and his chest glistened in the waning light. He'd catch a chill if he stopped, so he kept on chopping. May in Missouri could bring cold temperatures at night. The hard work of chopping wood wasn't an issue. He'd worked hard all his life. And although he preferred to whittle, this chore was necessary work, and he'd earn his keep.

He mulled over the story the reverend had told of the boy he called Thomas and wondered if this could be the same precious child he'd befriended years ago when a young family had stopped at their farm. He thought he'd remembered that boy's last name being Trexler, not Shankel, as the reverend had said. If it was the same boy, it would be a pleasure catching up with him if they crossed paths.

Not crossing paths with Joe was another thing. Joe had been a thorn in his side from the moment the vile man had half-carried his brother into camp. Joe had singled out Hans and seen him as the sole reason his brother had died, taunting him every time Hans had passed the fenced-in holding area they'd used for a makeshift jail.

"Couldn't handle a rifle, boy? Yellow-bellied sapsucker. Too chicken to fight like a man? Had to hide as a lowlife away from the action, huh? Imbecile. Why, I've got dogs smarter than you."

Cruel words, aimed directly at him, filled his mind. Joe had remained shackled in the makeshift prison at the field hospital until he'd been transported to Gratiot Street Prison in St. Louis. Yet somehow, he'd ended up in Shumard Oak Bend.

Hans swung the ax with more force. *Thump.* Sounds still filled his thoughts. *Thwack.* The ax connected harder than necessary with the standing wood at each blow. Joe's repeated words ran through his mind with each chop. *Worthless. Stupid. Lazy. Maggot. Waste of space. Cow dung.* He sank the ax into the stump, shoulders slumping in defeat. He felt those words deeply and struggled not to believe them.

Maybe staying here wasn't the best idea. He should go farther west, maybe Oregon. No one would know him there. Memories surfaced of the night he'd almost run, almost become a deserter.

Hans removed his gloves and placed them on the chopping block. With his hands on his trim waist, his thumbs massaged his muscles as he leaned back to stretch. His finger grazed over the scar Joe had left between two of his ribs. By standing up to the man, he'd created more problems for himself. Some in the camp had seen him as the hero who'd taken down an armed Confederate. Others had spread rumors that he wasn't right in the head and that was why he'd roamed the camp at night. Either way, he'd had enough and had been more than happy when the war had been over and he'd been able to return home.

Only, home wasn't the same. He had gone from one militant experience to another under General Edna's rule. He hadn't been in Shumard Oak Bend but for a few hours and already he'd started allowing others to push him around and decide for him.

He could leave in the morning. It wasn't like he'd set down roots here. He would miss the good food but had survived for years on less. He could do it again. One town was like another, but he'd miss the reverend.

Two emerald-green eyes flickered in his mind while a slow smile grew over his face. Aideen's niece was pleasant to look at when she wasn't scowling or spouting off something terse. That Katie had been pure vinegar at supper. She likely had somebody who was sweet on her. Paul? Even if she had a beau, they could still be friends, right?

A full smile formed. He could return the sass if that was what she wanted. Well, he could if he ever got his tongue to work in her presence. He'd had lots of time to learn from Edna. His mother would have quoted a proverb about catching more flies with honey than with vinegar. But since he wasn't trying to catch anything, he just might give back what she was dishing out. Just because his brothers were stoic didn't mean he had to be.

Who was he kidding? Skunks didn't change their stripes. They just left disasters in their wake. Just like him. The foul stench of past failures permeated his mind before his nostrils filled with the reek of unwashed bodies, decay, and death. He pushed the memories down, burying them deep. He'd been apathetic, never making friends with his comrades and washing his hands of war before heading back home, only to leave his brother, the best friend he'd ever had, as well. He shivered, not sure if it was caused by his thoughts or the fact that he'd stood still in the cooling night air too long.

After wriggling his tired fingers back into the smooth leather of his worn gloves, he placed another log on the chopping block and took a deep breath. With one swing, he split the log in two. His mind drifted. Those emerald-green eyes, blazing red hair, and freckles that danced on the bridge of a pert nose floated in front of him. Her fairy-like features had an almost ethereal quality.

Breathe, swing, chop. Breathe, swing, chop. Over and over, Hans repeated the process, his mind fluctuating between those eyes and those freckles. His breathing still labored, he filled his arms with wood and stacked it neatly on the now-growing pile near the kitchen door.

Nothing had changed since leaving home. He had immediately done what Aideen had asked, just like he'd done for Edna—just like he had done for his military superiors. Only, Aideen's words had been kind, her request almost uplifting as she'd focused on what he could do. Unlike Edna's harsh tone and demeaning words, Aideen made him feel needed, important. Her gentle tone was a balm for his hurting soul.

"I'm still following orders."

Breathe, swing, chop.

"Still doing what I'm told without standing up for myself or my dreams."

Breathe, swing, chop.

His back and arms ached as he took out his frustration on the log before him. Would he ever be his own man?

"I'll make my own decisions from here on out."

Breathe, swing, chop.

Why had he gone back to Johann's after the war? He should have set out then, knowing nothing about Edna would ever change.

Breathe, swing, whack.

The ax deflected off the stump, skidding to a halt in the dirt.

Tired. He was so tired. He was tired of doing everyone else's bidding. Tired of living under another's rule. Tired of lying to himself that he could change. Tired of being tired.

Hans rubbed his hands through his gloves before removing them. A blister had formed on his palm. The once-well-fitting gloves now rubbed his hands raw. Using his shirt to dry his chest, he felt his ribs sticking out. Tonight's meal had him feeling full for the first time in years. He could use a few more of those meals.

Hans shrugged into his shirt, picked up the ax, and sank it into the block. It needed a good sharpening. He'd do that tomorrow—if he stayed.

Chapter 12

Shumard Oak Bend

hat's got your attention, Katie girl?"

Katie felt Aideen peek over her shoulder and out the window at the fine specimen of a man arching his back and rubbing at the taut muscles. Katie supposed even an old woman could appreciate the view, but she did not respond, even though Aideen waited several moments.

"Quite a handsome young man."

Katie flinched at Aideen's words but remained quiet.

"Mmm. Ar chaill tú do chuid cainte?" Aideen teased, her Irish homeland's words flowing easily from her tongue.

Katie turned her head, eyes sending daggers. "No, Aunt. I did not lose my ability to speak. Good-looking or not, he is no different from any other man."

"Ach. Do you know many, lass?"

"Enough to know there isn't a man out there with enough sense to use the brains God gave him."

"Katie, girl. What's got you all riled up?"

Whirling on her aunt, Katie spoke more forcefully than planned. "They all lie and have no backbone. A man cannot make a decision and stick to it or his family."

"Ach. Your Uncle Paddy were no such man."

Katie saw the change in Aideen's eyes. Was she wrong to base her view of men on her absentee father? She broke eye contact with Aideen and turned back to the window, this time averting her gaze from the figure and doing her best to focus on the waning light in the distance.

"Not all men are the same, Katie."

Katie melted under the hand that now rested on her shoulder, her fight gone. She needed to remember she was a guest in this home.

"I best be telling that young man to head on in." Grabbing her shawl, Aideen headed out. "Goodness, but this door be needing a fresh coat of paint."

Katie stood at the window, watching Aideen and Hans deep in discussion. Her hand brushed away the stray wisps on her warm face, the realization that she found Hans to be a fine-looking man causing her to blush. Her father had been handsome once, too, according to her mother. Katie only remembered his wrinkled, ruddy skin, flushed cheeks, and wet eyes peeking out from beneath puffy lids.

When he'd been sober, he had been congenial but prone to

lying, which often made for entertaining tales but generated a lack of trust. No man she knew had enough backbone to stand up to the wrongs she had endured in Ireland. Even the landlord had made false promises, then skulked away like a beat dog when the Guardians of the Peace of Ireland had applied pressure. Katie winced when she pulled her hair in agitation. *No. Ireland is no longer home.* Missouri, America, was her home now, and she would make something of herself here.

Home. She felt loved and appreciated in Aideen's house, but could she consider it her own? She had always lived in rented hovels, several since they'd needed to move frequently and usually in the middle of the night. Home was the place where those she loved and cared for gathered.

Katie thought of the child now sheltered in the barn. Sam's small hands were so dirty a single washing would not remove their stain. Just this afternoon, those small hands had tugged at her skirt.

"Miss Katie, I'm hungry." Even now the remembrance of the boy's pleading eyes wrenched her heart.

Katie brushed at her skirt. She thought of the children and widows she had already helped. These people she secretly cared for were the ones who gave her a genuine sense of home. Seeing a need and fulfilling it gave Katie purpose and made her feel valued. Even if no one else saw her that way, she knew her solitary efforts were making a difference.

Anger stirred in her soul as she remembered the conversation with Mrs. Olivia Branch. Would this be the only way she could help the children? But what about their mothers? No. She was sure there had to be another way. Her muscles tensed, and she narrowed her eyes. She would do this her way. Aideen's words flashed through her mind, reminding her to seek God.

Katie moved to the settee, pulled the large family Bible into her lap, and opened to the verse Aideen had read the night before from Psalm 138. Marking the page was a blue-tatted cross. She knew the dainty piece had taken her aunt hours to create. She fingered the item before locating the verse she sought.

"In the day when I cried thou answeredst me, and strengthenedst me with strength in my soul." The verse had been on her mind since last night. Defiance changed to submission as she kneeled before the soft velvet cushion of the settee.

"God, I know you understand the desire of my heart." Katie poured her heart out to the Lord. "There are so many obstacles. Please, Lord, make a way. Give me the strength You've promised." There was no doubt God heard her prayer, and she knew He would answer it how He desired—and in His timing.

God's presence permeated the room. Katie quieted, listening for that still, small voice she knew was His. Silence filled the room and seeped into her heart. Why wasn't God answering? Knees sore, she stood and looked to the ceiling, searching for anything from God. She huffed when He continued His silence.

"If others in this community don't want to join in on blessing Your children, then that's their loss. I don't need approval or permission from anyone but You which You've given." She felt pricked in her spirit but continued. "I have a mission to accomplish, and You will provide the strength I need." Katie nodded her head once, letting God know she'd take it from here.

"Áiméan."

"Hans. You've earned more than your keep tonight, young man."

From the corner of his eye, Hans saw movement in the window. He wondered how long Katie had been standing there and secured the last button on his shirt before replying to Aideen.

"Yes, ma'am. Let me stack these last few pieces."

"I have a proposition since you haven't decided if you're staying or going."

She had his full attention, and his hostess hesitated only a moment before continuing.

"I've a need for some work a man of your strength and skill could easily do. Since you said at dinner you were looking, I'm offering. I'll give you a job without pay in exchange for room and board for one month. You'll need feed for your horse, but he's free to stay in the barn and roam in the pasture. I figure it'll give you time to seek employment in town or decide if you want to be moving on."

"Well, that's a generous offer. It would be foolish of me to turn you down." Hans surprised himself with the quick response, especially after all the contemplating he'd just done.

"Glory be! The Lord has smiled down on us this day."

Hans watched her jubilant expression turn firm as her facial features showed the words that followed would be all business.

"You'll need to abide by our house rules as a long-term guest. We don't tolerate drink or coarse language. No carousing, and you'll keep us informed if you'll not be at a meal." She paused. "I know I'm missing something." Her right finger tapped her temple.

"Yes, ma'am. I can easily keep those rules. I'll be no trouble to you."

"Then head on in, and we'll discuss what I be needing done, and you can begin first thing tomorrow."

"Yes, ma'am. I'll be right in."

A smile split his face. He finished stacking the cut wood and cleaned up the area. He slowed and mentally kicked himself. He had done it again. He'd not even given her offer more than a fleeting thought. What was wrong with him?

Hans cleaned the ax and looked at the dull blade. He guessed he'd be making a to-do list of his own. After brushing bits of wood and bark from his shirt, Hans headed to the barn to return the used items to their proper home. He needed to think of this as a temporary stay while he figured things out. In the dim light of the barn, he heard a rustling sound. Rauti made a low rumble in his chest.

"Is that you making all that ruckus, Rauti?"

Dorcas responded with a pleasant neigh. Hans shook his head and laughed.

"Rauti, you usually don't make friends with other horses,

but it appears you might have taken a liking to the docile Dorcas." Hans patted Rauti's neck. "Well, boy, looks like we've had some good fortune. How'd you like to stay here for a bit?"

The horse bobbed his head and snorted, turning it toward Dorcas as if to ask if she'd be staying, too. The laughter that bubbled up inside Hans was genuine and refreshing.

"She's a bit old for you, friend."

Dorcas responded by chattering her teeth like a young mare.

"You are something else, Dorcas. If I didn't know better, I'd think you understand every word I say."

Rauti blew out, loud and long, and it looked like the horse rolled his eyes.

"Well, boy. We've been offered a place to stay until we decide what the future holds. We just have to follow the rules. That means you need to be nice to this gal." He reached for the mare. Dorcas matched the light touch he placed on her muzzle with equal pressure.

"Following rules is something I've done all my life. I'm sure we'll do just fine. Besides, we can do anything for a month, right, boy?" He returned his focus to Rauti, who shook his head back and forth as if Hans had missed something.

"Do you know something I don't?" Hans scratched the stubble on his chin with his free hand and wondered if he'd just gotten himself into something he hadn't intended. "It's only for a month."

A new life was about to begin for him. He'd never been on his own, having gone from his father's home in Finland to his eldest brother's after months of travel to America. He was free to make his own choices now. He would take a month to see if he liked this town, but if he didn't, he'd move on. The thought was freeing and frightening, and the magnitude of the future weighed on his mind.

Hans secured the door to the barn, his past now behind and the uncertain future ahead.

Chapter 13

Shumard Oak Bend

"**N**o time for woolgathering, Katie dear. I'm expecting the stagecoach today. We need to be preparing for guests." Aideen's words were not cross but held a note of authority.

Katie did not move from the window. She lifted her hand to the hollow of her neck, missing the feel of her mother's necklace. She'd used it to pay for her freedom, but how would she pay for the care of the children?

The two women worked well together—little talk, much action—but today was different, with Aideen going on about mundane things more than usual. Katie usually didn't mind the chatter. It kept her mind as busy as her hands. Today she felt distracted and would have appreciated the silent camaraderie. She wiped the already-clean work area. "How many do you expect today?"

"Never know. There always seems to be a top rider ready to be fed. I'd feed them a hot meal, but it seems they either don't have the coin or don't feel comfortable at the dining room table. We'll make extra biscuits and fill them with bacon or ham if needed. That and some ginger switchel is not but a few cents. Surely riding atop that stagecoach warrants sustenance of some sort."

"I have no ginger, and there is only one lemon."

"You'll need to use the essence of lemon to make lemonade. It will be tart with minimal sugar, but I'll add molasses cookies to the list today. You know, I may have you take a few to the Gray sisters. The dear souls don't get out much anymore, and molasses is good for the bones."

Katie mixed the lemonade and placed it aside to allow the rough, granulated sugar to dissolve. The heavy mixing bowl made a clunk on the wooden surface. She began adding ingredients to the large bowl for bread.

"No answer?"

"I'm sorry. Did you ask me something?"

"I was telling you about how the sisters came to this fair town. Well-respected business owners, they were. I figured you'd have something to say about that."

"Didn't the sisters own the mercantile?" Katie asked.

"That they did."

"Isn't that unusual? Women owning such a business?"

"Well, now." Aideen stopped stirring. "I suppose so, but those two had powerful minds and stronger wills."

"But the magistrate. Didn't he . . . ?" Katie wasn't sure what she was asking.

"The magistrate hadn't arrived in town yet. The sisters gave him what for, and he knew where he stood. Those two could make a man cower; they could. But as they aged, it got harder to keep up with the store. They began praying God would send just the right family to take it over."

"The Taylors?"

"One and the same. George and Nancy Taylor, the new owners of Gray's Mercantile, were once weary travelers headed farther west. Mrs. Taylor needed a break from their journey and asked to stay and rest for a week. Being one of six people, two of them children, wedged into the metal box of a coach and sitting on wooden benches for days on end had been more than she could endure."

Katie understood being cramped and exhausted. It had been a long trip to Shumard Oak Bend for her as well, and she'd also crossed the ocean.

"After a week of hot meals and clean facilities, Mrs. Taylor had started praying right out loud for God to change her husband's stubborn heart. I had never heard such caterwauling, beseeching God to keep her out of what she called 'godforsaken country.'" Aideen laughed.

Katie couldn't imagine the reserved woman raising her voice, let alone wailing before God.

"Somewhere between the prayers, the meals, me hospitality, and the news that one of the Gray sisters had taken ill, Mr. Taylor agreed to remain an additional week until the next stage passed." Aideen put her finger under her nose to mimic the man's mustache. "It'll give me time to see if Gray's Mercantile is worth purchasing or if we be needing to go farther west to establish our business." Aideen snorted, and flour from her finger puffed in front of her.

"Mrs. Taylor, now, she struck a bargain with the sisters before sunset. The Taylors sent for their belongings by week's end, helped the sisters move into a right modest home behind Main Street, and took over the mercantile and their new home above the store. They've been here just over a year now, and Mrs. Taylor and I, well, we became instant friends, her and I. I figured if she be able to change a man's mind that quickly, I might learn a thing or two."

Why couldn't things with the magistrate fall into place like that for me? Katie's hand mixed the flour into the pool of liquid in the center of the bread bowl without thinking. She'd done it thousands of times, giving her mind more time to wander.

She wanted to establish an orphanage for needy children and provide a place of employment for women suffering from the effects of war. Why couldn't Magistrate Marley see the benefits, the possibility? She glanced at her aunt, who tested the split-pea soup before adding a pinch more salt. At least she had Aunt Aideen, who had generously taken her under her wing. Otherwise, she'd be in the same predicament as those she desired to help.

"Knead that dough anymore, and it will be tough as leather." Aideen's watchful eye had not missed the memorized motions Katie performed.

"Right. Woolgathering, as you say." Katie felt a sadness she couldn't describe. "Mama was strong once. Like the Gray sisters."

"Be thinking of Bridget?" Aideen used her apron to wipe her eyes even before tears had formed. "I miss me dear sister, too. She were a tough one; you're right." At Katie's nod, Aideen placed a work-worn hand on her niece's pushed-up sleeve. "You look like her, you know."

Katie returned the dough to the large ceramic bowl and, like when placing a shroud, covered it with a towel. She remembered her mother's final years as sickly, but then, at present, she also felt old and worn out, especially in spirit. She pulled the rough linen cloth from her apron waistband and removed the remnants of flour and dough from her hands.

Aideen reached out again and took the now-clean hand. "Come, let's sit fer a spell with a cup of tea while the dough rises. I've something to show you."

Katie poured the tea and placed the cups on the table as Aideen returned with a small book covered in deep red velvet. Katie wiped the last of the flour from the table's surface.

Aideen sat and exhaled, low and long. "This is one of me most treasured possessions. When your ma, me dear sister, learned of your coming, we knew life would change. We were poor, but I had a few coins tucked away since I was about to be wed. I used one of them to have this done." Aideen turned to the center page of the book. There, in a coal drawing, was the exact likeness of Katie.

Katie reached up and touched the hair slipping from her mob cap, recognizing the same flowing curls. She imagined the color of the hair in the image as her own. The bright eyes and smiling faces of the two girls, however, did not feel like hers. Those faces held genuine happiness, even joy, something Katie did not possess.

"See those smiles? It weren't because we were happy about our circumstances. I'd be journeying in a few days for America with me Pádraig and leaving me pregnant sister behind. She were but a child herself. She could not work in her condition, and your father was mostly absent. Me heart ached more than I can express."

"Then why the smiles?"

"Because we be knowing God were in control. We chose to have joy in our present circumstances rather than dwell on all that were wrong around us." Aideen pointed to a figure in the background. "See that boy sitting in the tree? That be your Uncle Martin. He were always where he weren't supposed to be. This one time, I were thankful he disobeyed. The boy made all manner of noises from that tree, and the artist felt compelled to capture the true spirit of the moment. He died not two weeks later after being overrun by a bull in a neighbor's field." Aideen's finger touched the drawing as if she could still feel the boy's presence.

"What of the rest of my kin? I thought we were alone."

"That you be. Bridget had nary a choice but to farm out the rest of our siblings. I'll always feel bad about leaving her with the responsibility. With our parents gone, there be no way to support anyone but herself and you. The oldest boys, Rayland and Farrell, left of their own accord. We never heard from them again. Jaxcy and Ida be old enough to get jobs in the landlord's kitchen." Aideen's hand reached over and patted Katie's. She spoke with a reverent tone. "Your mother did something very difficult because she loved you and believed in you, Kathleen."

Other than her mother, few used her given name. Tears formed, their wetness marring the table's surface as they fell unbidden.

"Why?" Katie figured Aideen thought she meant, "Why did all this happen?" But what Katie really wondered was, *Why would anyone believe in me when I'm not certain I believe in myself?*

Chapter 14

Sunday

Shumard Oak Bend

"This is the day the Lord has made," the reverend said with more energy and enthusiasm than Hans thought possible before a cup of coffee. Sitting in the chair at the head of the table, the man tucked his napkin into his collar.

"Let us rejoice and be glad in it." Aideen's cheerful reply was more than Hans could manage this early.

Hans nursed his coffee as Katie placed a plate of eggs, cornbread, thick-cut bacon, and fried potatoes before him. He reached for his fork, ready to dig in as the smells overtook his senses.

"Hans, would you do the honor of blessing our food on the Lord's Day?" Reverend Jenkins's eyes were keen and clear this morning.

Hans squirmed. To refuse would not be wise. Hans knew the

conscious act of prayer before a meal showed gratitude to God, whom many believed sustained them and provided for their needs. Hans knew the hard labor needed to put this meal on the table. It had not been God who had supplied it, but many hands that had toiled for long hours. As a guest in this home, he decided it was more important to keep the peace than stand by his convictions.

"Yes, sir," he responded before hearing what he thought was an audible sigh from Aideen. He caught Katie's gaze before bowing his head. *Hypocrite*, her eyes seemed to say. He lowered his without closing them.

"Lord, we thank You for this food these ladies have prepared." He paused, wracking his brain, unsure what else to say. He tried to rephrase the haughty prayers Edna had said over their meals, but nothing seemed appropriate. Deciding there was nothing else to add, he finished with an "amen."

He stared at his food. He was only three days away from home, and he'd already succumbed to the rules and wishes of another household. Would he never be his own man?

"Your eggs be gettin' cold."

Aideen's words entered the discussion in his mind. He looked at her and smiled before he took a heaping bite of the fluffy eggs, but they tasted like sand in his mouth. Hans knew neither what he wanted nor who he was. So much for opening the door to a new beginning. He had already slipped back into following the path others set before him.

"What will your sermon be, Reverend?"

Aideen's question had Hans's full attention. It was Sunday.

He hadn't been to a church service since he was a boy. Edna always required them to gather on Sundays for Bible reading and singing, but it was not the same.

"Encountering God. Speaking of which, as soon as I've finished this fine meal, I need to make my way over to the church and encounter Him myself." He chuckled lightly. "I always like to pray over the seats of each of my parishioners. You never know when the Lord will speak to someone's heart, and I want to extend an invitation to our Lord on this day He has created."

The man spoke of God as if He were a personal friend. Inviting God to anything never crossed Hans's mind. His hand moved over his shirt, checking to see if it was clean enough to wear to the service. He lifted his head, about to say something, when Katie spoke.

"You're dressed just fine." She raised a single eyebrow the same way her aunt might have.

He looked at her, and, if he could read her mind like she apparently could his, he would have guessed she was saying, "If I have to go, so do you." If he were a betting man, he'd guess this was the rule Aideen had forgotten the night he'd arrived.

"You are right, Miss Katie. Absolutely right." Reverend Jenkins turned from Katie to Hans. "We do not worry about our outward appearance here, son. Just like the Bible says, 'For man looketh on the outward appearance, but the Lord looketh on the heart.' The heart is all that matters. Yes, sir. All that matters."

Hans sighed inwardly. That was even worse.

Aideen must know every person in Shumard Oak Bend. There were more people in this town than Hans had first realized, certainly more churchgoers than he'd expected. His hand hurt from greeting each one, and he hadn't yet made it inside the building. He had dodged the magistrate but had still answered more questions than he'd thought possible.

His gaze swept over the area before the trio headed up the steps and through the wide double doors, at which point he glanced back. The horses at the hitching posts and those hobbled in the field farther out hinted at a full church service today. Wouldn't this crowd surprise his war buddy? A few men wearing tattered and repaired Confederate gray walked with canes or crutches, evidence of the war's effect on the town and reminders to Hans that Missouri had been a slave state.

Sweat ran down his neck into his worn collar. It wasn't hot inside the multi-use building with the windows open. Yet even with a cool breeze circulating the air, Hans was uncomfortable. He sat on the long bench seat, wedged between the wall and Aideen. There would be no escaping at this point.

Katie sat on Aideen's other side, her hands visible as she smoothed the fabric of her blue floral frock. Could she be just as uncomfortable as he? Mesmerized, he watched as she picked at the cuticle of a clean nail before clutching her hands together. Red tendrils fell around her graceful neck. His mouth went dry. He straightened his spine and focused on those in front of him.

Hans felt a brush against his back and turned slightly to

see a young man standing just behind their row. The scrawny lad turned his cap in his hands as if contemplating something important before sitting on the bench behind them. The brief look let him know the young man had eyes only for Katie. Could this be the Paul Katie had mentioned under her breath at dinner? If they were courting, wouldn't he walk her to church? It seemed odd, but then, Hans didn't know how these things worked here.

A well-dressed couple with two children, not quite teens, walked to the front and sat. The boy turned in his seat twice before his mother poked him in the ribs. Hans put his hand to his mouth to keep from laughing, not quite succeeding. He remembered his mother doing the same to him in church.

"That be the new mercantile owner and his family," Aideen whispered.

A tall, lanky man passed their row with a plump woman at his side. Two young men followed behind and took up the first bench on the right.

Aideen leaned over, angling her head in the family's direction. "Sheriff Adkins and his sweet wife, Martha. The two young men are Thomas and Gabe. They come one week a month for schooling from Martha. She be our school teacher at present and doing a mighty fine job of it."

Hans squirmed in his seat. Being inside the church building was difficult enough, but keeping track of the names of the dozens he'd met made his head swim. He tried to remember the faces that went with the backs of the heads in front of him. He felt Aideen tug at his shirtsleeve and realized everyone was standing. Reverend Jenkins stood before the congregation, arms raised, head bowed.

"Let us pray. Lord, we invite You into our midst. We ask that You fill our hearts and minds with Your words, that You might transform us into Your likeness. May we encounter You in a fresh, new way today. Amen."

Hans remembered sitting and hearing an occasional murmur of the crowd, but he didn't recollect a single word Reverend Jenkins said in his sermon. The reverend's prayer had unnerved him.

There wasn't room for words from God in Hans's mind. His thoughts were full of hurtful, hateful remarks from Joe, images of disappointed faces from his military superiors, sounds of Edna's exasperated sighs, and thoughts of what others believed him to be. All these voices fought for prominence in his head, and none would transform him into the likeness of God. There would be no fresh, new thoughts today, just reminders of what he really was—worthless.

Yet, even at the thought, Hans realized today could be a new day. He was starting fresh with people who had been kind and opened their home and hearts to him. Still, could he do it? Could he leave the past behind and start new? Not likely. He was who he was. He'd made his choices.

When the congregation stood for the last prayer and the singing of the doxology, his hands felt clammy, and his mouth felt dry. He couldn't keep up this ruse of playing at being a believer in God. He was an imposter.

Chapter 15

Shumard Oak Bend

K atie wondered what Hans was thinking. Rocking forward on his toes, forearms crossed over his chest, he looked as if he were having a hard conversation with—God? Himself? Katie had no trouble letting her words out when she had something on her chest. From the looks of it, Hans needed a reprieve.

"Aunt." Katie leaned in toward Aideen, so the woman could hear her whisper. "I'm afraid I might have put too much wood in the stove and fear the roast will burn."

"I should probably go as well," Hans said.

Katie saw him poke his head around Aideen's other side.

"True. If Hans doesn't go with me, you'll both be late returning since everyone will be trying to greet him." Katie's eyes caught his for the briefest moment before focusing once again on her aunt. Now she knew her hunch was correct. He'd been uncomfortable throughout the service. His eyes told her he was miserable. It was the Christian thing to do. Right?

Giving him an out?

Without a verbal reply, Aideen motioned with her fingers for the two of them to go. Katie reached around her aunt and grabbed Hans's sweaty hand in hers. She dragged him past the others in their row, pulling him out the door at the back of the building. When she heard the last words of the doxology, she released his hand, lifted her skirts, and broke into a run. Her mother would have scolded her for the unladylike act.

"Last one home washes the dishes." She glanced back, noting Hans's eyes focused on the ankles peeking out from beneath her lifted skirt.

The loud choral "Amen" inside the church brought his eyes up to hers. Like a schoolboy, he broke into a full run.

Hair flying, chest heaving, Katie flew down the hill and turned onto the deserted Main Street. Images of racing her childhood schoolmates home from Mass crossed her mind, and she ran all the harder. Determined to be the winner of this race, she glanced behind to see Hans getting closer. She squealed as she lifted her skirts higher and ran faster.

An orange tabby sat placidly in the middle of the road, licking its paw, then paused as a flurry of blue floral barreled toward its bathing spot.

"Shoo!" Katie said as the cat sprawled out, as if making itself bigger and more in the way was a good idea. Katie jumped over the animal, who reached up, catching a claw in her petticoat. Katie felt more than heard tearing but did not slow down. She looked back in time to see Hans only a few steps behind. The cat darted between buildings with a cry, causing Hans to stumble and giving Katie a slight lead.

With only a few yards left, Hans overtook her. He hopped the steps with a deep intake of breath and opened the door in one fluid motion.

"My lady." He bowed and swung his arm in front of him as if ushering her inside. "I'll not be doing any dishes."

"You'd likely break something if you did." Katie lifted her chin and schooled her features but surmised the flush she felt in her cheeks did not match her curt tone. She swished past him, skirts still hiked higher than appropriate, before dropping them and smoothing the fabric.

Breathing hard from the run, Katie followed the direction of Hans's eyes. She smiled when she realized the focus was once again on the hem of her skirt, which now covered her ankles. Excitement rushed through her, pooling in her stomach, which growled. Her raised brows challenged Hans to comment on the sound. The smell of roasted meat drew them inside the large kitchen to a pile of clean dishes ready for the noon meal.

"Do you know how to set a table?" She covered the question in a sweet yet condescending tone.

"Of course," Hans replied and picked up the stack of plates.

She knew the moment he realized she'd tricked him, yet he continued and moved toward the table.

"How many will there be today?"

"The reverend, of course, and Martha, Henry, and the boys. That makes . . ." The tip of her pink tongue stuck out from the corner of her mouth. "Eight."

HEIDIGRAY MCGILL

"The boys? You mean Gabe and Thomas?"

"Yes. Why?"

He ducked his head. "Um, no reason. Just trying to remember names." He placed the fork on the wrong side of the plate and continued around the table.

Katie's fingers itched to correct the placement. She arranged the candlesticks near each end and put the salt, pepper, butter, and other condiments at the corners, saving room for the platters in the center.

"We'll need more chairs. Where are they?" he asked, not meeting her eyes.

"You'll find two more chairs hanging on the far wall of the barn."

Katie watched him retreat like a lone soldier being advanced upon by an army. *Maybe Aideen shouldn't have invited so many for dinner.* She'd noticed how uncomfortable he'd been with only a few conversations going on over previous meals. He would have a hard time keeping up with today's discussions. *Maybe it will scare him off*, she mused.

That might be for the best, especially since his presence threatened to distract her from her mission. There was also the issue of his past—he seemed to be running from something. And it was obvious he knew nothing about setting a table. Katie righted the silver.

Chapter 16

Shumard Oak Bend

The horses whinnied when Hans entered the cool structure. Air flowed through the loft door, and a shaft of light illuminated Rauti's stall. As Hans's eyes adjusted to the dark interior, he scanned the area for the chairs he'd come to collect. Dorcas remained still while Rauti bobbed his head back and forth, begging for attention.

"All right, boy. I'm coming." He walked the few steps to scratch Rauti's moving head. The horse stilled as soon as Hans's hand touched the smooth hair of his muzzle. "Good boy." His gentle tone echoed in the quiet. "I saw a familiar face at church today."

The horse's ears swiveled back and forth as if not wanting to miss a word. Dorcas stretched her neck around her stall to get as close as possible to the conversation.

"Do you remember a few years back when a young family stayed with us?" Rauti blinked. "You partook of a few of the lady's biscuits if my memory serves me right."

Rauti's long tongue reached toward Hans's hand. Laughing, Hans shook his head.

"I don't have any of those biscuits now, but if there is a treat left over from our meal today, I'll be sure to save something for you." Out of habit and nervous energy, he grabbed the pitchfork and began mucking the stalls.

"Well, it appears this is that family's town. I think they settled close to here." Hans placed the offending load into the wheelbarrow. "The boy, Thomas, is coming for the noon meal." Putting fresh straw in the stall, Hans continued his comfortable banter with his friend.

"I remember Thomas as inquisitive and a talker. But boys can be boys. One wrong word, and, well, let's just say it wouldn't do for him to put questions in people's minds or spread the news of my loyalties. This town seems to be full of Southern Sympathizers." Hans's sides swelled much like Rauti's did when danger approached. He released his breath, reminding himself he was free to leave. Nothing was holding him here.

Placing the pitchfork back on the wall hook, he spied the two chairs. His gaze moved from the chairs to the wide-open door. He could run now, escape the interaction with all these people, but Johann's words hung in the air.

"You are running from something. Korhonens face their fears."

"I'd best be getting what I came for before that spitfire gives me the stink eye."

Dorcas snickered, and Hans had to laugh right along with her. He might enjoy having those pretty eyes focused on him, no matter the reason.

Hans placed one chair outside and returned to get the other. He watched the horses with their heads together as if conspiring before moving to the opposite sides of their respective stalls. Hans felt like he had walked in on a private conversation about him.

He wondered if the townspeople were talking about him as they left the service. He hadn't lied to them. He had simply evaded some of their prying questions. Hans knew the Ten Commandments by heart and knew the eighth condemned lying.

"God is the author of all truth, Hans," he heard his mother's voice say as if she were speaking to him now. *"We are obligated as followers of our Lord to honor the truth. Never intentionally deceive another by speaking a falsehood or not speaking when the truth is needed."*

Hans felt heat creep up his neck. So much for keeping that commandment—and others. He hadn't even given a second thought to mucking the stalls on the Sabbath. And, if his thoughts of the red-haired sprite continued, he would be breaking another, at least in his mind. Hans ran his hand through his hair as his eyes followed the dust motes floating through the stream of light.

"You up there, God?" No sound followed. He hadn't expected one, but it would have been nice if he'd received instructions on what was forthcoming.

He needed some clear direction. Should he be forthright in sharing his loyalties? Should he tell Aideen he wasn't certain he would stay? Was deciding from day to day deceitful by not speaking up when he knew he was contemplating leaving?

Grabbing the second chair from the wall with more force than needed, Hans took one last look at the ceiling of the barn, as if God were glaring down at him.

"Expect nothing from me. You're not even listening."

Chapter 17

"Hans?"

Hans turned at the sound, the light coming in from the open barn doors causing him to squint. It only took a moment for his eyes to adjust. There stood Thomas, and Hans knew him immediately—those bright blue eyes so like his own and that wave of dark hair falling over his forehead. Only he was taller now.

"Hello, Thomas. My, how you've grown. How old are you now?" Hans longed to reach for the boy and embrace him as he had the day his family had left his brothers' homestead.

"Fourteen." The now-young man moved his arm from behind his back.

There in his hand was the cow Hans had whittled and given as a gift.

"I kept her, Hans."

If it embarrassed the boy that he still carried the trinket, it didn't show. The tail was missing, and the wood was smooth, showing how much the boy had loved the treasure.

"I missed you." Thomas took a step forward, his head cocked, his gaze roaming over Hans's frame. "You've lost weight. Were you in the war?"

"Yes."

"Confederate or Union?"

There it was. The direct question Hans had expected but had hoped would not come. His mother's words ran through his mind again. *Truth. Speak the truth.*

"Union." The word came out in a whisper.

Thomas made a slight nod before closing the distance. The boy extended his hand, and Hans took it. But when they connected, Thomas continued forward and wrapped his arm around his friend.

Hans enfolded Thomas. The absolute acceptance, not questioning, touched him deep in his soul. Was it really that easy? Would others be as understanding? Leave it to a child to show him the way. He hadn't needed to bother calling out to God after all.

Thomas closed the barn doors, and Hans picked up one chair and turned. The sun glinted off the badge of a tall man in front of him.

"I'm Henry Adkins. I apologize for not greeting you before church." He reached over and placed a large hand on Thomas's shoulder. "We were running a few minutes behind today."

The hand Hans shook was much larger than his own, and the grip held as much meaning as the man's eyes.

"I've already forgotten most of the names," Hans admitted, "so meeting you now, I'll remember yours."

"What brings you to these parts?"

Truth, speak the truth. The man only wanted clarity. It was natural to ask such questions of a newcomer to town and less unusual since the one asking was the sheriff.

"My brothers have both married, and it was time I made my own way, a new beginning. I'm hoping to find work and sell a two-wheeled cart I've designed. Well, technically, my brother Johann designed it while I crafted it." Nervousness had him blabbering like an old woman.

"I'd like to see that, but I know better than to be late for dinner." He leaned in. "Don't eat the pound cake. Fair warning, my friend."

His conspiratorial wink set Hans's nerves at ease.

"I carried it, and it's a fair bit heavier than a pound. I thanked Mrs. Swanson just the same for her generous gift. She brings me something every Sunday in exchange for my keeping her husband locked up over the weekend. But that's another story." The man's good-natured laugh drained away the last of the stress Hans felt.

"Can I carry one chair for you?" Thomas moved toward the well-crafted item.

"That would be great, little man," Hans said.

Thomas beamed at the familiar term of endearment before hefting the chair and moving to the house. Hans followed, his resolve firm to speak the truth in all things from here on out.

Hans leaned back in his chair, his waistband feeling a mite bit tighter than earlier in the day. He had not heeded the sheriff's warning and had eaten the pound cake, feeling obligated when Aideen had set a large slice before him. He was regretting it. The boy, Gabe, had eaten three slices. Gabe must have a hollow leg like he'd had at that age.

Throughout the meal, the boys had been quiet unless spoken to, except for the occasional grunt. One or the other enjoyed seeing who could kick the other under the table harder without their tablemates becoming aware of their game—if the wincing was any indicator. It reminded Hans of dinners with his brothers as young boys.

"Aideen, why don't you lie down for a bit? Katie and I can get these dishes." Martha's gentle tone ended the conversation, to which Hans had only been half-listening.

Reverend Jenkins pushed his chair back and stood. The sheriff took the man's arm when he wobbled. "Steady there, Reverend. Can I help you to your room?"

"That would be right nice of you. . . ." The reverend stumbled over his words as well as faltered in his step.

"Henry. I'm the sheriff in this town."

"Right." Glassy eyes focused past the man, a look of concern creeping around the edges.

"I believe I might close my eyes on the settee for a few minutes as well after I get you settled." At the sheriff's smile, the reverend's look of confusion softened, and he reciprocated as the two headed to the stairs.

"Well, I don't plan on doing dishes." Hans looked straight into Katie's eyes. Hers held mirth—his held resolve. He turned to Gabe and Thomas. "How about if the three of us head outside before Corporal Katie here conscripts us into cleanup duty? I saw a tabby this morning, and I bet he'd appreciate a morsel if we can find him. He may even be in the barn. I heard something earlier."

Hans swiped a small piece of meat from Aideen's plate, still on the table. Katie's eyes went large, and her coloring turned pale. It wasn't that big of a deal to feed the cat. He'd seen her set a plate out with more on it than the small amount he'd taken.

It didn't take long to find the cat. The animal came quickly, wasting no time in consuming the morsel.

"I wonder if he has a name?" Hans questioned.

"Marmalade." The word had an undertone of laughter. It was the first thing Gabe had said with expression.

"Marmalade? It sounds like there's a story there."

"Aideen once made a batch of orange marmalade to sell at the mercantile. That cat jumped through the window and licked the spills on her counter. She swears she had all the lids on the jars before that happened, but I'm not eating any." Gabe's hands clasped his throat as if he were choking, all while making gagging noises.

Hans felt like a young man as he laughed at the dramatic scene. It had been years since his cares had felt far away.

"Hey, wanna go to the creek and skip rocks?" Gabe found his voice.

"Sure." Hans shrugged as if it didn't matter, but it did. He had done nothing just for fun for a long time.

Sunlight shone, and a gentle wind blew their hair as they walked. Gabe's dark locks gleamed in the sun. Cut short like Thomas's, a slight wave bounced on his broad forehead. The boy's coloring was more bronze than tanned. It embarrassed Hans when Gabe caught him staring.

"Were you injured in the war?" Gabe asked.

The direct question pulled Hans back from his musings. *Injured? Probably not like Gabe expected. Truth, speak the truth.* If he couldn't be honest with these boys now, he knew he'd not be honest with others later.

"Well, the short answer is yes." Neither boy interrupted when Hans paused. He took a deep breath before continuing. "I didn't see action." He swallowed and forced himself to continue. "I served at a field hospital."

Men's faces clouded the path, and he stumbled over a rock. Neither Thomas nor Gabe seemed to notice or were at least thoughtful enough not to acknowledge the misstep.

"My wounds are different. I suffered from frostbite, and although I've gained a good bit of weight back, it took time to get my strength back. I feel like I've lived a lifetime in my twenty-six years. But those maladies pale compared to what others suffered."

Missing limbs, vision and hearing loss, bodies wasted away

—Hans could not get the faces out of his mind. Joe's hawk-like nose, askew from being broken by his own hand, and the man's beady eyes devoid of color but full of evil, jeered at him. Hans shivered. This time, Thomas noticed and commented.

"Does it hurt?"

How did this boy get right to the core? *Does it hurt? Does it?* Hans had to be honest, not only with Thomas but also with himself.

"Yes, Thomas. It hurts. I watched men die, go crazy in their minds, and become so bitter and full of rage that they killed others and sometimes took their own lives. The suffering in the hospital was, well, devastating." The three veered off to the right on a deer path before Hans continued. "If men didn't suffer from a physical malady, they suffered from boredom and the demons of their own creation."

His words described how he felt about himself. He'd felt trapped in that field hospital as much as those in their beds. He would long for the freedom to be in the field like his brothers until a new load of wounded would come and tell of the horrors they had seen and experienced. He'd heard more than once that freedom cost dearly. The war may be over, but there was no freedom for those now enslaved by their scars.

Picking up smooth rocks, they skipped them across the swollen creek. Thomas showed his competitive side and counted every skip before challenging himself to do better. Gabe took the time to study how Thomas and Hans threw, then mimicked the motion, improving after a few tries.

"So, what are your plans now?" Thomas stopped skipping

rocks and looked at Hans.

Plans. Another thing he hadn't completely resolved. He only knew he'd been desperate to get out from under Edna's rule, be on his own, and start fresh. Now, he wanted to make something of himself, be his own man, prove to himself he could do more than just follow rules and orders.

"Do you have a job yet?" Gabe interjected.

"Aideen has asked me to do some work for her in exchange for room and board. That's something, I suppose. I'll talk to Mr. Finch tomorrow to see if he needs some help at the livery." He smiled when his rock went farther than Thomas's.

"He's a good man," Thomas said. "Where did you get the cart in the barn?"

His cheeks felt taut as a smile spread across his face even as the warmth from the sun beat down on his shoulders. "I made it."

Thomas stopped mid-throw. "Truly?"

"Truly. I'd like to start a business and sell them." There, he'd said it. He'd dreamed it and listened to Johann encourage him to do it, but he'd never voiced it. "I'm not sure if anyone would buy it."

"I know they will. Why, Moses, he only has one horse, so he has to borrow my dad's buggy and an extra horse every time he comes to town."

"Who's Moses?"

"The blacksmith. He lives on our land but comes to town

once a month to work. He's got a place near the livery."

"Is he good?"

"Good?" The word held a note of astonishment. "He's the best. He can make anything, not just horseshoes. And he's as strong as an ox. He's the biggest man I've ever seen, and I thought your brother Johann was big."

Hans laughed at Thomas's exaggerated tone. "I'll have to speak with him, then."

"He'll be here until Friday when he takes Gabe and me back home."

"Thomas and I come once a month for schooling from Mrs. Adkins," Gabe added. "Mrs. Shankel and Ms. Delphina help us the other weeks. My dad says book learning is fine, but he thinks there is more to learn in the doing."

It surprised Hans that Gabe sounded as if he would prefer to learn from books. Well-muscled with work-worn hands, the boy was clearly no slacker like Edna's son.

"Race ya back!" Thomas was off in a flash before Hans realized the boys were already well ahead. Typical youngsters, always rushing for the next best thing.

Hans remained motionless. Is that what he was doing, rushing forward without thinking? No, he would earn his living making carts. Whether he'd do that in Shumard Oak Bend or another town was yet to be determined.

Chapter 18

Shumard Oak Bend

"Did you have a good time with the boys while I slaved in the kitchen?" Katie asked as she entered the barn.

"Have you ever wrangled two boys at the same time?" Hans peeked from behind his horse but continued brushing. He wasn't certain of her mood since her tone gave no indication.

"As a matter of fact, yes. And a dozen girls as well."

Hans stopped and looked from beneath Rauti's neck to see if Katie was teasing him.

"Doubt me?"

"I'm guessing you were a teacher?"

"Ha! No. I've barely an education myself."

Hans continued brushing Rauti as he watched Katie cross her slim ankles as she leaned back against Dorcas's stall.

"Quit staring at my ankles." She crossed them in the other

direction.

Hans felt the heat rise in his neck and remained behind the horse.

"So, not only are you capable of cooking, cleaning, and taking care of multiple children at one time, but you can also tell what someone is doing without looking?"

"There are many things you don't know about me, Mr. Korhonen."

Hans set the brush away and came around to witness Katie switch to a more lady-like posture.

"And what might those things be?"

"Oh, no you don't. I'll not be sharing my secrets with the likes of you."

"Secrets? Now I'm curious." He found he did want to know. He pulled the two chairs from dinner back off the wall and gestured for her to sit.

"Thank you."

"I'll make you a deal. I'll share something about me, and you share one thing about you," he offered.

"What makes you think I want to know anything about you?"

He hadn't planned on that but saw a sparkle in her eyes and pressed on. "I'm from Finland. Have—had—three older brothers. Otto died in the war."

"I'm so sorry."

"Thank you. Johann and Franc married mail-order brides. Johann is my eldest brother—his wife came with her son." He smirked.

"I take it you didn't care for this?"

"Let's just say I was tired of babysitting and was ready to move on and not be under Edna's thumb anymore. I want to be my own man."

Hans watched as a shadow crossed over Katie's eyes. He wasn't sure what he'd said, but she dropped her chin and took a deep breath.

"Your turn."

"I'm from Ireland." She folded her hands in her lap.

"...And..."

"You said one thing." She paused before she winked and continued. "Before my mother passed, she asked me to come live with Aunt Aideen. My father was absent most of my life. I had nothing to keep me in Ireland. And, as far as keeping children, the town's children all seemed to find me when school was out since there was no place else to go and nothing to keep them occupied."

Hans listened to her matter-of-fact telling. He'd figured she'd be more like Edna and shed tears as a ploy for sympathy.

"Do you like it—sorry, I made the mistake of asking that earlier. I know the answer. I guess my question is, isn't there anything here you enjoy?"

She stared at him as if judging how much or what to say.

A sound came from the back corner. Marmalade chose that moment to jump from the rafters and into Katie's lap.

"Hello, Marmalade. Are you hungry?"

"Hungry? How much can one cat eat?" Hans asked. "I saw the leftovers you kept for him."

"Her."

"What?"

"Marmalade is a female." Katie stood, placing the cat at her feet. She took a quick look around before hanging the chair.

Hans stood and did the same.

"How much longer will you be out here?" she asked.

"I'm done, I guess." Hans watched Katie's gaze roam the barn as she spoke.

"Very good. Good night, Mr. Korhonen."

"Hans. Please."

A small smile graced her face, but she did not respond. He watched her retreating form.

"Quit looking at my ankles."

Chapter 19

Monday

Shumard Oak Bend

"**I**s the reverend still not feeling well?" Hans sat at the table as Aideen placed a steaming cup of coffee in front of him.

"He's got no fever, but he says he aches clear to his bones. And tired, so very tired." Aideen used her apron to wipe wayward flour from the back of her hand.

"Is there a doctor in town?"

Aideen rolled her eyes. "Yes, but he's more likely to prescribe spirits than sound medicine. Shumard Oak Bend is large enough now that we need a good one, but until Doc retires, I don't think . . ." Her words trailed off, and a flush covered her face. "Forgive me. I be speaking pure gossip." Aideen looked to the ceiling as if seeking something from its rafters.

Hans watched the woman, her lips moving without sound before they formed a slow smile. Then she winked. *Winked?*

He looked up to see if something might have floated down and into her eye, but she did not raise her hand to brush anything away but a single tear. As if nothing had transpired, Aideen continued.

"We be needing Robin. I told you about her. She be Pete's wife."

"Robin?"

"Aye. Pete's Arapaho Indian wife and Gabe's mother," Aideen clarified. "She's saved many a life from an early departure. I bear witness to her healing ways."

Hans looked at the plate Katie brought in and plunked before him. She juggled Aideen's and her own before placing theirs on the table with a much lighter touch.

Aideen's eyes followed Katie's form until the girl took her seat. She held out her hands.

"Where two or more gather in His name . . ." Aideen smiled at Hans and took his hand, which was poised over and ready to pick up his fork. She lifted her chin to Katie, who sighed but accepted her aunt's hand before reaching across the table.

Katie's upturned hand showed a calloused palm. Hans stared until she wiggled her fingers. He looked up and read the *Let's get this over with* look in her eyes. Aideen wasted no time starting her conversation with her God.

The warmth of Katie's fingers moved up his arm, spread across his chest, and settled. . . . His eyes shot up from their hands to Katie's eyes. Her face did not show she felt the same, but he noted the slight spread of red across her neck where she'd opened her collar. Perhaps the heat of the kitchen was causing the color.

"Áiméan." Aideen released his hand and lifted her apron to wipe her eyes. "Well. That's settled, then." She placed her hands on either side of her plate.

What? He hadn't heard a single word of the prayer.

"Finish up your breakfast, Hans, then head over to Gray's Mercantile to see if anyone up near the Shankels' land has placed an order. You can show off your cart if there's a delivery to be made. Katie girl, when you've finished eating, please pack Hans some provisions."

"Yes, ma'am." Katie fixed her eyes on the man across the table before glimpsing down at their still-touching fingers.

Hans withdrew his, placing the burning appendage in his lap, and turned to get clarification from Aideen. "Ma'am? Aideen? I'm not sure I'm following you."

"I'll draw a map. You get your bedroll ready. It's a two-day journey. That cart of yours will be a mite better than a wagon, so you'll arrive early evening."

"Yes, ma'am." The familiar phrase escaped with his long exhale as he picked up his fork and finished his meal.

"Well, be on with you, then. We've not got all day." Aideen used her hands to shoo both statues into action when they finished eating.

Katie stood and pushed in her chair. Those fingers brushed a wayward red lock back into her mob cap. Hans watched in fascination. Breakfast felt heavy in his stomach, and he swallowed the last of his now-lukewarm coffee before standing.

"Well, thank you, young man," Mr. Taylor at Gray's Mercantile said. "Now, I can't pay you for delivery until you return, but I'll pay the same wages I would have given Horace had he been able to make the trip. The timing of your going out there is a godsend. Horace has been sick for a week, and I wasn't sure when I'd get that load delivered."

"Mr. Taylor, I appreciate the offer," Hans said. "I'm happy to do it and am already heading that way, so no wages are needed. But if you would be so kind as to spread the word about my carts, I'd be much obliged."

"It's George," he offered as he inspected Hans's craftmanship. "It holds more than expected. You still have a good bit of room. The tall sides were a good idea. Wheels look sturdy, although I think they'd be able to bear more load with metal covering the outside edge. You should speak to Moses. He's the blacksmith and is very knowledgeable. I'm guessing he'd have a good idea of what you might need."

"Thank you, George. I meant to do that today, but it will have to wait." Mounting Rauti, he leaned in and patted his friend before fully sitting in the saddle, causing a familiar creak of leather.

"Wouldn't have been able to, anyway. I heard Moses left before daybreak to see to a broken wheel down south. He'll be back by late this afternoon, I'm sure."

"I'll have to catch him when I return. Thank you for the information." Hans pressed Rauti's sides with his legs. "Let's go, boy. We've some miles to cover today."

As he rode up to the boarding house, he noticed Katie standing on the porch, a basket in hand.

"Taking the cart, I see." Katie twirled a loose strand of hair, the motion turning Hans's stomach into a similarly tight spring.

"Yes," he choked out before dismounting.

She placed the basket in the cart. "I have another item for you to take." She held her other hand out to her side, and Hans watched in amazement as a young boy ran from the barn and wrapped himself in her skirts.

"Mr. Korhonen, this is Sam." She pushed the boy forward and used the tip of her finger to lift his chin.

"Sam?" Hans asked.

"Yes." She squared her shoulders. "Sam, Mr. Korhonen will take you to Aunt Delphina, who will get you to family."

"But . . ." The boy's simple word sounded like a plea.

"Remember, Sam?" Katie kneeled. Hans watched in amazement as she placed both hands on the small boy's shoulders. "We discussed this. Aunt Delphina will find a family for you."

A family? Had he heard that correctly?

"Mr. Korhonen." She was all business now as she stood.

"Sam will give you no trouble. He can ride in the cart and fetch kindling when you reach the halfway point." She patted the boy's shoulder. "If you don't get a move on, you won't reach it until dark."

"I'm not sure . . ." Hans started.

"Katie girl?" Aideen called from inside the house.

"Please." Katie's breathy word came out as a plea. "Please, Hans."

One nod and the boy scrambled into the cart and covered himself with the oiled cloth tucked in the side. *Is he hiding or afraid of me?* Hans rubbed his forehead.

"Coming, Aunt Aideen." Katie lifted her skirt and spun.

Hans followed her form with his eyes as she hurried inside.

She called me Hans.

Chapter 20

Shumard Oak Bend

Katie stood at the window, watching the muscles of Rauti's rump pull the cart carrying Sam. Rauti climbed the hill behind the boarding house and headed north to the Shankels' land. She'd heard it was a beautiful, wide-open country full of tall prairie grass. All she knew was this dull town. Dry, dusty, and full of children like Sam who needed a family.

He's five years old, Lord. Five. Please help Delphina understand. Prepare her heart, Lord.

"Katie, please grab those cookies and take them to Mr. Taylor. Bring back a new wooden spoon. The big one seems to be missing, and I need it to finish this recipe."

"Yes, ma'am." Katie grabbed the basket from the table and rushed out the door, hoping for a final glimpse of Hans.

"Morning, Miss Murphy. Lovely day, wouldn't you say?" The magistrate fell into step beside Katie.

It had been. Katie wet her lips, willing them to hold in the words. She pulled the basket of cookies closer to her right, forcing distance between them.

"You're looking lovely today."

Katie glanced down at her work dress. A streak of flour dusted the front where she'd leaned over the counter.

"I haven't seen you out lately. Is everything going well?"

"Is there something I should know about, Magistrate? Am I missing some key point of information?"

"No. No." Pudgy fingers smoothed his mustache. "This coming Sunday is the fourth Lord's Day of the month."

"Yes, it is. The reverend is already at the boarding house."

"I wonder if the Gray sisters will feel up to attending. I probably should visit them. Have you seen them recently?"

Katie slowed her step, and the pieces fell into place. She would not give him the satisfaction he sought. She tapped the basket, and an idea formed.

"I was on my way there now. Dear me, I've missed the turnoff to their home with this delightful discussion. Good day, sir." Her precise turn would have impressed a military commander. Turning between buildings, she started when a flash of orange darted across her path.

"Marmalade, you have the worst timing." Katie's free hand tapped her chest. "You gave me quite the fright." The tabby meowed, tail swishing, before sauntering over to an upturned crate and jumping up.

"I've nothing for you today. I'm on a mission." She reached to pet the animal between the ears, but the cat turned as if perturbed by her answer and unwilling to allow human contact. "Contrary feline."

Blue shutters came into view. With the cat forgotten, Katie entered the garden and strode up the front steps. She knocked, but there was no answer. "There is no hiding from me, you scoundrels," she whispered into the dry air. A faint sound came from the back. Katie followed the stone walkway to find both ladies pulling weeds.

"Hello, ladies."

"Oh," one exclaimed as her hand flew to her wrinkled neck. The other fell flat on her backside from her crouched position. "Oh, sister dear, are you quite all right?"

"I'm fine, Fidelia. My dress, however, will require a good cleaning." She scowled at the intruder, then sobered when she recognized Katie.

"I'm glad to have caught you." Katie placed the basket on the back porch, then adjusted her skirts to sit on the top step. She wasn't going anywhere, and she knew the sisters wouldn't leave the yard, not with kerchiefs over their hair. Katie watched as the two held a silent conversation before Elizabeth removed her gloves and helped her sister to her feet.

"I'm supposing you are here about the other day?" Elizabeth inquired.

"You suppose correctly." Katie stood and came down the steps, then offered her vacated seat to the ladies. The two sat like scolded schoolgirls as Katie towered over them, arms crossed. "Enlighten me."

A flurry of words from each lady, one talking over the other, the sound like fighting birds.

"Enough." Her word was quiet but firm. "You first." She pointed to Elizabeth.

"That woman came out of nowhere. She knocked on our door and told us to send for you."

"And she left just as quickly, like a vapor." Fidelia's gnarled fingers fluttered around her face, causing wisps of gray hair to move.

Katie leaned forward with her silent request for more information.

"Miss Katie, we hadn't a clue of what she wanted. Had we known she was such a . . . well, never mind the name-calling. If we'd known her character, we would not have allowed her in our home." Elizabeth shook her head, and Fidelia patted her sister's hand.

"What I'm trying to figure out is how she came to think I was—what were the words she used—available and suitable?"

The ladies shook their heads but did not make eye contact.

"Ladies? What aren't you telling me?"

"I don't have the energy, Elizabeth. You tell her." Fidelia sighed.

Fidelia patted the small space beside her, scooting closer to her sister. Katie picked up the pail of weeds and hefted the contents over the fence before turning it upside-down to sit and face the two.

"That works as well. Now, what did you want to know?" Elizabeth tapped a finger to her chin. "Oh, yes. Magistrate Marley visited us last week, and he said his sister was coming for a visit and wanted to meet us. We were, of course, delighted to have the company. Only, when she arrived, she was not as agreeable as the magistrate led us to believe."

"That's right," Fidelia interjected. "She sent Elizabeth off to fetch you and took over our parlor." Her words, full of indignation, ended with a loud *humph*.

Katie watched the two exchange more silent words before she spoke. "So, you mean to tell me Mrs. Olivia Branch is Magistrate Bill Marley's sister?"

"One and the same." The deep sigh from Elizabeth and the shake of her head were comical.

"You don't think . . ." Fidelia's fingers slowly lifted to her throat. "He wouldn't stoop to . . ." She turned to her sister. "Do you?"

Elizabeth must have responded, but Katie had not heard.

"Think what?" Katie asked. "That Bill Marley is trying to get rid of me?"

Both ladies sat up straighter, their faces ashen.

"Oh, dear. You don't think we were . . . I mean . . ." Fidelia wiped at her eyes as Elizabeth patted her sister's hand.

"No, ladies," Katie said. "I do not hold you responsible. I'm sorry the magistrate involved you, but I'm certain he knew it was the only way I'd speak to the woman. I'm sure he expected me to jump at the chance and had not bargained on my saying no."

A sly smile crept to Elizabeth's lips. "Sister?"

"Yes?" Fidelia asked. "Oh, dear. I know that look."

Elizabeth's gaze locked on Katie's. "Two can play that game. We may be old, but we're not done for yet." She reached for the railing and pulled herself up. "This calls for tea. I'm hoping that basket contains molasses cookies?"

"That it does," Katie said.

"Fidelia, you start the water. I'll get the paper. We're going to need a battle plan."

Chapter 21

Shumard Oak Bend

"Revenge?" Katie gulped.

"Not exactly." Elizabeth moved her teacup to the side and laid the crisp sheet of paper on the table. She licked the tip of the graphite pencil. "I see it more like a challenge to accomplish the unexpected. If Bill Marley has his mind set on not having an orphanage in this town, then we have to succeed in creating one."

Katie wasn't sure she followed, but the devious looks between the two sisters gave her a glimpse of what they had been like as young women on the frontier alone. One thing she knew for sure—these two women may be old and stooped over, but they still had backbones.

"So, are you saying you support an orphanage?" Katie noticed the silent exchange between her hosts.

"We support a tenacious female like yourself who will blaze a path through history," Elizabeth replied with a smile.

"Sometimes that means going against convention," Fidelia added.

Katie's head swiveled left and right as she listened to the two women talk over each other.

"Being self-confident helps," Elizabeth chimed in.

"Being feisty and headstrong is a must. A woman who sees possibilities and works to change things will survive in these parts."

"One who tackles obstacles head-on, going against the wishes of others, and has fun doing it."

Katie liked the way these ladies thought. "So, what's the plan?"

"Let's start with the basics, dear. It isn't so much a plan of action as an infiltration of minds, one in particular." Elizabeth tapped the pencil on the table.

"Magistrate Marley's?" Katie offered after a moment's silence.

"Exactly. Now, let's start with a list of people you feel may be inclined to support your cause and why. This is an essential detail since subversion takes many forms."

Katie guarded her pocket and its contents like a spy crossing enemy lines. She still wasn't sure what all had transpired but knew she not only had allies in the Gray sisters but also friends. Her first victim, as the sisters referred to those on the list, would be Mrs. Taylor. All she had to do was wait for an opening.

"Good morning, Katie. I'll be right with you," Mrs. Taylor said as she assisted Mrs. Kilpatrick. "This calico will look lovely on your girls, Mona. You know, we will soon be carrying Mrs. O'Sullivan's tatted collars. They would truly set your girls apart from the others. She has a lovely blue that would complement this fabric and match the color of their eyes beautifully."

"I've seen Aideen's handiwork. Please let her know I'll take two." Mrs. Kilpatrick paid for her purchase. "Do you have anyone who might deliver these items?"

"I'll have Mr. Taylor drop them off this afternoon if that suits you."

"That will be fine. Thank you," Mrs. Kilpatrick said. "Oh, how do you do, Miss Murphy?" The woman offered a hug that Katie readily accepted.

"Quite well, thank you. I'll be sure to pass on your thoughtful compliment of Aideen's work. She is quite gifted," Katie replied.

"That she is. Well, I must be on my way. I've baking to do. Oh, Mrs. Taylor, might I have the baking powder? Goodness, that's what I came in for. One can't make cookies without it."

"Of course, here you are. Enjoy your day." Mrs. Taylor turned to Katie. "What might I help you with today?"

"You've already been a help. Thank you for suggesting the collars for the dresses. I'll let Aideen know to get started on two right away. I also need a wooden spoon." Katie flushed. "I got a little overly excited at seeing a mouse, and my weapon of choice failed me miserably."

"Oh, my. Well then, I suggest we look at a sturdier variety." Mrs. Taylor did not hide her chuckle. "I'd like to have seen that," she muttered as she led Katie to the crate of utensils.

The bell over the door played a happy tune.

"I'll be with you in a moment. We've been quite busy lately. I need another pair of hands."

Katie inhaled the scents of pickles, tobacco, and leather. Now was as good a time as any.

"Have you ever considered an apprentice?" Katie nearly ran into the woman when Mrs. Taylor stopped and turned to face her. Had she overstepped her boundaries?

"To be honest, I hadn't considered an apprentice. Mr. Taylor doesn't want to hire anyone until the town grows a bit more, but someone in training who could also do deliveries might not be a bad idea. I'm just not sure who that might be."

"I'll keep my ear to the ground for you. God does seem to put people in our paths at just the right time. This spoon looks good." Katie smacked the flat edge against her hand, making Mrs. Taylor jump. "I think it will do the job."

"I do hope you mean stirring and not whacking." Mrs. Taylor winked. "I'll put this on your bill, and we'll settle up at the end of the month."

"Thank you." Katie lifted the spoon in a wave.

She'd planted a seed and seen it take root. God would have to do the rest.

Chapter 22

Shankel Farm

"You awake back there?" Hans made a quarter-turn in the saddle and peered into the cart where the boy sat wedged between boxes.

"Yes, sir."

"We should be there in another hour. Would you like to ride up here with me for a bit?"

Hans heard scrambling and pulled Rauti to a hasty stop.

"Whoa, boy." He meant it for both the horse and the youngster clambering to get out of the cart. "Let me give you a hand, son."

"Your horse is really big, mister."

"Hans. Just call me Hans, remember?" Familiar silence followed. The boy had spoken little on the trip, followed directions when given, and slept a good bit as they'd traveled.

"Do you know Aunt Delphina?" Rauti's ears perked up at the boy's unfamiliar voice.

"No. Can't say as I do."

"Me neither. Miss Katie told me she'd help me find a family."

Hans wanted to ask outright for clarification but kept silent even when the boy offered no more. Could this be a war orphan? Things began to fall into place in Hans's mind. The full plates of scraps Katie had taken from the kitchen. Her presence in the barn when he'd cared for Rauti. Her urgency when Aideen had called. Even the boy hiding himself in the cart as they'd left.

"Sam, where have you been sleeping?" Hans felt the boy tense.

"Are you and Miss Katie friends?"

Friends? Are we? He was doing her bidding by carting this boy, but did that make them friends?

"Yes. New friends."

"I heard you and Miss Katie talking in the barn and that boy, Thomas. You sure have lots of friends."

The conversation with Thomas had been on Sunday, meaning Sam had been in the barn for several days. The sounds of cattle and men's voices interrupted his musings as they crested a hill.

"Wow. That's a big ranch."

"That it is." Hans took in the two-story home with its wrap-around porch. A woman hung laundry while two children ran around, ducking under the flapping fabrics. Hans felt the boy stiffen, his small hands turning white as they grasped the saddle horn.

"Are they nice folk?"

"Let's make our presence known. I'm sure they're friendly folk. Hello, the house," Hans called as he waved his hat at the woman.

She lifted her hand to the white kerchief tied around her head before shooing the children onto the porch.

"We've a delivery from Gray's Mercantile for a Mr. Shankel." Hans figured that bit of information was all the woman needed for now.

"Take it to the barn. Mr. Shankel will meet you there in a moment." Her speech was sophisticated, as if she had a regal upbringing, but firm.

"Yes, ma'am. Thank you, ma'am." He watched a wary smile form on her face.

"Is that Aunt Delphina?" the boy whispered.

"I don't rightly know, Sam. We'll find out soon enough. Let's get this cart unloaded and take care of Rauti." Hans helped the boy to the ground. If Hans had been wearing a skirt, he imagined Sam would have hidden behind it. The boy stuck so close that Hans struggled to move.

"Welcome. I'm Clint Shankel. What can I help you with?" A muscled man with dark hair streaked with silver came from the barn.

"Hans." He offered the man his hand.

"Quite the cart you've got there."

"Thank you, sir. That's part of the reason I'm here. Mr. Taylor needed a load delivered. I believe this is for you?" Hans moved to unload.

"Good timing. We're leaving at the end of the week to drive cattle to market. We needed these supplies. What's the other reason?"

"This." Hans took the shoulder of the boy tucked behind him. "Katie, I mean, Miss Murphy, said he'd find his Aunt Delphina here."

"Did she?"

The question confused Hans. "Yes, sir. Sam here is looking for his family."

"My guess is Delphina isn't your aunt. Am I correct?" Clint's question was gentle, yet the boy shook under Hans's grasp.

"Miss Katie told me to call her Aunt Delphina. She said she'd help me find a family."

"I'm sure she will."

Hans followed the direction of Clint's raised hand as he motioned for the woman with the kerchief on her head to approach. As she neared, her tanned face became clear, and Hans realized why Clint had said she was likely not the boy's kin.

"You're a negro," Sam said matter-of-factly.

"That I am. And what's your name, young man?"

The woman was gracious. Hans had to give her that. He chanced a glance at the stern face of Mr. Shankel and understood a bit of what the boy felt. Hans wondered if he could hide behind one of the sheets drying on the clothesline.

"Are you Aunt Delphina?" Sam's wrinkled brow made it look like he was scrutinizing the woman.

"That depends on who you are."

When Sam did not respond, Delphina moved her focus to Hans.

"Katie—Miss Murphy asked that I bring the boy up to his Aunt Delphina. Apparently, he is looking for a family."

"I see. Does the boy have a name?"

"Sam." The boy stuck out his hand, his prior concern gone.

She shook the offering. "Well, Sam, if Mr. Shankel will allow it, let's head into the big house for milk and a cookie."

Mr. Shankel tipped his head, then turned to Hans as Sam and Delphina walked away. "Any idea what that's about?"

"Well, sir . . . " Hans started.

"Clint. Please call me Clint. Let's finish unloading, then sit on the porch. This leg doesn't always cooperate."

Hans watched the man's uneven gait as he followed with multiple loads to the barn. Once the items had been stored, Hans sank into a well-built rocking chair, enjoying the break.

"Well, Clint, as best as I can figure it, Ka—Miss Murphy's been hiding the boy in the boarding house barn. I didn't get much out of him, but I know he's been staying there for a few days."

"I'll let the women folk figure out the details. I didn't realize Katie had gotten involved. There are several families needing help these days." He rubbed his hand over the day's growth of stubble on his face. "Anything else bring you here besides the boy?"

"Yes, sir. Horace is ill, so I offered to deliver your supplies from the mercantile. But the biggest reason is Reverend Jenkins is ill. I'm to head to Pete Manning's to inquire if his wife is available."

"I see. Is it critical?"

"I don't believe so. Aideen's concerned and doesn't trust the local doctor."

"I don't blame her. We'll talk to Rachel—that's my wife— before sending you to Pete's." The man rocked for a moment before continuing his questions. "Quite a contraption you've got there. Does it travel well?"

"It took these roads just fine. Lulled the boy to sleep many a time, but I'm guessing he may not have slept much in the barn. The nights are bitter." He waited for Clint to speak, but when he didn't, Hans continued. "I heard you have a man here by the name of Moses who's handy with iron and anvil."

"That would be Delphina's man."

"Married?" Hans's voice went up a notch. He hadn't considered the fact that Moses might be black. No one in town had made the distinction. He realized it did not matter to him either, and the pace of his heart slowed.

"The law didn't allow it, but now that they're both free, we shall see. Missouri may not recognize their union, but I married them two summers ago with God as the witness. I'm not a preacher, and Reverend Jenkins stays busy on his circuit, but Moses insisted that, as a God-fearing man, he wanted to do as best he could in the eyes of his Savior."

Hans did not want to get into a discussion about God, religion, or marriage. He changed the subject. "Did you serve?" He tipped his head to the leg the man continually rubbed.

"Union Cavalry. In my former life, I was a US marshal. Patrolling, scouting, guarding supply trains and railroads, and providing the ever-dreaded escort to generals seemed like a good fit for me. You?"

"Union soldier. I've seen my fair share of partial bodies. I served at two different field hospitals." The shiver he felt was not from the cooling temperatures.

Clint slapped his leg. "No more talk of war. What work are you doing now?"

Hans pointed to where his cart rested under the barn's lean-to. "I make these carts, and I do odd jobs for Aideen in exchange for room and board. I moved to Shumard Oak Bend just this week, so I haven't secured work yet."

"So, nothing permanent?"

Hans shrugged.

"Let me show you around."

Hans wondered why the owner of a large ranch would give such personal attention to a stranger. They moved to the paddock and stood at the rail, watching Rauti settle.

"I'm short several hands. I lost some of my best men in that war. But since we aren't mentioning it . . ." Clint let his breath out in a long stream. "Fine animal. Can he cut?"

"Sir?" Hans rubbed his chin.

"Cattle. Can he keep cattle in line?" Clint pointed to the far field. "Those boys are riding some of the finest cutters in the west. The horses react as quickly, if not quicker, than the rider. It's an amazing thing to watch." He rubbed his leg. "We've got to get cattle to market, and this thing isn't interested in making the trip." He lifted his leg to the railing and rubbed deeper.

"I don't know about cutting, but he's strong and rides well."

"Clint, supper's ready," a tall woman called from the house.

Something was familiar about her, and Hans wondered if he'd met her at church on Sunday.

"Rachel, I'd like for you to meet Hans." Clint turned to him. "I'm sorry. I didn't ask your last name."

"Korhonen. Hans Korhonen."

"Oh, lands sakes!" she squealed.

The woman nearly knocked him off his feet when she threw her arms around his shoulders.

"Hans, it's me, Rachel. Rachel Trexler. Melvin and I stayed at your farm when we traveled this way. Look." She pointed to the far side of the field. "Otto's trees. They all survived."

Hans could barely see the small orchard in the distance.

"How is Otto?"

Rachel would have had no way of knowing. Hans cleared his throat. "He didn't survive the war." He heard her intake of breath. "Johann and Franc are back at the farm, each married now."

"And you?"

Clint interrupted. "I thought you said something about supper. How about we talk over whatever it is that smells so good coming out our door?"

Chapter 23

Traveling back to Shumard Oak Bend

He'd done it. He'd said no to Clint Shankel at his request to join the cattle drive. Hans sat straighter in the saddle.

"Rauti, if I was able to turn down a job from a man of that influence and still sell him a cart, I can do anything."

The satisfaction Hans felt at having accomplished so much in two days washed over him like a fine rain.

"You think Robin is in the family way?"

Rauti bobbed his head.

"Me, too. Did you smell those herbs she gave me? Made me shudder. I'll find outside work when Aideen brews those. I may even break down and say a prayer for the reverend. If the taste is anything like the smell, it will be bad enough to gag a snipe."

Rauti swayed his head back and forth after whinnying.

"And what about Melvin? Rachel's story of his passing and all she went through was some tale. I tell you, that brother of hers, Charlie, sure did well. I saw some of the horses he and his wife are raising. I saw you eyeing one of the mares at Clint's."

Rauti made a low rumble deep in his chest.

"You do beat all, boy. Did you make any friends, or are you still pining after old Dorcas?" Hans tightened the reins when Rauti reached back to nip at his pant leg. "That's what I thought. Well, I did. Clint's hired some hardworking hands. Hey, that kid from church that I thought might be Paul? Name's Connor. He's Pete's hand. Gangly fellow. I'm not sure why I thought Katie might see something in him. She'd walk all over that boy. It still doesn't solve the mystery of Paul and his intentions."

Visions of Katie danced before him. Not only was she beautiful but she was also tough. Her courage and boldness impressed him, as did her ability to make things happen. He doubted he'd be willing to risk being found out about hiding and feeding Sam.

Rauti's ears perked up as Hans spoke his thoughts. "You know, Clint was mighty clear about the magistrate. That man wants nothing to do with helping those less fortunate. He's warned Katie more than once, according to Clint."

Rauti pulled on the reins, and Hans loosened his tightening grip.

"Now, don't you worry about Sam. He'll be fine, boy. Delphina has already found a home for the lad. The wife of one of the hands leaving on the drive welcomed the boy into her home and said she would gladly take more. Delphina said the first thing Sam asked was, 'Can I have a dog?' And the second was, 'Can I call you Mama and Papa?'" A lump formed in Hans's throat at the telling.

A low rumble emanated from Rowdy's chest.

"Feels good being a part of something like that, like I'm making a difference." He wasn't making a difference. Katie was. He was just an errand boy. He did what he was told. She made things happen. All he had done was use his cart to do her bidding. The elation of earlier faded, and doubt clouded his mind. Hans watched as the sun began its descent behind the land, his heart going with it. Even Rauti's steps slowed. It took a moment for Hans to realize Rauti hadn't slowed because he sympathized with the likes of him—he'd heard voices.

A deep, haunting sound settled in the surrounding air. He wasn't certain he could make it to the safety of the boulders ahead before he was seen. Rauti's ears swiveled and locked on the path. His breath came out hard, and he whinnied, which was returned. The air stilled.

"Who goes there?"

The deep voice from earlier reached Hans's ears and froze his thoughts. He'd been so engrossed in his own world that he had not given thought to safety. Hans struggled to make out the features of the dark man atop the buckboard seat. Everything but the whites of his eyes, which bore into Hans, was as black as night. The wagon he pulled stopped. They waited as if in a standoff. Rauti sidestepped and again blew out a long breath.

"My name is Hans. I'm traveling from the Shankel ranch back to Shumard Oak Bend." The voice he'd lost returned.

"Hans?" A head popped up from the bed of the wagon.

"Thomas?"

"You know him?" the big man asked.

Thomas jumped from the cart with Gabe not far behind. Hans dismounted as well.

"This is Moses." The boy pointed behind him. "Moses, see, that's the cart I was telling you about."

"It's a pleasure to meet you, Moses." Hans took a deep breath. "I've just had the privilege of meeting your lovely wife. She's some cook."

Moses pulled the team to the side, and both boys began unharnessing the horses.

"That she is."

The man stood taller than Hans and was much broader. Hans reached out his hand in greeting and hoped the man's massive one wouldn't crush his. It was the direct eye contact that settled the remaining angst in Hans's heart. This man was a gentle giant. When Hans released his grip and smiled, the man returned the gesture. Even his smile was big.

"Cup of coffee?" Moses pointed to the kindling Hans had replaced on his way up. "The boys will take care of our horses. Let's you and me make some grub."

Soon, they were eating and laughing. Hans leaned his head back and patted his full stomach as he listened to Moses share his story. With the calming night sounds and Moses's deep bass voice, even a third cup of coffee wasn't enough to keep his eyes from drooping. The sun agreed as it dipped behind the horizon.

"Mr. Shankel, Sr., gave me my freedom. Hooking up with him was a God-ordained moment."

The man interjected God into every other sentence. God allowed. God purposed. God willed. The man was intelligent, an excellent cook, and good company, but the way he sprinkled God into everything was getting to be a bit much. He mentioned God more than Reverend Jenkins.

"So, I'm thinking if we straked your wheels with iron, it would protect them against wear on the ground and help bind the wheel together, God willing."

"Strake?" Had he missed that much of the conversation? Perhaps he'd fallen asleep.

"It's a method of nailing iron plates onto the felloes. Not hard to do with the right equipment. In the morning, you can see how I did it on Mr. Shankel's wagon. Sure makes the wheels easier to service when I'm not around."

"What will I need? Or, of more importance, what will it cost me?"

"Well, it requires flat iron for the strake and nails to pound through the steel and into the wood. The hardest thing is getting the iron and coal. There are ways to make charcoal out of burnt wood, but that takes time. Don't you worry about the cost right now. God will provide."

"Can you get what you need?"

"Me? Nah, even Scranbury Iron Furnaces in Pennsylvania

won't sell to a black man, freed or slave. The war may be over . . ." His voice trailed off. "Mr. Shankel—he orders it for me. His men will bring home a load after they drop the cattle at the rail station."

Hans tapped his feet in the dirt, having a difficult time containing his excitement. The tiredness of earlier was gone, and it felt like his insides were jittery. Of course, that could be the coffee kicking in.

"Clint ordered a cart. I can have it assembled in a week or so. Should I bring the wheels to you?"

"I bring the boys to town for schooling with Mrs. Adkins once a month. If you have the cart ready, except for attaching the wheels, we can work on them together, and I'll deliver the final product to Mr. Shankel when I return home."

"Thank you, friend." Hans stuck out his hand, which the big man accepted.

"Don't thank me. Thank the Lord."

Chapter 24

"Reverend Jenkins isn't leaving this weekend either?" Hans asked Katie Friday morning.

"The church he visits on his circuit on the third Sunday is the farthest. He says he feels better, but he's not sure he can travel that distance." Katie cleared the table, filled her cup, and joined Hans.

"Didn't those horrible-smelling herbs from Robin help?"

"Two weeks of that nasty concoction, and we've seen no change. Aunt Aideen said she tried it and said if it were her, she'd rather stay sick."

"Where is your aunt?" Hans took in the room, realizing the two had been alone all morning.

"On the porch with the reverend, taking advantage of the warm day. They've an interesting friendship. It's nice knowing she has someone near her own age to talk to."

"Kind of like us?" Hans winked.

"Nothing like us."

Her deadpan expression squelched all hope of friendly banter until she laughed, which was followed by a snort.

"You do beat all, Hans Korhonen." She slurped her coffee. "I don't think I ever thanked you for taking Sam."

"Have you had any more stowaways?"

She glowered at him over her mug.

Hands raised, he leaned back in his chair. "Truth be told, I felt a part of something bigger than myself. I think it's what gave me the confidence to say no to Mr. Shankel when he asked me to join his crew on the cattle drive. If I'd done that, I wouldn't have met Moses when I did."

"God incidence."

"God what?"

"God incidence. There are no coincidences when you are a believer. It's a supernatural part of being born again. You may think you have it all under control or that things happen by your own hand, but the Bible is clear. 'A man's heart plans his way, but the Lord directs his steps.' That's Proverbs 16:9."

"I hadn't planned on church this morning."

Katie kicked him under the table. "That verse is the reason I know helping the widows and orphans of war is something I'll do despite having no support. Don't look at me that way. Magistrate Marley made it very clear I'm not to 'encourage peddling behavior.' I may not be able to start an orphanage like I'd hoped, but I can help those less fortunate one at a time."

"Orphanage?"

Once again, he felt her scowl on him, and he squirmed in his seat. She stood and put her mug in the wash basin.

"I'm genuinely interested," he said. "What would it take to start an orphanage?"

She leaned back against the counter, the green in her eyes intensifying. "No judgment?"

He stood, placed his mug beside hers, and tilted his head to the door. "Let's not waste this beautiful day. How about we walk while you tell me all about it?"

Katie was not sure what to think. She pondered all that had transpired as she walked to town. Hans had listened, his full attention on her as she'd shared her heart. He'd asked thought-provoking questions, even hinted at helping her when it came time to build. Even though she wanted to believe Hans was in earnest, Katie could not let go of all the empty promises her father had made over the years. Perhaps Hans was placating her to get out of doing morning chores.

Yet, when they'd returned from their walk, Hans had worked twice as fast and hard, making up for lost time. She'd had to get busy as well. Baking cookies for the mercantile to sell was one small way she earned a few coins of her own.

Katie focused her attention on sidestepping the horse dung in the street as she walked to the mercantile. Laughter drew her focus to the outdoor seating area where Hans and Moses sat discussing something that had the larger man making a hammering motion with his massive arm.

"Oh, excuse me." Katie gasped, the handle of the basket full of cookies she'd made to sell at the mercantile slipping from the crook of her arm. She caught it in her palm.

"Watch where you're going."

She'd been so engrossed in watching Moses and Hans that she hadn't seen the men directly in front of her. But she smelled them. Katie lifted her hand to her nose to cover the stench wafting off their dirty clothing.

"Yeah, watch where you're going," a second man slurred.

Katie stopped, appalled at the men's actions. There were six of them. She followed their wake of destruction as they barreled through town, straight toward the mercantile. She couldn't decide if she should give them a piece of her mind or head to the bank to stay out of their way. She did neither. She stood, unable to move when she heard the first man speak to Moses, using words that made her heart ache.

"Come along, Miss Murphy. No need for your ears or eyes to witness any rough goings-on." The magistrate guided her to the other side of the street. "You head on to the bank or my office now."

She did as she was told but not before hearing more words that made her stomach churn. Surely Hans would stick up for his friend. A shot rang out, then another. She dared not turn but heard the sheriff's voice.

"You boys simmer down now. Hans, you and Moses have a seat."

Katie turned, unable to keep her attention in check any longer. Hans looked like a dejected dog. Moses wore no expression, his focus straight ahead, not landing on anything in particular.

"Sheriff," the magistrate spoke up. "I'm certain you'll handle whatever is going on between these men. I'll not have any fighting in my town."

"Joe, is there a problem here?" Sheriff Adkins kept his weapon drawn but pointed downward.

Joe spat, and his sidekick followed suit. "That nig— northern sympathizer was being a mite friendly with . . ."

Katie watched Henry lift his palm. "I suggest you stop before you say more than I'm willing to hear. You boys be on your way. We'll not have any trouble today."

The look the man shot at Hans gave Katie the willies. That man was pure evil. Katie felt a tug to go to Hans, but she resisted. With the men gone, Mr. Taylor stepped out of his shop.

"Thank you, Sheriff." He turned to Moses. "Are you all right, Moses?"

Katie watched in disbelief. Hans sat, bent forward with his forearms on his knees, hands clasped and following the bounce of his legs. It dawned on her he had not stood up for his friend and, even now, had retreated into his shell. Pressure built in her chest, and she forgot to breathe. Anger and disappointment warred with each other. Moments earlier she'd wanted to console him, stand by his side. She bristled. Now she wanted to take him down a notch, the lying, mollifying . . . oooh! She stomped her foot.

Just like my father. I knew he was no different from any other man. Well, Mr. Korhonen, you're about to be very sorry you ever crossed paths with the likes of Kathleen Orla Murphy.

"That was a quick trip." Aideen flinched when Katie slammed the basket on the table.

"I changed my mind. I may eat those cookies myself." Katie banged the cupboard door. She sloshed the coffee, her hands shaking as she poured.

"Dearie, I'll wipe that up. You sit." Aideen pointed to the chair. "Want to talk about it?"

"No. Ooo." The liquid burned her tongue. "He's just like Father. I knew it."

Aideen joined her at the table.

"Well, if he thinks . . ."

The door opened, and a wide-eyed Hans entered.

"Well, dearie. It will work out." Aideen patted her hand.

Katie thought she heard the woman snicker as she tapped her shoulder on her way out the door.

"Pour it yourself," Katie quipped when Hans glanced at the coffee on the stove. He did, then sat in the chair Aideen had vacated. She watched him. It dawned on her he likely hadn't seen her in the street. She switched tactics. Placing a smile on her face, she asked, "How was your day?"

"Mine?"

He was flustered and had no idea she knew why. She was going to enjoy this. "Yes." Her tone turned sweet. "You said you were going to meet Moses today. How did that go?"

"Oh, that, well, yes."

"Yes?" She tapped her foot under the table, her hand gripping and releasing its stranglehold on her mug.

"We finished straking the wheels and loading the cart into his wagon."

"I see. Anything else?" She watched the pupils of his eyes become darker, larger under his furrowed brow. He looked around the room and his gaze settled on the basket.

"I wondered why the mercantile didn't have any cookies. You haven't taken them yet."

"Oh, were you at the mercantile?" If he didn't come clean, she might burst into flames.

"Yes. Moses and I . . ."

"Moses? He's such a lovely man. Loyal. Honest. Trustworthy." She knew she'd gone a bit too far.

"All true."

The finality in the breath that escaped him made her heart catch. Was he feeling remorse, guilt? But he still had not told the truth of what had happened. He'd not stood up for his friend. In that one non-act, he had proven he could not be counted on. Her heart ached, and her eyes burned. She was more disappointed than angry. She'd wanted him to be more than he was. She'd wanted him to be different.

What she'd wanted was for him to intervene and prove he desired more to alleviate the pain and suffering of others than care for his own self-preservation. More than anything, she realized he would not—could not—fight for her, the orphans, or the widows.

Not able to bear being in his presence any longer, she slammed the basket in front of him on the table and stomped out of the room. His dazed look at her abrupt change wasn't enough to melt her frozen heart.

For two days, she found excuses to be absent when Hans was nearby. She sat with Reverend Jenkins on the back porch and endured his stories. She visited with the Gray sisters to formulate more plans to put positive thoughts about an orphanage in people's minds. But even weeding the garden and doing the laundry could not get thoughts of what Hans had done, or rather, had not done, out of her head. Only during meals did she have to tolerate his stare. If he tried to start a conversation with her, she found ways to ignore him. She knew Aideen wasn't pleased, but nothing would change her mind.

"You've become an island, Katie girl. You've no ship and no supplies."

"That's how it's been my entire life, Aunt Aideen. It's no fun, but it's familiar."

"Talk to him, Katie."

Katie whirled on her aunt. "Talk to him? What would you say to a man who has no backbone? He cannot even stand up for his own friend. He didn't even fight in the war!" She was yelling now. "If he couldn't fight then, he'll not fight ever."

She watched her aunt flinch at her cutting tone and sharing of gossip. She followed the woman's gaze to the open kitchen door. There stood Hans, mouth agape, all color drained from his face.

He'd heard enough and bolted. Collapsing at the base of a tree, he pulled his knees to his chest and tucked his head. His lungs burned from running up the hill, his muscles cramped. The pain in the back of his throat didn't hurt nearly as much as his broken heart. One choice, the decision to not be a man, had cost him dearly. He wasn't sure how she knew, but he'd lost the respect of Katie and Moses in one day. He could not even face the reverend. He had no one else.

Katie might believe in God incidences, but this one was all on him. He had created this mess. He did not deserve help from God or anyone else for that matter.

"I'm a fool—an idiot. What was I thinking? Johann was right. I'm running. Always running."

To go or to stay? Whether right or wrong, the best thing he could do now was leave. He and Rauti would pull out at first light. They would find a new town where he could start over.

"Hans?" Reverend Jenkins called from his room across the hall early the next morning.

All he'd wanted to do was pack and leave. He did not have time nor patience for a lengthy conversation, but perhaps the man needed help.

"Yes, sir?"

Hans watched as the man patted the chair beside the bed where his form moved the blankets in the warm room. Hans plopped down, resting his forearms on his thighs.

"You've been on my mind this morning." Reverend Jenkins closed his eyes for a moment. "I'm not one to ask for help, but I'm in need, and I believe you've been heaven-sent."

Again with more God talk. Hans wriggled in his chair, and his heel bounced up and down as if preparing to bolt. When he looked up, Reverend Jenkins's eyes were clear and boring a hole into his soul.

"What's going on with you and Miss Katie?"

"Pffft. Nothing. Absolutely nothing."

"I see. You know, the Lord is more pleased when we do what is right and just. Says so in Proverbs twenty-one, verse three. Seems to me you're willing to destroy a friendship rather than make things right."

Hans was sure he was referring to his friendship with Katie, but it was his friendship with Moses that felt like a lead weight on his chest. They had connected, and the man now felt like a brother. Or had.

"The Bible is clear about making it right with your brother."

Hans stilled. Had the man read his mind?

"That's what I thought. I've a proposition for you, Hans. I need to get to a little town north of here called Blythewood this Sunday, but I don't have the energy to sit on a horse for that long or continue on my circuit. I would like you to take me." He put up his hand. "Now, before you go giving me every excuse, give this some thought. If you carry me in that cart of yours, I'll be able to rest. You, on the other hand, will have a month to figure out what you would like to do without making a rash decision and running off on a whim."

Hans watched the reverend scrutinize his facial expression.

"Mm-hmm. That's what I thought. Don't make a decision based on a season of life that will alter the rest of your life." The man gave him a knowing look. "Do the hard thing first, Hans. Fix things with Katie, settle whatever business you have in town, then let Aideen know you've agreed to go. She'll pack provisions for us."

His legs felt as if he were slogging through heavy mud. He wasn't sure what he would say to Katie. She had hurt him deeply with her words. But, putting that aside, he'd hurt her as well, probably just as profoundly, if not more. He rubbed his arm, blew out a deep breath, and swung open the kitchen door.

"Aideen?" He looked around the empty room before seeing her bent near the oven. "Is Katie here?"

Aideen put the bread in, shut the door, and wiped her hands on the towel. He watched as she folded it into a perfect rectangle and draped it over the oven door handle before turning.

"She's not here, Hans." She rested her bulk against the counter.

"Do you know when she'll be back?"

"I'm not certain. She left this morning on Dorcas."

"Ma'am?"

"She's gone to stay a while with Delphina."

His emotions and thoughts twisted together like his mother's yarn ball when the cat got a hold of it.

"I tried to get her to clear things up with you before she left, but, well, she's a proud woman. It's not my place to say more than that."

It was his own pride that had caused this.

"Aideen, I'm sorry." The breath that escaped felt final. He'd ruined everything. But he could at least make it right with Moses. The mud sucking at his feet had risen. "I've got some business in town."

"You'll be back by lunch?"

"Yes, ma'am."

"And you've decided to accompany the reverend?"

Up until this moment in time, he had not decided. But now, there was no reason to stay, and he would be even more miserable in this house without Katie in it. Even if she weren't speaking to him. He nodded in the affirmative.

Putting one foot in front of the other, he trudged to the barn. Rauti shook his head when Hans entered.

"Don't start with me. I'm already miserable enough."

The horse pawed the ground. A foul smell filled Hans's nostrils, and he wondered if Katie had a new stowaway.

"Hey, boy."

Hans turned, dread filling his body with the motion. Only one person he knew could put so much venom into so few words. Rauti continued to paw the ground.

"Joe. I see you brought your gang of misfits." He regretted it as soon as he'd said it. The false bravado did nothing to shore up his confidence.

"Came to finish what we started earlier."

The last thing he remembered was the eerie roar of Rauti trumpeting and a very loud crash.

Chapter 25

Shankel Farm

God? Katie looked out over the water as she sat on Delphina's front porch, Bible on her lap. She wore the heaviness of her heart like a woolen cloak. "God, does it ever get easier?" Hope seemed like an unattainable goal. Resting her head against the high back of the chair, she rocked, allowing her breathing to match the motion.

"Habakkuk 3:17–18." Delphina stepped out and took the other chair. "Look it up."

Katie's eyes focused on finding the passage. "Although the fig tree shall not blossom, neither shall fruit be in the vines; the labour of the olive shall fail, and the fields shall yield no meat; the flock shall be cut off from the fold, and there shall be no herd in the stalls: Yet I will rejoice in the LORD, I will joy in the God of my salvation."

"That verse carried me through many a day." Delphina looked to the horizon. "I'd lost my first husband, didn't have papers saying I was a freed woman, my child needed nourishment, and I'd gone dry—yet." She stopped rocking.

"Katie, I know it seems God is not hearing or answering your prayers, but yet . . ." Delphina resumed the heel-toe, heel-toe motion, and the chair creaked.

Katie watched the waning light form a halo around the woman's wiry, unruly head of hair. "Delphina, I know I'm supposed to rejoice in the Lord. I just can't seem to muster the energy."

Delphina laughed. "You've missed the point. It isn't in the rejoicing, it's in the yet."

"I don't understand."

"When our identity comes from anything or anyone other than God, we will fail. It's in the time between when we ask and God answers that He brings to light what we value or what has become an idol. Look deeper into that scripture, and stop at the yet. When you've figured that out, you can move on to the rejoicing part." Delphina stood. "Goodnight, child."

Katie reread the words and thought of the things she'd asked but God had not yet answered. "'Although the fig tree shall not blossom, neither shall fruit be in the vines; the labour of the olive shall fail, and the fields shall yield no meat; the flock shall be cut off from the fold, and there shall be no herd in the stalls: Yet' . . ."

Her breath caught in her throat even as she fell to her knees. "God, forgive me. If Habakkuk can see you in the everyday waiting and come out rejoicing, not because of his circumstances but because of the history he has with You, then I should strive to do so as well." She sobbed. God wasn't telling her no—He was telling her to live in the 'yet'—that transitional time where she could grow and learn until He was ready to fulfill His will.

As she prayed, asking God to forgive her for her lack of trust in Him, she knew God was telling her she needed to ask forgiveness of Hans. Forgiveness was not dependent on his actions. She needed to ask forgiveness for hers.

"Are you sure you're ready to return?" Rachel placed her hand on top of Katie's as Delphina refilled their cups.

"Yes, ma'am." Katie glanced at Delphina. "The Lord and one of his angels helped me see that I need to ask forgiveness of someone, so I can walk in harmony with Christ and be ready when He opens or closes the door on my dreams."

"Dreaming is my middle name. Good morning, ladies." Clint walked in, putting his hat on the peg before accepting a cup of coffee from Delphina.

"Katie was just about to tell us hers, darling," Rachel said. "Please join us."

Katie had not planned on sharing details, but since they'd already helped with Sam, she figured it was only fair. Explaining what she had done so far to help the widows and orphans who had come to town flowed easily from her tongue. "What you all did for Sam means so much to me. Delphina, thank you for understanding the need and finding a home for the child. I needed to be careful and not send a note in case the magistrate somehow intervened. I don't want to keep doing this in secret. I want to establish an orphanage."

"Bill talked to me at our last town meeting," said Clint. "He's pretty adamant that building an orphanage would bring unsavory folk to town. You don't see it that way, I'm surmising?"

"Would you call Sam riffraff, Mr. Shankel? The purpose of an orphanage is to care for abandoned children or those whose families are unable to care for them. It could also provide housing and jobs to women who need work. I know children grow up best in families, whether extended families or other arrangements, but someone needs to help them find these homes. Most importantly, when you leave individuals homeless, they become a drain on society, the ragtag and bobtail Magistrate Marley refers to. If their basic needs are met and they are educated or trained in a trade, they grow up to be responsible, healthy adults who give back to the community they live in instead of taking away from it." Her heartrate had increased, and she knew her face was flushed. At some point, she had stood and begun pacing. She took her seat.

"Miss Murphy, I do believe you've thought this through," Clint said.

"Just a bit." She chuckled and took a deep breath. "Sorry, I get a tad excited."

"Passionate." Rachel smiled.

Delphina added, "Mm-hmm."

"Let's say the magistrate changed his mind. What would you need to get started?" Clint asked.

"If"—Katie emphasized the word—"I started an orphanage, I would need a large house or land to build one on." She touched one index finger to the other. "Staff, such as a cook and caregivers." She moved her finger to the next as if ticking off her list. "Supplies." She sighed as she realized the rising cost involved.

"Go on. Pretend money is no object."

"Right. We are dreaming." She smirked at the absurdity but continued voicing her dream. "Each child would need basic necessities. Oh, and schooling, no matter their color." She looked around the table and saw acceptance in their faces. "They'd need religious training, and as they got older, they'd need mentors to provide trade skills as well." She struggled to remain seated. "Mr. Taylor at the mercantile could train a clerk. Aideen could help the girls learn to cook and clean. Mr. Finch could show the boys how to care for horses." She picked up speed. "And Moses—he could apprentice a boy to become a blacksmith." Her excitement was almost more than she could contain. "And perhaps one or more of the widows would have a particular skill they could teach the girls in addition to the work they do around the house. I plan on providing work for them as well."

"Sounds to me like all God's people need to have a part of this child-raising idea," Delphina offered.

Clint ran his hand over his mustache and down his neck, sticking his finger in the top of his collar and moving it from left to right. "So, let me get this straight. Rather than those widows and orphans being a drain on society, you plan on raising up God-fearing, educated, respectable, working citizens."

"Yes," she yelled as she slammed her hands on the table. The sting brought her to her senses.

Those at the table burst into laughter.

"Young lady, have you ever thought of running for president?" Clint wiped his eyes with the back of his hand.

"What's all this laughter I hear?"

"Moses." Delphina rushed to her husband but slowed just as she got within reach. "You weren't supposed to be back until this evening." She swatted at his arm.

"I can go back." His deep voice rumbled before he wrapped her in a bear hug and kissed her forehead. "Boys wanted to get back to see if the dog had had those pups yet. I knew there'd be no sleeping, so we drove through the night." Moses shook Clint's hand and nodded to the other ladies, stopping at Katie.

Something changed in his expression. Whatever it was made her feel as if someone had doused her in an ice bath.

"Miss Murphy, might I have a word with you?"

It took a moment for Katie to realize the others were leaving. She felt glued to her chair yet still grabbed onto the table to steady herself. "Is Aideen all right?"

"Miss Aideen is just fine."

"The reverend?"

He pulled out a chair, and she noticed Delphina standing behind him, her hand on his shoulder. "Miss Katie, it's Hans."

She'd made a terrible mistake. She had misjudged Hans. It had been a struggle to sit still long enough to hear Moses's retelling of the story at the mercantile. The explanation of how he'd asked Hans not to make eye contact or do anything that might cause more trouble rolled around in her mind, making her dizzy. Then, hearing how Moses had found Hans's bloodied and unconscious body in the barn, made her stomach roil and body tremble.

"Oh, Lord. If Rauti hadn't broken out and chased those men into town, it may have been too late." A sob escaped. She went over the scenario hundreds of times as she journeyed back to Shumard Oak Bend.

"Miss Murphy," Magistrate Marley called as she pulled into town. "Nice to see you. Did you have a nice visit with the Shankels? How is Clint these days?"

He was the last person she wanted to talk with; being pumped for information made her blood begin to boil. *Lord, help me here. I'm willing to grow in the "yet," but I'd rather get the "right about now" over with.*

"I'm sure you've heard about Hans?" He made it a question, and Katie knew he was hoping she'd not heard, so he could have the honor.

"Yes, sir. I left straight away when I heard. I'm headed there now to see if there's anything I can do."

"Do? Why, you haven't heard, then. He's gone. Up and left

yesterday morning."

Katie did not want to hear his version. The urgency to see Aideen increased. "If you'll excuse me, Magistrate. I'm quite tired from my journey." She didn't wait for a response. Dorcas seemed to understand and began walking before she gave the command.

"Aunt Aideen?" Katie called from the foyer. "Aideen, I'm home."

"Oh, me dear girl." Aideen's eyes were puffy, her mob cap askew, and apparently, the flour bowl had won a war in the kitchen. Katie looked down to see traces of white on the floor. It looked like her aunt had been pacing if the white footprints were any indication. She wrapped her aunt in a hug. The connection released a flood gate in the woman. Katie worked to keep her own tears at bay as she led Aideen to the settee.

"It's awful, just awful." Aideen patted her face with her hankie.

"Moses told me about Hans, but what's this about him leaving?"

"Reverend Jenkins asked him to accompany him on his circuit."

"The magistrate made it sound like he'd done something awful."

"That's the thing. Rumor in town has it that Hans is running from something. Henry asked me to let you know that he wants to speak with you."

"What? The sheriff? Why? Should I go now?"

"It's too late tonight. You can see him in the morning. But, as far as why, I was hoping you could tell me."

"And he told you nothing of this Joe fellow from the war?"

"No, Sheriff. He never mentioned him," Katie said. "Is there a problem?"

"There wasn't until this showed up." He slid a piece of paper across the table that showed the likeness of the man everyone knew as Joe.

Joseph Tallmadge Clemons, Age 34
Wanted for desertion from the Confederate Army
Escaped from Gratiot Street Prison
Considered armed and dangerous.

Katie looked up.

"I'm as shocked as you are. Figured he was just another cocky lowlife. It's the first time I've been down on my watch." Sheriff Adkins leaned on the back two legs of his chair.

"Where is he now?"

"Joe? Good question. Rauti made some permanent hoof print markings on one man named Larry. He'll survive but may not ride again. The others got away, and Larry isn't talking. Says he met Joe and his gang in the woods outside of town. Apparently, Magistrate Marley wasn't as thorough in his questioning with this bunch."

"What does any of this have to do with Hans?"

"That's the problem. I'm not sure. The magistrate has it in his mind that Hans was a part of this group, but it just doesn't add up. It's my job to figure out the truth."

The walk home from the opposite edge of town felt longer than usual. Deep in thought, she paid no mind to what she stepped in. Her mind missed the sounds around her as she wracked her brain for any remembrance of seeing Hans spend time with anyone in town other than Moses, Mr. Taylor, or Mr. Finch.

"Did you have a nice chat with the sheriff, Miss Murphy?" Magistrate Marley drew up beside her, keeping pace, which was a challenge given his girth. His breath came out in big puffs.

Katie picked up her pace.

"We had another mother and son come through while you were away."

Katie stopped. The magistrate had to turn back to see her. The sun was now in his eyes, and he squinted.

"Young woman, perhaps in her early twenties. The boy couldn't have been more than two. I didn't know what to do with them, so sent them on their way. Now, should that happen again . . ."

"What are you not saying, Mr. Marley?" Katie emphasized "Mr."

"I'm simply stating a fact, Miss Murphy. I'm giving you a bit of information and asking you to do likewise. There's a decent piece of land with a small house on it that has recently become available."

Was he dangling the orphanage like a carrot in front of her nose?

"It's not too far out of town, close enough to walk to the church, yet . . ."

Yet. That one three-letter word was all she needed. The magistrate was not the one to say whether or not there would be an orphanage, nor where it might be located. That was up to God.

From the depths of her being, she conjured up the sweetest tone she could muster. "Mr. Marley, I've nothing to say. When Hans returns with Reverend Jenkins, he can speak for himself. In the meantime, I suggest you focus your energy on ensuring riffraff like Joe and his gang don't get past your perusal. Good day." She schooled her features as she turned.

Fabric bunched in her hands. She couldn't decide if she wanted to lift her skirt and skip after giving the magistrate a piece of her mind or tear the fabric in frustration.

Oh, Hans. What is going on?

Chapter 26

Blythewood, Missouri

"**H**e's such a quiet, unassuming young man."

The woman was rail-thin with a tight bun. She reminded Hans of Edna in more than looks. She whispered like a toddler who didn't yet understand a concept, was all up in his business, and had a grating tone. Even so, he could not close his ears to her words.

"To have cared for the reverend enough to transport him in his weakened state on his circuit. I can only imagine what he endured to receive those bruises. I'm certain the reverend is thankful for that boy's protection."

Hans let out a slow breath. He didn't have the energy or the inclination to correct the woman. Wincing, he shook out the oiled cloth and began folding it. His ribs ached, his neck was stiff, and the stitches Aideen had placed over his eye and in his lip pulled when he scowled. He tried to relax his eyebrows, which were pinched together at the moment. A younger voice joined the discussion.

"Did you see how gently he helped the reverend from that cart he built? You knew he crafted that, didn't you, Mother? My, but he is handsome in a rugged sort of way." A sigh escaped the lips of the girl who stood beside the woman.

He shook his head, the motion making his stomach heave. A bitter tang filled his mouth, and he spat. It wasn't just the pain. He knew he needed to put an end to the not-quite-truths these gossipers were spreading. He looked about, wishing to be anywhere else but here.

"What a beautiful piece of workmanship." Hans's ears perked up at the praise, but he did not look to the gossiper. Another woman's voice joined in. He remained focused on folding the cloth, this time taking care to be quiet. He didn't want the ladies to know he was listening. He may not have wanted to hear them extol his personal attributes, especially since most were a lie, but he craved the feeling he received when someone noticed and admired his craftsmanship.

"You know, Wilhelmina, he'd be able to support a wife with skill such as that. Why, with the attention to detail I see in that cart and the care I witnessed him give the reverend, he'd be a catch for any young lady."

"Quite a shiner you've got there, son." A wiry man with white hair that stuck out like the quills of a porcupine interrupted Hans's eavesdropping. "Elder Timpe." The man stuck out a gnarled hand, his twisted fingers making Hans cautious about giving him a firm handshake.

"Pleased to meet you, sir." Hans placed the folded cloth on

the cart bed and ignored the mention of his bruises.

"You've chosen a fine man to follow. Reverend Jenkins has served us well for many a year. It's a blessing to have you with us."

"My pleasure, sir. He's been very good to me." Hans realized his words were true. Reverend Jenkins had become a very close friend and treated him with kindness. The reverend had a gentle way of helping Hans see God's truths, even if Hans didn't want to accept them.

He looked up to see Elder Timpe glance at the gathering of women. Hans groaned.

"Not interested?" Elder Timpe gestured with his head to the group.

"Not in the least. I'd rather read my Bible." Hans kept the laughter begging to be released to himself. Reading his Bible had been the most detestable task on this journey. Reverend Jenkins read scripture out loud for hours. All those thees and thous made Hans's head spin.

"Well now, that's a wonderful thing to hear from a young man. Each generation seems to get further and further from the Lord. It's good to see a fine youngster like yourself standing up for what's true, honest, just, and of good report, as it says in Philippians, but I'm sure you're quite familiar with that passage."

Hans stilled. The man had misunderstood. If he only knew how far from truth, honesty, and justness he was. Hans rubbed the back of his neck.

"And humble." The man reached out to touch Hans's shoulder but must have thought better of it.

Hans rubbed the place where the man would have touched. Everything hurt.

"You and the reverend will be bunking with me. I've the space since my wife and son are both gone from this world. You take your time finishing up here. You can put your horse in my barn over there." The man pointed to a rough-looking shed. "Weather's nice, so we'll be having services outside tomorrow." He pointed to the field beside the barn. "Do you feel well enough to help put out the pews in the morning? Nothing but some logs and boards."

"I'll do my best to help with whatever you need. I can head over to your place now. I just finished up." He followed the man.

"Pews are in the lean-to. But we'll deal with that first thing in the morning, so the dew doesn't cover them in the night. Mrs. Shuster and her four daughters provided a stew for dinner this evening. She's quite the cook. If I were a younger man . . ." Mr. Timpe gave an impressive wink. "Let's get cleaned up."

Hans enjoyed the stew, biscuits, greens, dessert, and quiet. He looked at the reverend, realizing the man had spoken not a word during dinner.

"Are you feeling well, Reverend Jenkins?" Hans asked. The man still had food on his plate.

"Are you sure you don't care for some apple crisp?" Mr. Timpe offered when Reverend Jenkins didn't respond.

"I don't believe so. I think I'll turn in early, but it would do this old man's heart good if you'd read a passage before I retire, Hans."

Hans tried to discern what the man was up to. Was that a twinkle in his eyes, or was something truly wrong? He'd never known the reverend to turn down a sweet of any kind.

"Yes, son, that would be wonderful. No need to get your Bible. Mine is there on the table." Mr. Timpe pointed. "I'll pour us another cup of coffee while you retrieve it."

Hans tried to slow his breathing as he picked up the heavy book that felt like a burden, the load almost more than he could bear. He flipped to the front pages as if perusing a gem of great worth. There it was—an index. He looked at it studiously, running his shaking hands over the page as if to smooth a non-existent wrinkle.

"John 8:31–32, if you would, please, Hans. I do love the fourth book of the New Testament," the reverend offered.

Hans gave the man a nod of appreciation and found the passage without issue. Tension spread up his neck, and he rolled his shoulders, wincing when the motion pulled at his ribs. Licking his lips, he cleared his throat.

"Then said Jesus to those Jews which believed on him, If ye continue in my word, then are ye my disciples indeed; and ye shall know the truth, and the truth shall make you free."

Hans reread the words. He didn't understand their meaning.

"The perfect three-point sermon," Mr. Timpe offered.

"Yes. Yes, it is. John is good at reminding us that if we continue, or abide, in God's Word, then, one, we will truly be His disciples; two, we will know the truth; and three, the truth will make us free." Reverend Jenkins seemed to have found his voice and energy.

Elder Timpe bobbed his head like Rauti. "My mother often reminded me that abide is an action word. Always the schoolteacher. If we dragged our feet to obey, she'd say 'endure without yielding and accept without objection.' Obedience was important in my day. Oh, that the youth of today would heed those same words. Seems to me rebellion is rampant."

"Not just outward rebellion," Reverend Jenkins added with exuberance. "Young people today don't take action. It's a new kind of rebellion—idleness."

Hans struggled to breathe. The tightness in his chest moved up his throat. His hand rubbed the front of his neck as if the motion would help him swallow whatever was lodged there. He listened to the men discuss the two short verses for what seemed like an hour but did not comment.

"Well, it's time I turned in for the night."

"Let me help you, Reverend." Hans jumped from his chair. The movement was too quick, making him grab at his side.

"You take care of those ribs. You're still healing, and no one knows what tomorrow may bring."

Chapter 27

Hans wanted nothing more than to breathe deeply of the crisp morning air, but his ribs would not allow it. He took care as he rolled the logs into place, then carried the first plank, struggling to place it on top.

"Need some help, mister?" A gangly teen in overalls picked up the other end of the board before Hans could answer.

"Thanks."

"You the new preacher?"

"I'm Hans. Reverend Jenkins wasn't up yet when I started this morning even though I'm slower than usual these days."

"Nice to meet you. I'm Larz."

Larz lifted the next plank onto his shoulder with ease. He looked Hans over but didn't comment on the bruises or stitches.

"Sunday's the only day of the week I don't have to wait around for my sisters before heading to town. They take forever getting ready. I usually set up the pews. You beat me to it this morning." The lad looked up at the rising sun as if to judge the time.

"That's the last one." Hans rubbed his back with his thumbs and heard his stomach growl. "Have you eaten, Larz? I could use some breakfast. Looked like my host had plenty if you're hungry." Hans had to pretend to wipe something off his pant legs so the boy wouldn't see the laughter about to burst forth. If the boy's eyes were as big as his stomach, the food may be gone before Hans had an opportunity to fill his plate.

"You betcha. Elder Timpe is a good man, and the womenfolk—they're always trying to get his attention by feeding him." The two walked into the small house.

"Well, hello, Larz. Thanks for helping Hans. You two sit down. Let me get another cup of coffee." He placed the full one in front of Hans. "Drink up, son. You'll need to get changed before service."

Hans looked down at the smudges on his clothing. Aideen had given him two of Paddy's shirts and told him to keep them clean for Sundays. He would change into one of them as soon as he'd finished eating.

"Where's the reverend?" Larz asked around a mouthful of ham biscuit.

"In his room," Elder Timpe said. "Hans, since you've finished, get yourself ready, then let's head on to church."

Hans drank the last swig of coffee, then headed to his room and changed his shirt.

"Looking good, Preacher," Larz said when Hans stepped out.

"I agree," Elder Timpe added. "You clean up nice. Now, you've a field full of parishioners waiting to hear from the Lord."

"But I—I'm not a . . ." Hans blanched.

"The reverend explained the church did not sanction you, but he believes in you. Told me as much last night. No time to waste." Mr. Timpe opened the door.

Panic seized Hans. *Lord, help me.* His mute plea filled his ears as he slumped onto the bench next to Larz.

"You'll do just fine. We all get nervous. I know I did my first time," Larz offered.

"Let us begin with a word of prayer." Elder Timpe stood in front of the crowd. "Help us today, Lord, as we learn how to walk closer to Your Son, Jesus Christ. Help us in our understanding of how to connect with You. We want to honor and glorify You today. Amen."

Hans didn't know how to walk with Christ, let alone connect and become closer. Mr. Timpe wedged himself between two older ladies after introductions and motioned for Hans to stand. He did not want to disappoint anyone—the congregation, the elder, and especially Reverend Jenkins. Larz said he'd done it before. Surely, Hans could as well.

"Just act like you're talking to me, Hans," Larz leaned over and whispered. "That's what I always had to do when giving a recitation at school." Larz grabbed his elbow and pushed him forward.

Speak truth. That's all I have to do. Later, I'll speak truth of a different kind to Reverend Jenkins. The thought made him smirk and erased his nerves for a moment. Taking a deep breath, he took the heavy Bible Mr. Timpe was holding out and moved behind the makeshift podium. It wobbled more than he did when he grasped its sides.

"I'm no preacher, so I'm just going to share God's Word." The Bible slipped, and Hans caught it before it reached the ground. He continued as if his clumsiness were not nerves. "I'll do my best to explain what I think God is trying to tell us." His voice changed pitch and a quivery, twitchy feeling started in his stomach and moved to his head.

He cleared his throat. "Everyone, please turn to John 8:31–32." He was thankful the elder had marked the passage they'd discussed last night. One of Aideen's tatted crosses lay across the underlined passage. Had the reverend given one to Elder Timpe, or had the reverend marked the spot himself? He struggled to bring the words into focus as his hands shook the podium. Hans repeated what he'd heard the men discuss the night before. His confidence built as he realized he did believe what he was saying—until he got to his third point.

"The truth will set you free."

For hours the previous night, Hans had watched a fly buzz around the ceiling where a moonbeam had confused the insect. Freedom was something Hans did not understand. He had fought against slavery, but it was his own enslavement that he did not know how to master. He knew powers imprisoned him beyond his ability to break free. Someone cleared his throat, bringing Hans back to the present. He wiped his hands on his pant legs, looked up, and, with finality said,

"The end."

A row of girls giggled as Hans made his way to his seat. He felt heat rise in his face, and uncertainty coursed through his veins, ending at the stitches on his forehead. He reached up and touched the spot, letting his head fall into his hands as he sat forward.

"Amen. Thank you, Hans." Elder Timpe coughed, removed his handkerchief, and wiped his brow. "Mrs. Beecher, would you please lead us in a hymn?"

Hans stood but did not sing. He was an embarrassment. *The end.* What was he thinking?

"Fine sermon, young man. You have a bright future." A man grasped Hans's hand and pumped it.

"What a wonderful way to show the finality of sin when saved. The end. So very moving." An older woman patted the back of his hand.

"You're a natural. God will use you mightily." This came from an elderly man.

One after another, the church people shook his hand and offered words of praise. His shoulders began to straighten, his chin lifted, and a satisfied smile graced his face. He felt taller somehow. Yet deep inside, he felt like a fraud. He looked at Larz to garner his reaction to the accolades. The boy grinned and gave him a thumbs-up.

Except for Reverend Jenkins's blessing on their lunch, the man hadn't said a word as they'd traveled to their next destination. Hans was angry enough with the man to, well, he wasn't exactly sure what, but it wouldn't be God-honoring—that was for certain.

"Right up there on that knoll, Hans—to the left is a small cabin. We can bunk there for the night if it isn't already occupied."

No "I'm sorry" or "thank you"? Hans's jaw tightened, and he felt heat rising up the back of his neck.

Hans checked the dwelling. Besides a few rodents and spiders, it was empty and dry and had ample floor space for two bedrolls—on opposite sides of the table. He flung both packs into their respective corners.

"I've got to care for Rauti." He did not offer to assist the reverend in getting down. He figured he was being kind to at least wait until the man was out before unhitching the cart from the horse.

As in his military days, he walked. Demons fought for space in his mind. He clenched and unclenched his fists as he marched toward an outcropping of rock. The struggle to climb felt good, and his chest heaved from the exertion. Hans took in great gulps of air when he reached the top. For what might be miles, he saw rolling hills, blue streaks of streams, and clumps of dark brush dotting the landscape.

Settling into a natural groove in the rock, he massaged the area around his sore ribs. He had overdone it when he'd climbed, and he was suffering, but it had been worth it. The scene before him was breathtaking. He glanced back to the small cabin and marveled at how far he had walked. He whistled to Rauti, and the horse responded, letting him know he'd be able to get back in the dark. Hans settled into the hollow in the rock as the sun continued its descent, creating myriad hues of purples and pinks. A burst of yellow sprang forth, illuminating the ground until the sun nestled itself in for the night.

Hans remained on the rock. The light buzzing of night sounds calmed him. He swatted at a flying insect and counted the chirps and clicks of various frogs and toads as they called out to each other. His laugh silenced the music when it dawned on him that while all God's creatures were searching for a mate, he'd called to Rauti.

Katie's green eyes flashed before his own. Leaning back, he closed his eyes. Freckles danced in his vision while skirts swished past, creating a gentle breeze that exposed slim ankles.

"Hans. Hans." Someone was calling to him. "Wake up."

He didn't want to report for duty. He'd just finished his shift. Enough dead bodies for one evening. *Lord, please just let me die!* Warmth covered his face, but no light shone in his eyes. Where was he?

"Hans, son, please," the gentle voice pleaded. "Can you come down?"

Come down? Hans felt the hard rock beneath him. He tried to focus, but his vision blurred.

"Hans. It's Scott Jenkins. You've had a bad dream. Can you wake enough to come down from there?"

Consciousness returned in small segments. He was traveling with the reverend. Anger had propelled him to this rock, but beauty had made him stay. "I'm coming, Reverend," he cried out as he descended.

"Looks like you've opened that head wound with all your thrashing. Let's get you taken care of."

A brightness burned his eyes, and he lifted his hands to shield the offending light.

"We've quite a way to walk back. Can you make it?"

"Yes." One foot in front of the other. It was how he'd moved for years.

He heard Rauti snort, letting him know he only had a few more steps to go. Reverend Jenkins helped him onto his open bedroll, then hurried away. He wasn't sure how long he lay there.

"Can you sit up, son?"

His head throbbed, his ribs ached, and the smell of something acrid wafted around him when he moved.

"I cleaned your wound as best I could," Reverend Jenkins said as he handed Hans a cup of coffee. "How long have you had these nightmares?"

Hans sipped coffee with one hand and held a damp cloth to his forehead with the other.

"Since the war." His response was slow.

"Does anything seem to trigger them?"

"Stress." If looks could kill, he'd be digging a hole for the man's grave about now.

Chapter 28

Shumard Oak Bend

"Marmalade, what's gotten into you today?" Orange hair clung to the bottom of Katie's skirt as the cat wove around her legs.

"Miss Murphy?"

"Hello, Mr. Finch," told the man. "Dorcas is looking happy with her new shoes. You didn't need to bring her, though. I was on my way to you."

"I . . . um . . . needed the exercise and wanted to ensure she was walking properly."

"How very thoughtful of you. Aideen is inside. Might you have time for a cup of tea and a cookie?" Katie watched the man's face flush. Could he be sweet on her aunt? Perhaps the age difference didn't matter to a widowed man.

"Will you be joining us?"

Her heart sank. Oh, dear. Were his intentions for her? She needed this man as an ally, not a suitor. He was one of the few she had not yet spoken to about the orphanage.

"That you, Mr. Finch?" Aideen stood on the top step, her hand shielding her eyes.

"Hello, Mrs. O'Sullivan." His gaze flitted from Aideen to Katie.

"Mr. Finch and I were just discussing date nut cookies and a cup of tea." Katie gave her most pleading look possible to her aunt and shook her head. She prayed Aideen would catch the hint.

"But, of course. Please, Mr. Finch, do join me."

Marmalade chose that moment to show herself. Katie reached down and petted the tail that brushed against her brown skirt.

"That your cat?" Mr. Finch wrinkled his nose, and his upper lip twitched moments before a forceful sneeze caused his hat to fall from his head. "Those creatures make me sneeze."

Katie smiled on the inside as a thought formed. "Oh, Marmalade? She's the sweetest thing." She reached down and picked up the cat, hoping that, for a rare moment, the feline would allow herself to be caught. Hair floated on the breeze as a soft purr emanated from the animal.

"Achoo. Achoo. Achoo." Mr. Finch pulled his hanky from his pocket and blew his reddened nose, then picked up his hat, which had once again landed on the ground.

Katie felt a kinship with the cat and whispered her thanks into the animal's soft ear. Orange hair flew as the cat leapt from Katie's arms and darted for the barn.

"I believe I'll pass on that cookie. My head's swimming, and I've work to do. Thank you for the offer, Mrs. O'Sullivan, Miss Murphy." He stretched his arm as far as possible and handed the reins to Katie before taking a step back.

"Thank you again for bringing Dorcas. You are most kind." Katie noted the man looked a bit dejected as he turned to go.

"Kathleen, what in tarnation was that all about?" Aideen hissed between tight lips.

Katie used one hand to brush the fur from her blouse and waited until she was certain the man was out of earshot. "I have no idea what you're referring to."

"Mm-hmm."

"If you don't mind, I'd like some fresh air. I thought I would take Dorcas for a ride. She needs the exercise and a chance to try out her new shoes."

"Sun's setting, so mind you don't go far."

Katie heard Aideen mutter Marmalade's name as she went back into the house. Marmalade must have heard it as well, for she peeked her head out the barn door.

"You, my friend, get an extra treat at supper tonight," Katie said.

She saddled and mounted Dorcas, then led her out of town to a flat area. Red curls whipped behind her as she urged the animal into a gallop. Sweet smells filled her with each deep breath. She felt free and unencumbered from life's cares. Dorcas slowed more quickly than Katie wished, but when Dorcas made a decision, there was no prodding or cajoling to convince her to do otherwise. Katie let the animal do as she pleased. Reverend Jenkins had warned her to let the horse have her head and to trust her instincts.

Thinking of the reverend brought Hans to mind. She willed herself to keep images of the handsome Finn away. Dorcas stilled, as did she. Focusing on the horizon, she took deep cleansing breaths and blew them out, along with Hans's image and the lilting sound of his voice.

"Ma'am?"

Katie jumped. Dorcas exhaled.

"Ma'am?"

Katie searched for the voice in the waning light. There, near a scrappy tree was a huddled figure wearing a bonnet. Dark gray skirts billowed, making her look like a rock. A carpetbag rested in a heap beside her, and another lump completed the outcropping.

Katie took in her surroundings. There were no other places close by for someone to hide, but a good shot from the trees in the distance could take her out. She willed to make herself smaller and chose to dismount and put Dorcas between her and those trees.

"Sorry, old girl." Katie's whisper came out louder than she'd hoped.

"Ma'am? Can you help us?"

Us. Katie's blood turned cold. What if this was Joe's gang setting a trap? Her earlier breaths did nothing to help as Katie's vision swam from lack of oxygen. She stumbled when Dorcas nudged her forward. The action forced her body to inhale.

"Not now, Dorcas."

Dorcas continued to nudge her.

"Please, ma'am. It's my boy. He needs help."

Dorcas nudged once more, then moved toward the voice.

Frozen and with her eyes closed, Katie worked to calm her nerves. The reins in her hand pulled her forward as Dorcas led the way. A child rested his head in the woman's lap. Even in the diminishing light, Katie noticed the sunken eyes and cracked lips. She pulled her canteen from the saddle and handed it to the woman.

"Take slow, small sips," Katie cautioned.

The woman drank before her shaking hand dribbled the liquid into the child's mouth, missing the mark.

"Here, let me." Katie poured water into her hand and brushed it against the boy's dry lips. The child did not respond, and Katie's pulse quickened, her stomach churning with fear. She wiped her hand across his warm skin, a faint breath tickling her palm. "Can you get atop my horse?"

The woman didn't respond but moved the child from her lap to the ground, then attempted to stand. Katie caught her arm as the woman wobbled.

"My legs are tingling, and I'm lightheaded." The woman's fingers sank into Katie's arm.

"Steady now."

"My boy."

"Let's get you on Dorcas, then I'll hand him up to you. Can you manage?"

"Yes." Her breathy reply seemed to diminish her energy, but her lifted chin showed her resolve.

Katie lost track of time as they headed to town. The lantern on the porch was a welcoming sight. How she had managed to get the mother and son back to Aideen's, she could not recollect.

"Katie, oh me dear girl," her aunt called. "I was so worried. Are you all right? Who do you have there?"

"Aideen, please come help me get them down."

Exhaustion settled over Katie. Hours of changing the damp cloths to lessen the boy's fever had her yearning for sleep.

"You get some rest. I'll watch over him for a bit." Steaming cup in one hand, Aideen placed the other on Katie's shoulder.

"How is Clara?"

"Sleeping. She was able to keep down some tea and bread. You go rest now. You can spell me in a few hours." Aideen nudged Katie's shoulder.

"Dorcas. Oh, my." Katie staggered as she rushed out the door.

Dorcas was not where she'd left her near the hitching post,

and Katie's throat tightened. "Oh, Dorcas. What have I done?" Marmalade came from the barn, her irritating meow grating on Katie's frayed nerves. "Not now, Marmalade. Go on with you." Katie's gaze followed the cat to the open barn doors. "Dorcas?"

There in the open stall was the old mare, bobbing her head and smiling as if it were natural to put herself to bed. Katie removed the saddle and brushed the horse. Weary in body and spirit, she placed her forehead on Dorcas's shoulder and wept. She was only one person, and there were so many in need.

"Lord," she choked out, her words echoing in the darkness. "Lord, what am I to do? Now I've pulled Aideen into this." Worry wrapped around her heart and squeezed. If Magistrate Marley found out, he would be furious. The ache in her chest increased, and she crumpled in the straw.

Katie woke. Warmth enveloped her. She reached for the covers and felt them move. Her eyes popped open to darkness and breathing.

The rumble of Marmalade's purr and the soft breathing of Dorcas settled around her. Katie realized the horse was asleep at her side. Katie was curled up beside her prostrate form with Marmalade tucked in tight. Slowly, she stood so as not to disturb the horse and risk injury to herself. Dorcas may be a gentle soul, but she still outweighed Katie. If she tried to rise and took one step with those new shoes, Katie would sport quite the bruise—or worse.

Outside, the moon was making its descent. The cool night breeze caressed her face. The birds would be up soon. Aideen and the events of the evening came to mind. She swept straw, cat fur, and wrinkles from her clothing as she hurried to the house.

Fresh coffee was on the stove, and biscuits were in the oven. Aideen's red-rimmed eyes peaked through the door. "I wondered where you'd gotten lost."

"Aideen, I'm sorry. I fell asleep in the barn. I'll take over, so you can rest now."

"The boy woke about an hour ago and sipped some water. Children heal quickly. See if you can spoon more into him each time he wakes or every hour, whichever comes first. His mother should be able to care for him when she gets up."

"Yes, ma'am."

"I'll bring you coffee and a biscuit when they're done, and then I'll head on in to get some rest myself."

Katie crept into the room where the boy's sleeping form rested. Shallow breaths came and went like the ticking of a clock. She changed the damp rag, picked at her biscuit, spooned water into his mouth, drank her cold coffee, and repeated the process until well after the birds and sun had risen.

"Danny?" a shaky voice, raspy and dry, called.

"Please come in. Your son is doing well." Katie watched as the boy's mother dropped to her knees. Her shoulders shook, and sobs escaped her mouth but no tears fell. "I'll bring coffee and a biscuit. Here, please take my seat." She helped Clara from the floor.

"Thank you." The woman grasped Katie's hand with more

force than she would have thought possible in the woman's weakened state. "God sent you. I know He did. Thank you."

Katie nodded as tears pricked at the backs of her eyes. Was that how God worked? Whenever Katie made plans, things didn't always work out as she'd hoped. But when she had no plans, God seemed to work in them just the same.

"I have much to learn, don't I, Lord?"

Chapter 29

Shumard Oak Bend

It could work. It might work. It had to work.

"Good day, Mr. Sneed." Katie wiggled her fingers as she picked up her pace. The banker waved back from where he stood and held the door for a patron. Katie let out a sigh of relief when he followed the man inside. She quickened her steps more and continued through town.

The bleating of goats pulled her attention to the back of the livery. There sat Marmalade, tail swishing over the fence, taunting one of the smaller goats. Zacchaeus—she believed was his name. "Marmalade, you are a nuisance."

"That you, Miss Murphy?" Mr. Finch came through the barn doors into the corral. Even with the fence between them, Katie took a step back before gathering her resolve.

"Hello, Mr. Finch." Words stuck in her throat, and she didn't recognize their sound.

"Did you need something? Dorcas having trouble with the new shoes? I should have stopped by last week to check."

"No. I mean . . ." She exhaled and let the practiced words fly. "Mr. Finch, Aideen and I would like to invite you to dinner this evening. We aren't expecting the stagecoach and thought you might appreciate a homecooked meal."

"Why, that would be right nice. Thank you." The smile that spread across his face made Katie feel guilty for the small deception. "I usually close up shop around six. Do you need me to lock up sooner?"

"Six thirty for dinner is fine." Katie wanted to turn and run, but Marmalade chose that moment to brush up against her skirt.

"That cat taunts me and my goats near every day. She won't be coming to dinner as well, I'm hoping?"

"No, sir. Aideen would never allow an animal in the house."

"Good to know. Achoo. Just seeing the thing makes me sneeze."

"Good day, Mr. Finch. Come, Marmalade. Let us leave the man to his work."

She had done it. Her heartbeat slowed, and she smiled at the townspeople blurring in her vision as she passed—until she saw Magistrate Marley step out and into her path.

"Well, Miss Murphy. Out for a stroll? Did I see that moggie cat following you just now? Menace, that thing. That varmint likely carries all forms of disease."

"Marmalade? Quite the opposite. Get rid of that sweet cat, and you'll see your vermin population increase. Why, we've not had a single critter in our cellar since Marmalade took up residence on our side of town."

"Well, keep that vile animal away from me. I don't abide by freeloaders of any shape or size. Do I make myself clear?"

He did, and it made her sick to her stomach. "Animals tend to steer clear of those they don't like, Mr. Marley. I'm sure you'll have no trouble." She knew the moment the words escaped her lips that they shouldn't have. His shock allowed her the moment she needed. "Enjoy the rest of your day, sir." Her skirts felt heavy and cumbersome as if they were holding her in place. She fought the urge to lift the weight and run as she plodded home.

The slight lift of her skirts brought Hans to mind. She remembered turning to see his shocked expression at her hiked-up skirts as she'd run from church. He'd been so carefree, playful, and oh, so charming. She opened the door to Aideen's and recalled his arm ushering her in as he'd bounded up the stairs before her, those white teeth surrounded by—

"Penny for your thoughts?"

Katie wiped the expression from her face and glared at Aideen, who was smiling at her like she knew exactly what Katie was thinking.

"Best save your penny. You may need it." Katie smoothed her skirts and brushed past her aunt. "The deed is done. Mr. Finch will be here at 6:30."

"A man," Danny pointed. "Pretty flowers."

Katie scooped up little Danny from the window and handed him to his mother as a knock sounded on the door. "I'll get that. You keep Danny boy here in the parlor."

Katie squared her shoulders, checked to see that Clara and her son were out of sight, and opened the door.

"Mr. Finch." No other words would escape. She took in the clean-shaven man. Silver streaks glistened in his still-wet hair. He lifted the flowers in his hands.

"For you. And Aideen. And Aideen," he repeated.

So, it was her he was interested in. Well, that was all about to change if she had anything to do with it.

"These will look lovely on our table, Mr. Finch, and you are right on time. Come, meet our guests." He looked confused, then deflated before her eyes. She took the flowers in one hand and ushered him into the parlor with the others.

"Guests?"

"Did I not tell you? What a treat. It will be a surprise." Katie needed to be jovial to hide the mirth she knew to be dancing in her eyes.

"Mr. Finch. Thank you for gracing our home with your presence this evening." Aideen joined them. "Widow Easton, I'd like to introduce you to our dear friend William Finch. William, this is Mrs. Clara Easton. Oh, let me retrieve a vase for these lovely flowers. What a thoughtful gesture, Mr. Finch. Wouldn't you agree, Clara?" Aideen headed into the kitchen.

"Hewwo."

Katie watched as Mr. Finch's gaze darted around the room, trying to determine the source of the muffled sound. A child appeared, a thumb in his mouth, from behind his mother's skirt. Katie saw Clara tap the boy's shoulder with one finger, and he quickly withdrew the thumb.

"Hello," he said more clearly this time.

"Hello?" Mr. Finch's single word came out almost as a question.

"This here be our Danny boy." Aideen returned empty-handed.

"Daniel." The child stuck his hand out like a man to Mr. Finch.

"Nice to meet you, Daniel."

Dark circles still hung beneath his cloudy eyes, but the boy's voice was strong. Mr. Finch shook the offered gift, then stared at the wet mark on his hand.

"Mr. Finch, how thoughtless of me. Did I not tell you of Clara and Daniel?" Katie squeezed her hands behind her, digging her nails into her skin to keep a straight face.

"Well, no bother. He knows now, me Katie girl. Come now, dinner is on the table." Aideen showed the man to his chair. "Mr. Finch, please have a seat." Aideen placed him at one end, with Clara and Daniel on either side. Katie sat beside Daniel while Aideen checked the table for missing items before sitting at the other end.

Katie placed her hands on the table, palms up. Daniel slipped his small one into hers. Her heart yearned for a child of her own, but until that time came, she would love on the ones who needed her care and intervention. For now, this child needed shelter, love, and a father. Katie glanced at Mr. Finch. *The latter is up to you, Lord.*

"What are they doing?" Aideen whispered.

"Shh . . ." Katie peeked through the door, hoping to get a glimpse of the back porch where Mr. Finch, Clara, and Daniel sat. "Daniel's opened the crate, but I can't tell what it is."

"Well, hurry and help me fix this tray so we can take it out there. That's the third time this week he's come by, and Clara hasn't shared a word." Aideen fussed with the tin. "Oh, I can't get this thing open."

"Here, let me." Katie turned and forgot to ease the door shut. It creaked. She tensed, her neck muscles becoming tight under her collar. She wiggled the lid until all four edges released at the same time with a scraping sound. Cinnamon filled her nostrils. "Mmm, snickerdoodles."

"Danny boy loves them. I'd not remembered how much boys can eat, even at three. There, let's go."

"Both of us? It's one tray," Katie said.

"It's a beautiful day. No need to waste this sunshine."

Lord, You seem to be doing just fine. Help me to not get in the way, Katie prayed as she followed Aideen.

"Miss Katie, look—a train!" Daniel's exclamation brought joy to Katie's heart.

"Oh, Mr. Finch. Wherever did you get such a toy? What a treasure." Her hand reached up where her once treasured item no longer hung.

"It was my boy Billy's. I figured Daniel might enjoy something to play with other than the loud pots and wooden spoons you give him, Aideen." The man smiled, his own joy evident. "I can hear the boy on my end of town."

"Oh, surely you jest." Aideen winked at Mr. Finch.

"It's a nice sound, Mrs. Easton. Take no offense," he quickly added.

The smile Mr. Finch bestowed on Clara and the shy drop of her lashes made Katie's insides tingle.

"No offense taken, Mr. Finch," Clara said.

"William, please. Remember?"

"Thank you, William."

Aideen placed the tray on the small table between the two. "Let us know if you need anything. Dinner will be ready in an hour," Aideen said as her wide-eyed gaze connected with Katie's.

They shut the door behind them, and Katie did a little tippy-toe dance while Aideen lifted her hands and face to the ceiling.

"Thank You, Lord," Aideen whispered.

"Yes. Thank You, Lord." He'd done it—if the past moments were any indication. And she'd not broken a rule. She'd simply introduced a "friend" to a lonely widower and allowed the rest to happen naturally. The magistrate had questioned her of Widow Easton. Katie's response had made it sound like they'd met on her travels, satisfying him enough for her to avoid more questioning.

Later that evening, Katie brushed her hair in the dark and thought over the day. Mr. Finch was a good bit older than Clara, but the woman seemed not to be bothered. Katie often heard her praying late into the night. She hoped the accompanying tears were healing ones. Each morning, Clara came to breakfast with puffy eyes but a light spirit about her as she hummed while helping with breakfast and throughout the day with chores.

The women had not asked more than Clara offered, but they'd gleaned enough information from her crying out in the night to know the death of her husband had been horrific, and she'd likely been the one to find him hanging from the tree she cursed in her sleep.

Did Hans suffer from the effects of war as Mr. Easton had? Hans was on her mind more often than not. *Lord, please keep him safe. Heal his mind. Heal his wounded heart. Heal our friendship.*

Friendship. She wanted it to be so much more.

Chapter 30

On the circuit

ell, son, our next stop is our last before heading home."

Hans didn't respond. Today, the reverend was having a good day. Some mornings, the reverend awoke clear of mind and, although tired in body, able to carry on as if all were fine. Other days, especially those when Hans needed the man to be at his best, the reverend seemed unclear with a general malaise that had not been there the night before.

"Have you given any more thought to what we discussed?"

Thought? Yesterday, the man had not even remembered Hans's name. Today, he was recalling the discussion from two weeks ago after their argument. Two could play that game.

"Discussion? I'm not sure I know what you mean." Hans knew his tone hinted at his frustration with the man.

"I see. Well, it will come to you. Things like that have a way of burrowing deep and then surfacing when you least expect them. Yes siree, it will come to you."

Hans knew that all too well.

"Quite an offer you had at the last church. You seemed to enjoy the festivities on Saturday night. Yes siree, quite an offer."

Enjoyed? More like endured. The mothers in town had presented every single lady on a silver platter. He'd danced until his feet had hurt worse than his head. The town leader had even hinted at an empty house with an attached shop if he found one of the town girls to his liking.

"You know, that community is large enough for their own preacher now. I'm thinking that Beecher boy will do just fine," Reverend Jenkins said.

"He won't have a choice if his girl's mother has anything to say about it. That woman is determined that her daughter will marry a preacher." Hans had dodged that bullet. Becker Beecher had let him know in no uncertain terms that "that pretty filly is spoken for." Good thing, too, because Dorcas had better teeth than she did, and her bray rivaled any horse he'd ever known. Hans smirked. Who named their boy Becker Beecher? That kid had been doomed from the get-go.

"Serving the Lord is not a laughing matter, Hans."

"No, sir. I agree with you there." About the only thing he'd agreed on with the reverend of late. It was also one of the few times he had laughed since he'd started this ridiculous trip. No, this trip had been fraught with hours of travel listening to the droning of an old man with selective memory, except when it came to scripture. That was one thing he never seemed to forget. Hans felt sorry for Dorcas. When Reverend Jenkins had said the horse had listened to more sermons than a preacher's boy, it had been pure truth. After three weeks of listening to the same sermons and scriptures, day in and day out, Hans knew them by heart. But by heart was different than in his heart.

"Are you getting hungry, Reverend? Or need to stop?"

"No, I believe I'll rest my eyes a bit."

Hans knew what that meant. The man would close his eyes but not his mouth. *Mouth.* Katie's came to mind. The thin line of freckles at the top ridge was like the distant horizon—far away.

"You know, I was thinking of Katie just now," Reverend Jenkins called from the cart.

As was he. He couldn't get those green eyes and full red locks out of his thoughts.

"She sure could use a nice man to help her settle down."

"Settle down?" He'd not like to see her settle down. It was her spunk that made her eyes twinkle just so, her sass that made his blood run hot.

"Yes. I believe that would be good for Katie. Settle down, raise a family of her own."

"A family?" Red curls bounced before his eyes. A child in a white dress raced to him, arms outstretched.

"William Finch might be a good match. He's still of an age to raise a passel of boys."

Hans's heart skipped a beat, and his attention became focused on the present, not some vision of a future that would never be.

"But, if I understand correctly, she's given her life to the service of others."

That got his attention as well. "Service?"

"Why, yes. Running an orphanage will be a full-time job. Full time for sure. As a God-fearing woman, she's set her mind to upholding the scripture of helping the fatherless. That is, if she can get the idea past the magistrate. Set in his ways, that man. Yes siree, set in his ways. He told me . . ."

Hans tuned out the words. Katie was strong and independent. She likely had no need or desire for a husband and certainly not the likes of a man old enough to be her father. But Hans wasn't any better. He may be young, but he had nothing to offer her. Supporting a family on a cart-maker's salary would not do. But if she were his wife . . . Was that what he was thinking? What was he thinking? She was God-fearing. He was . . . What was he?

He thought back to the discussion the reverend had referred to earlier. Touching the still-unhealed wound he'd reopened on the rock that night, he chilled and lowered his hand from his forehead. Hans had shared the nightmare with the reverend but had held back one small detail, an aspect he wasn't ready to share.

"Have you given any further thought to what we discussed?"

So, they were back to that. He had enjoyed an hour of silence while Reverend Jenkins had slept. Not true. *I should be honest with myself as well as others.* The silence had been torture.

"You know, I believe I feel well enough to walk a spell. Would you mind?" Reverend Jenkins asked.

Rauti responded for him, stopping and turning his head to get a good look at his rider.

"Mm-hmm, I see how it is. Traitor," Hans said to Rauti.

The horse blew air and lifted his lips, showing his teeth in a cheeky grin. Hans dismounted and stretched, taking in the clear air around him and hoping it would do the same for his mind as it did for his body.

"Thank you, son." Reverend Jenkins swung his feet over the now-open end of the cart and stood. His body trembled. "Give me just a moment to get my sea legs." He laughed, the familiar sound a part of who he was.

"Does everything make you laugh?"

Without hesitation, a smile spread over the whiskered face all the way to his cloudy eyes. "That's a good question. A very good question."

"Whoa there, Reverend. Steady on your feet now." Hans kept a firm grasp under the man's arm.

"Might need a little assistance for a bit. These old legs don't seem to agree with my request for a walk."

"Take in some of this crisp air, and I'll fix us our lunch. We can walk in a bit. For now, you stand here, and get some blood flowing." Hans traded his support for the cart, and the man leaned heavily on the edge.

Whispers of "Glory to God," "Thank you, Lord Jesus," and "Praised be Your name," came from the man with each intake and exhale.

"Already praying over the food, Reverend?"

"I was giving God His rightful dues. We've seen no trouble on this trip, and God has provided for our every need. I was also thanking Him for you."

"For me?"

"Yes, son, for you. Why, you've been a blessing to me."

"Me? A blessing? Parson, I just sat the horse. You can give your thanks to Rauti." Hans removed the straps for the cart and let the horse graze near the water's edge.

"You've done more than you realize, Hans. Why, I'd never have made the trip without your ministrations and care. You've prepared our meals, cared for your horse, set up camp each evening, gathered wood and replaced it for the next traveler, and, more than once, saved my sorry hide from a fall. I'm not as young as I once was."

"Ah, you're just worn out."

"That I am. That I am, but perhaps not in the way you think."

The quiet was uncomfortable, but Hans could not think of something to fill the void. Except for the prayer Hans offered when he realized his companion was staring at his food, they ate in silence.

"Thank you," the reverend said.

"Sir?"

"I let you know how you were a blessing, but I didn't thank you." Reverend Jenkins flicked the crumbs to the ground, folded the cloth, and handed it to Hans.

"Here, let me help you up."

"See? Truth is, Hans, you bless others without thought because you have a servant's heart. You desire to please others. It's in your nature. God can use that gift if you'll allow Him."

Hans dipped his head in acknowledgment that he'd heard, but he didn't have to agree. Rauti stood still as Hans reconnected the cart. He held out his hand to help the reverend up.

"I believe I'll walk a bit if you don't mind."

"If you need a change from the cart, Rauti would be happy to carry you."

"Again, being thoughtful. You know, you've the making of a fine pastor."

"I'm no preacher."

"Ah, I said pastor. You know, the word 'pastor' means 'shepherd,' as in caring for a flock. You have the innate desire to care for others."

"My mother used to say that."

"Wise woman," Reverend Jenkins said.

They continued to walk. It was unusual for the reverend to say so few words and to walk so far.

"We've walked a fair piece, Reverend. Care to ride now?"

"See? There you go again. A natural desire to help others."

"Hmph. Not always."

"Care to elaborate?"

He didn't really, but something tugged at his heart, and he knew he needed to get it off his chest.

"Moses. I didn't stand up for Moses," Hans said.

"Ahh, but you did."

"Excuse me?"

The reverend's head lifted, and laughter poured out. "You like that phrase, don't you? Full of questions. That's a good thing, a very good thing." He wiped his eyes with his handkerchief. "Moses said he asked you not to say anything, and you didn't."

"Yeah, a total coward."

"Son, you asked me earlier if I always laugh. It isn't just laughter. It is choosing to find the good in everything. You're seeing your failure. I'm seeing your worth."

MATTERS OF THE HEART

Worth. He wasn't worth anything.

"You were honoring your friend's request. It may not have turned out as Moses would have liked, but you respected his wishes and didn't draw more attention to the situation than necessary. Moses might be big, but he avoids public attention— as if that goliath is capable of such a thing." Again, the man had to brush at his eyes.

"I hadn't thought of that, I guess."

"You guess correctly. In fact, I believe if you look back over what brought you to this point in time and search for the good, you'll find it. A change of perspective does a body good. Like now, I've been watching the world pass in that cart as I sat backward. Now I'm walking forward. A very different picture. Yes, every step forward changes the view; it never remains the same."

Every step forward changes the view. He let the words sink in. Could this be true, and could he have been lying to himself as well?

Chapter 31

Darkness began to settle, and Hans looked for a place to set up camp. "I see smoke up ahead. Campfire, I'm guessing." He turned and spoke to the reverend as he checked to ensure his gun was at the ready, even though it had not moved from its spot since they'd started this never-ending journey.

"Wonderful. Marvelous. We'll share some of the bounty from the good church folk at . . ." The man paused as if thinking. "The folk at that church we just left, in exchange for whatever smoke might keep these pesky mosquitos away." *Swat.* "Never understood why God made these tormenting creatures," he mumbled loud enough for Hans to hear.

The laugh that followed made Hans cringe. Who knew what they were approaching? A quiet entrance was preferable to him.

"I just had the funniest thought. God told Noah to take every creature onto the ark. Poor Noah. He wouldn't have been able to swat these pesky creatures." The reverend's laughter increased in volume.

Hans struggled to keep from joining him, but a crashing sound pulled him back.

"Stupid girl. Use that sorry excuse for a dress to lift the pot next time. Don't you have enough sense to know the thing's blazing hot?"

Hans dismounted and helped the now-quiet reverend out of the cart. Both peered through the sparse covering of trees. A small-framed man sat cross-legged, his back to them, barking orders at a dark-skinned girl. Hans couldn't tell how old she was, but from her height and frame, he guessed her to be around twelve or fourteen. She didn't speak, but her rigid body performed calculated movements, attesting to her heritage and the ingrained memories of years following orders.

"Hello. May we join your fire?" The reverend moved into the clearing.

"Who goes there?" The man staggered to his feet as the girl stood motionless on the far side of the fire.

"Reverend Jenkins and my transport . . ." He paused and looked at Hans. "Might we share your fire?" He continued to move forward a few steps.

There would be nothing Hans could do should the stranger become violent. He was too far from both men to use his sorry excuse for fists. The more he studied the man, the more he realized he'd be hitting a moving target. The man swayed on his feet. Hans would do what he needed to in order to protect his friend but didn't abide by killing or maiming.

"We'd be happy to share our provisions." Reverend Jenkins continued moving forward.

"Girl. Get over here."

Hans watched in horror as the man reached over the fire and grabbed the girl by the arm. She jumped to keep the fabric of her dress, or worse, from being scorched by the heat. The foul man may be drunk, but he was not one to be trifled with. Hans felt his blood boil even as his resolve faltered. His desire to help the reverend was all hat and no cattle, as he'd heard said. The reverend didn't know what he was talking about. Hans was no blessing. He hadn't stood up for Moses and knew he'd not change his stripes now. *Coward.* More of Joe's words filled his mind, continuing to weaken his determination to intervene should the need arise.

"Young man, would you be so good as to get provisions from the cart to share with our new friends?" Reverend Jenkins looked at Hans.

Hans stood unmoving as the reverend shook the man's hand and patted him on his shoulder. This wasn't good. One never knew what the reverend would say when he became forgetful. And how had he gone from strangers to friends with these people in a few moments? Though still wary, Hans chuckled. The poor man and the girl had no idea what accepting the reverend's friendship meant. *Sure hope they can tolerate the barrage of words they'll hear before the night ends.*

Rauti whinnied into the night.

"Coming, Rauti," Hans called to his friend.

"Girl. Be of some use, and go help the man." The drunkard spat the words.

Hans heard her light footsteps behind him but did not turn.

"Mister? You got anythin' I can carry for you?"

Her voice was childlike in tone but mature at the same time. He studied her. Grime covered her dark skin, making the whites of her eyes appear brighter. Matted hair clung to her scalp. The collar of her dress hung lower on one side, the torn edges exposing her slim neck. The dress was both too big and too matronly for her slim frame.

"Here." He handed her an apple. "Eat this while I gather our things." She didn't move. "Go on now. If you're going to help me carry this load, I need you to have some strength to do it."

He took his time going through the well-organized items until he heard no more chewing. He turned to see her outstretched hand. In it were four seeds and a stem.

"You want these, mister?"

His brother Otto would have liked this girl.

"Do you have a pocket?"

She searched her dress and found one near her knee when it should have been at her hip. She pointed. Hans didn't notice the pocket. He noticed the jagged scars around her ankles and her broad feet with wide-spread toes inconsistent with her slight frame. *Did someone shackle this child? Have those feet ever seen a pair of shoes?* Katie came to mind, and he understood her desire to help "the least of these."

"You keep those. Never know when you might want to put down roots and plant a tree."

She stared at them. He turned his head. It was as if he'd given her a treasure worth more than gold. Placing a hand on his chest, he felt the familiar beat, beat, beat. The scene stirred him. The reverend had spent hours telling Hans how the Bible spoke of the heart as the center of life and strength. Hans felt his physical strength renewed each day, but his heart felt empty, drained of any life. Until now. His small act of kindness in giving the apple and then the seeds to the girl stirred something inside him. It was as if the seed she held had been planted in his heart and started to grow, filling him with new life. He looked up to see her still looking at the seeds, turning them over in her palm before she placed them in the pocket of her dress.

"Here you go. You take that on back, and we'll eat a fine meal. I'll take care of Rauti here and be there in a moment. Reverend Jenkins will tell you what to do."

He broke his stare, nodded, then noted she now stared at him. All the slaves he'd ever met averted their gaze when speaking to a white man. Not this girl. Her look didn't evoke a challenge. It was as if she were trying to discern Hans's worth and character.

She'll come away lacking if that's what she's seeking.

The girl took the crate while Hans cared for Rauti, settled the cart, and started back to the clearing. Reverend Jenkins's voice carried over the gentle breeze.

"Good, you're back. Our young friend here . . ." He looked to the girl.

"Essie, sir," she said.

"Yes. Essie here has warmed our meal."

"Burned it," the drunkard said. "Good for nothing—"

"Louis, might you like to do the honor of blessing this fine meal the Lord has provided?" Reverend Jenkins interrupted.

"Ah, no. Don't believe I would." The man picked a piece of golden cornbread from the pan with dirty fingers and popped it into his mouth with a smile.

Hans hoped the man choked. And he did.

"Here you go." Reverend Jenkins picked up the man's coffee cup, filled it, and handed it to him.

Essie stood several paces off, not moving or acknowledging their presence until Hans saw her finger the seeds he knew to be in her pocket. Her eyes closed, and her skirt bunched up around the treasure.

Reverend Jenkins said he had a servant's heart. Then why had he not stepped in to help when the man had choked? He'd even felt a jolt of satisfaction when the sorry excuse for a human hadn't been able to stop coughing.

What was this war going on inside him? He shouldn't pick and choose who to be kind to. He wanted to be the man Reverend Jenkins thought him to be. Maybe if he tried harder, pretended even. Maybe then? It was worth a try.

"Sit, son. Sit." The reverend patted the ground beside him.

Hans remained standing, his thoughts and focus on the girl. *I wonder if that's how slaves managed all those years. Did they just pretend to be subservient? To be what their masters wanted?*

"You dumb, boy?"

The man reminded him of Joe. All thoughts of kindness from moments before blew with the wind.

"Well, the Lord can hear you just fine from your position." Reverend Jenkins locked his gaze on Hans.

He understood full well. He would pray over the meal but not with the fervor he knew the reverend desired. "Lord, thank you for this bounty we are about to receive. Amen." Short and to the point. He had no desire to say more, at least to God. "Essie?" Her gaze shot up, fear evident in its depths. "Would you care to join us?" A somewhat noticeable shake of the head was all he received.

"Dumb and stupid." The man spat crumbs onto his lap.

"Excuse me?" Hans felt heat rise in his neck and rolled his head back and forth, attempting to loosen his muscles as if preparing for a fight.

"Nothing." Louis shoved a spoonful of beans into his mouth. Dark juice dripped down his unkempt beard as he lifted one side in a smirk.

Hans looked to Essie. The girl shook her head, eyes wide, hands grasping at either side of her too-large skirt as if preparing to lift it and run. Why was she so frightened?

"Come, now, young man. Eat with us," the reverend said. "Essie's thoughtfulness in ensuring we have all we need before serving herself is an admirable quality."

Hans heard the words but couldn't believe his ears. He shot a glance at his friend, only to recognize the unsaid *bide your time, boy* look. Hans fixed himself a small serving and ate as if he were the one getting ready to run. In a way, he was. He was on the run from God.

"Dearly beloved. We are gathered today to pay our final tribute of respect to that which was mortal. . . ."

Hans kicked his leg at the offender. Were they trying to pull him down to Sheol with them?

". . . Almighty God, our Heavenly Father, we come into this sanctuary of sorrow, realizing our utter dependence upon You."

He continued to kick away the hands of the dead men, their fingers scraping as they grabbed at his legs. He raised his voice louder to the heavens.

"Then I heard a voice from heaven say, 'Write this: Blessed are the dead who die in the Lord from now on.'"

"Mr. Hans, sir. Mr. Hans, sir."

Now they were calling to him. He hit them and kicked them, but they did not retreat.

"Mr. Hans, sir. Please wake up, sir. Oh, Lord Jesus, hep me now."

Hans bolted upright, pulling his legs underneath him. The girl stood before him, stick in hand. She poked him once more for good measure.

"You awake now, Mr. Hans, sir? How them other two ain't, I

don't rightly know. You preach a loud funeral."

Hans stared and wiped his eyes, hoping to clear the vision.

"Come now. I made you some coffee when you was just gettin' started with your hell fire and brimstone talkin'."

Hans shivered, his shirt damp with sweat. Hair fell in his face, and he brushed it away, hitting the mark he had received the last time he'd had the dream—the one where he hadn't been the preacher but the gravedigger.

"You drink that."

She placed a cup a few paces from him. Still holding the stick, she stepped back. He tried to thank her, but his throat was too dry. His hands shook as he sipped the steaming liquid, drawing in the aroma as he attempted to calm his racing heart.

"Thank you, Essie." The steam rose like incense, the fragrant offering he should be giving to God. *Please, Lord. I don't understand. What do You want of me?* He flinched. His arms wrapped tight around his knees as he rocked back and forth. Red marks formed where the liquid sloshed over his hand. Tears streamed down his face. When no more burning sensation came, he felt a calm fall on him like fog. A hum came from nearby, then words.

> "Nobody knows the trouble I've been through
> Nobody knows my sorrow
> Nobody knows the trouble I've seen
> Glory hallelujah!" ("Nobody Knows the Trouble
> I've Seen")

A girl's voice. Essie sat to his right, her form imitating his.

When he slowly uncurled his legs, she rose and reached for the coffee again, offering to pour.

"Thank you, Essie. That song. What does it mean?"

"Why, just what it say, Mr. Hans, sir. Nobody know what I been through, 'cept God. He knowed. My Jesus—He done been beat, treated all kind of wrong, but He knowed God was watchin' out for Him."

"I understand that part. But why the ending? Why the 'Glory, hallelujah'?"

"Mr. Hans, sir, you gots lots to learn. Just 'cause it don't look like God be payin' me no mind, don't make it true. You think Jesus happy God don't make Him not hang on that cross? But He don't complain. He hold His head high. That make me say 'Glory, hallelujah' right there."

This simple, uneducated slave girl who had experienced life in a way Hans could only imagine was able to see the good and glorify God. Reverend Jenkins's words ran through his mind as the girl continued to hum and sing the song.

Lord. Lord. He hung his head and wept. Would he never find peace, contentment, and joy?

Chapter 32

Shumard Oak Bend

"Y ou've been sullen today, Katie girl." Aideen tasted the soup, adding a generous dash of salt.

"Boredom."

"Boredom?" Aideen's laughter filled the room. "We haven't had a moment's peace for days, and the stage should be here at any moment. God has blessed us beyond measure with travelers but not so many that we can't keep up with the laundry and dishes. Now, if it's variety you be needing, we'll be starting the canning soon."

Katie groaned.

"That's what I thought. I was thinking it might be nice to do something a little bit different this evening. We haven't had much time to enjoy something frivolous. Perhaps you could read aloud while I work on those collars for the Kilpatrick girls."

"Would you consider giving your eyes a rest and taking a walk?" Katie hoped her aunt would agree. Their reading options were *The Farmer's Almanac, The Bible,* a copy of *Little Women* that a boarder had left behind and was missing several pages, or *Alice's Adventures in Wonderland,* which neither she nor Aideen could follow. She missed the penny-dreadful stories. She'd read dozens of those books, most more than once, on her trip across the ocean. By the time she'd reached land, the entirety of the ship seemed to have read them.

"That sounds like a fine idea," Aideen agreed. "We'll go as soon as we clean up our supper dishes."

Katie helped Aideen with her shawl as the two stepped into the warm evening air. Katie noticed how pale her aunt was. The woman had spent every extra moment tatting to bring in just a few more coins each week.

"You are working too hard." Katie put her hand under her aunt's elbow to help her up the hill behind the boarding house.

"Ach, you've taken so much off of me; I have plenty of time to do what I enjoy."

"I'm trying to figure out how we are going to get all the canning done and keep up with everything else. It will be a challenge."

"The Lord will provide. He always does."

"If He provides more boarders, we won't be able to keep up."

"Katie girl, I trust my God enough to believe He will provide exactly what we need at the moment we need it. Not a second early, nor a minute late."

Katie hoped God would do so, but she wasn't sure how.

"Do you think God sent Clara? I mean, she's a help in the kitchen, but she naps nearly every day and sometimes sleeps later. . . ."

"Katie, that is gossiping. We do not know all Clara has endured. She is doing what she can and is a most gracious guest."

Katie felt heat rise in her cheeks.

"Danny is an obedient child," Katie said, trying to think of something positive to say.

"That he is. He does like spending time with Mr. Finch and the goats. I think Mr. Finch enjoys having his company."

Katie nodded. The conversation felt stiff, and she wondered if Aideen had something on her mind.

"Katie, might I ask you a question?"

Stiff changed to uncomfortable.

"Yes, ma'am."

"When I'm gone . . ."

"Aunt, are you ill?" Katie stopped and turned, looking her aunt in the face.

"No, me dear girl. I'm not ill. But I've been wondering how many more years I can keep doing what I'm doing if you marry . . ."

Katie snorted. "Not likely to be an issue. I'm more apt to be an old maid caring for other peoples' discarded or orphaned children than to be raising a passel of my own."

"I would not give up on that dream yet. God is always working under the surface. My real question is, if I am not able, would you be willing to take over the boarding house?"

Katie stopped again, but this time, Aideen had to turn to face her.

"You are my only kin, so it is rightfully yours when I'm gone."

"Please, can we talk of something pleasant?" Katie's chest tightened.

"You know, the boarding house would make a fine orphanage."

The tightness in Katie's chest lessened as excitement began to build.

"Now, mind you, I'm not dying yet." Aideen put her arm through Katie's and pulled her close like a schoolgirl telling a secret to her closest friend.

Yet. Peace washed over Katie as she felt God's gentle reminder to wait in the yet. They had reached the top of the hill. The sun was beginning its descent, giving them a dazzling display of colors. Neither lady spoke as they watched the colors change on the horizon until the last burst of orange dipped behind the earth.

"Thank you," Aideen said.

"For what?" Katie asked.

"For getting me out of the house to see the splendor of my King. For showing up on me doorstep exactly when I needed you. For bringing life and excitement into me life when I'd lost the love of me life. For reminding me of the importance of having a passion for a cause. But mostly for being you." Aideen squeezed her arm. "You bring joy—and exasperation—to my life." She leaned into Katie's shoulder and laughed. "I wouldn't have it any other way."

"Thank you," Katie choked out.

"Ready to head back?"

Katie nodded.

"One more thing." Aideen took Katie's hand in hers as they walked. "Don't be getting any ideas too soon. I plan on living a good long while yet."

"I hope you do." Katie lifted their hands and kissed her aunt's knuckles. "I hope you do."

Chapter 33

Hans ached all over. A melody played in his mind, accompanied by the sounds of crackling. His gaze followed the direction of the noise. Essie crouched at the edge of the fire and pulled bacon strips from a cast iron pan, placing them on a tin plate. She poured a yellow mixture into the hot grease and returned the pan to the fire.

"Good morning, Mr. Hans, sir." The whispered words flowed with the song she continued singing.

"Ahh-hmmm." Reverend Jenkins's yawn stretched over the group.

Hans echoed a yawn back.

"This is the day the Lord has made. Let us rejoice, and be glad in it." Reverend Jenkins rubbed the shoulder he'd been lying on. "Well, I'm awake, but my arm isn't."

Hans stood and helped his friend into a comfortable sitting position. Snoring came from the bedroll on the far side of the fire.

"He'll sleep another hour or so," Essie offered as she handed them plates of steaming food.

"Thank you, dear," the reverend said. "It's Essie, correct?"

"Yes, sir. That be right, Reverend Jenkins."

"Wonderful. Well, Essie, I'm sure Hans appreciates your thoughtfulness. He didn't know he was signing up for cook as well as transporter on this trip."

"I don't mind," she said. "This here is nice fine cornmeal. Where I's come from, we use coarse cornmeal that takes longer to cook. This done been ground real good and has a nice citrus flavor."

"You do know your cornmeal—and your bacon. You cooked this to perfection. Absolute perfection."

"Person who done cured it did it right. Not too much salt, jus' enough smoke."

Hans marveled at the girl. Her words appeared uneducated, but she was knowledgeable. He took a bite of the cornbread. She was right. It did have a slight citrus tang, subtle like an apricot he'd once eaten. Essie poured each man a mug of coffee, using the bottom of her dress as a potholder. Her smile was sweet, but her eyes looked tired. She must be exhausted. He'd gone to sleep hearing her voice and woken to the same sweet tune. He watched the girl fix a plate, set it aside, then fix another, but, unlike at the previous meal, she began eating. Before Hans had taken a sip of his second cup of coffee, Essie stood.

"When you two finishes eatin', we'll leave."

Hans stopped midbite. Had he missed something?

Reverend Jenkins didn't seem phased by her pronouncement. "We may want to wait for Mr. . . . um . . ."

"Louis," Hans interjected.

"Yes, right you are. We may want to wait for Louis to wake to discuss the particulars."

"He don't own me," Essie said. "He ain't got no say."

"Even so, we will be forthright in our discussions."

Essie glared at the man, then turned her frustration on Hans. He held up the three fingers not holding the cornbread and gave her a *Don't look at me* look. Her hands did their familiar bunching of her skirt. Each squeeze lifted the fabric to reveal her scarred ankles. His cornbread turned to sand in his mouth.

Essie closed her eyes and squared her shoulders. When she opened them, Hans saw a fire in them he'd not seen before. She focused squarely on the reverend. Her voice came out strong and clear. Gone was the natural cadence of her song. Now, she spoke with conviction and determination.

"And Ruth said, Intreat me not to leave thee, or to return from following after thee: for whither thou goest, I will go; and where thou lodgest, I will lodge: thy people shall be my people, and thy God my God: Where thou diest, will I die, and there will I be buried: the Lord do so to me, and more also, if ought but death part thee and me."

"My, my." Reverend Jenkins pulled out his handkerchief and wiped the beads of perspiration that had gathered on his upper lip. Whether from the steaming coffee or the fervent tone of the recitation, Hans wasn't sure.

"I've waited my whole life to say that." Essie pulled her lips tight.

Hans knew that feeling. She was proud of herself, as she should be. But did she mean it? He glanced over to the still-sleeping form. What if this man laid claim to her? The law may say slaves were now free, but not all men abided by the law.

"We've nothing to offer you, Essie, but you may journey with us," the reverend said. "God will provide for your needs as He has ours."

Hans finished his meal in silence. What in the world would they do with a girl? In practiced motions, she cleaned the supplies, banked the fire, and placed new wood for the next traveler.

"Best pack up. We'll wake Louis if he doesn't come to on his own." Reverend Jenkins attempted to stand.

"Here you go, Reverend." Hans offered an arm. "If you'll put up our bedrolls, I'll get Rauti and the cart ready."

"I got that." Essie hurried over and began packing up Reverend Jenkins's things. "You finish that coffee." Reverend Jenkins eased back onto his sitting log.

Hans moved to hook the cart to Rauti and repack their gear.

"What do you think, Rauti?" Rauti replied to Hans with a huff and blow, then his ears perked and swiveled toward camp at the sound of the reverend's voice.

"Now, now, Louis. Enjoy your coffee and this fine breakfast.

We'll talk when you've had a chance to fully wake."

Hans attached the cart. If the girl came with them, she'd either have to sit with him or with the reverend in the cart. He rearranged a few things to make more room. Would she really join them? What if Louis wouldn't let her go? Those scarred ankles made his own hurt. Essie deserved to be free, fully free. Was he willing to help her, no matter what?

"Fight for her."

Hans shot a glance at Rauti, but the stallion's ears did not move.

"Fight for her."

"God?" The whisper stuck in his throat. He lifted his hands to his neck and rubbed his rough palms across his weathered skin, then squeezed, trying to force out the words. An image of shackles around the girl's ankles formed. Hans lowered his head. "God." The name flowed like warm milk but tasted like defeat. He hated fighting.

Hans checked the fittings, steeled himself with a fortifying breath, then reentered the campsite. Fire blazed from Louis's eyes while bits of cornbread stuck in his unkempt beard, competing for space with last night's beans. Hans shuddered when the man licked his filthy fingers of the bacon grease.

"Louis, I have a proposition for you." The reverend patted the girl's shoulder as she sat huddled beside him on the ground. "This girl here has asked to accompany us on our journey."

"She ain't goin' nowhere." Louis tossed the last of his coffee into the ashes. Sparks flew and sizzled like Hans's resolve.

"Now, I know she's been a burden on your supplies and slows you down as you traverse this rough, rough land," the reverend continued.

Hans watched as Louis followed the man's hand from the scrub and rock to the clear blue sky of the morning. He marveled at the change in Louis, as if he were being mesmerized by the cadence of the words and the beauty around him.

"I'm thinking we can be of service to you. Helpful, if you will. We'll provide you with provisions to continue on your journey, which won't last as long if you need to feed two. If you think it best, and a man of your understanding most certainly would, we'll help you by taking the girl off your hands."

Louis's gaze shot to Essie. Hans held his breath. Would the man agree, or would his refusal force Hans to fight for her freedom? He needed to be the man he wanted to be—the man the reverend said he was. The desire to prove to himself that he could stand up for what was right and noble, even if it was difficult, spread across his heart.

"Take her."

Hans hadn't realized he'd closed his eyes. They popped open, and he worked to bring the man into focus.

"Just take her, and go, but I expect a good price."

"Oh, we're not buying her from you, Louis. No siree. We are thanking you for the gift of her presence. Hans, would you please gather the remainder of the provisions we have? Include the coffee."

His hands shook as he pulled the crate containing the food, coffee, and supplies from the cart. Was the man crazy? What would they eat?

"Now, my friend, carrying this crate will be a mite difficult, so you take what you can in your pack. Don't be shy now. You take what you see fit, for the Lord will provide for our needs."

"You old fool," Louis mumbled under his breath. The man was like a rabid dog, rifling through the goods. Joe came to mind and old feelings of worthlessness surfaced—until he noticed the sly grin forming on the man's lips. Louis thought he was getting the better end of the deal.

No person's life should be traded for food.

Chapter 34

"**W**here are we headed?" Essie asked.

Hans tapped the cart, and Essie moved her swinging legs from the edge to under her skirts. He secured the end panel of the cart, then winked at Essie, who became wide-eyed.

"Well, my dear, Hans here and Rowdy, of course, are taking us to our last church on this circuit." Reverend Jenkins situated himself amongst their belongings. "I am right in that, aren't I, Hans?"

"Yes, sir. One more church, then we head home."

"Church? Oh, my. Do you think they'll let me sit close enough to hear?" Essie wiggled in excitement.

"Young lady, if I have anything to do with it, you'll have a front-row seat. The best seat in the house. Truth is, all of God's creation is His cathedral. No matter where you sit, you are in His presence."

Hans listened as Essie soaked up everything the reverend

said over the next hours of travel. The man's gentle teaching and questioning probed into Hans's heart as he listened. This young girl asked questions, was bold enough to stop Reverend Jenkins and ask for clarification, and even offered her opinions, which were deep and thought-provoking for a girl so young.

"All my life, they done trained me to be obedient. How do I know if I'm really followin' God from my heart or just doin' the right thing 'cause that's what I knows?"

"Essie, that is an excellent question, excellent question. Many people follow the rules of the Bible."

"Like the Ten Commandments?" Essie interrupted.

"Exactly. So, being a Christian is more than believing you are saved by your good works. Let me ask you this, why did you obey your master?"

"Had to, so I guess I obeyed out of fear."

"Mmm . . . see, there is the difference. When we serve God, it is our desire, our deepest longing, to serve Him. When obedient, we never need to fear God. Did you ever go against what others asked of you or rebel?"

"I drug my feet a few times on purpose."

"I remember doing the same when I had to do chores for my mother." The birds stopped their singing at Reverend Jenkins's boisterous laughter. "When we give our hearts to Him, we desire to please Him, and something changes. We don't become perfect, mind you. Far from it."

"I knows I'm not perfect."

"None of us are. We are forgiven, but we are not perfect in all we say and do. But, when we give our hearts over to Christ, we know, oh, we know, Essie. There is no doubt He is our Lord because He gives us the Holy Spirit."

Hans wished Rauti's hoof falls were quieter. He didn't want to miss a word being said. His heart was stirring.

"Being born again, saved, a follower of Christ—whatever you call it—can only happen when the Spirit of God dwells in us. If God has changed your heart, your life will show signs of that change."

"But what if those changes are only on the inside? Doin' what I'm told is a part of who I is. Nobody sees what I be thinkin' in my mind."

"Very observant, Essie. When one goes from death to life, the heart shows signs of that new life."

"I ain't never been to church. Our preacher man—he teach us what he know, but he couldn't read or write. I wanna go to heaven and be with my mammy. Not right now, mind you. I've a life to live."

"Oh, Essie, you are refreshing. Absolutely refreshing. Questioning where you stand with the Almighty allows you to evaluate your heart. The one thing I believe helps people know if they are truly saved is if they turn their backs on sin. Repentance means exactly that, and if you are saved, you will live a new life in Christ."

Hans's body felt heavy. His head drooped and shoulders slumped. He'd always assumed he would go to heaven. He did his best, and except for being angry at God, he was a good person. But was that enough? He tried so hard. His efforts must count for something.

Rauti pulled back on the reins, which Hans had tightened without realizing. Surely, he must be a Christian. Rauti bobbed his head, and Hans focused his attention on the horizon, where he saw the outline of a town. The sun was well past its peak. They'd traveled the day with no need to stop for a lingering lunch.

"Reverend, I believe we are coming up on the town of Huntsville," Hans said. "Is there a specific place I need to go?"

"If you'll be so kind as to stop this contraption, Hans, I'll stretch my legs a bit and give you the directions."

"I need a privy bush." Essie darted off when Hans released the gate.

"She's quite the girl. I pray we can find her a decent home in this town." Reverend Jenkins staggered, and Hans held him upright until the man's legs appeared able to hold him. "Not feeling myself at the moment."

"Oh, no you don't. You preached a fine sermon all the way here. You can do it again tomorrow."

"Nice to know you've been paying attention."

Hans wasn't sure if the reverend meant his listening to the hours of chatter with Essie or recognizing that the reverend seemed to choose when and where he didn't feel well. He was about to say something when the man stumbled.

"Whoa there, Reverend." Hans wrapped his arm around his friend's waist. The age spots on the man's hands blanched as he grasped the side of the cart. "Reverend, you feel a mite warm. Let's get you to the creek for some cool water."

"That sounds right nice, young man. Thank you."

"Young man." That wasn't a good sign.

Hans sat on the front row, listening to the squeak and warble coming from the robust woman. Every fiber of his being hurt as she started another torturous verse of "All Hail the Power of Jesus' Name." Hans wondered if the ringing in his ears would be permanent. Movement caught his attention, and he looked to the door of the little house where Essie remained to care for the ailing reverend. There she stood, face and hands to heaven, her entire body in full worship.

Shame on me. He focused on the words rather than the war cry. He knew he'd never fully crowned God as Lord of his life and couldn't fathom that all it took was accepting God's grace to be saved.

"Thank you, Mrs. Patterson, for helping us worship today." The man at the front's round spectacles moved up and down as he looked from his notes to the congregation.

Like at the other churches, benches had been placed outside in a flat, grassy area. Behind the house where Essie retreated was a not-yet-completed church. The structure was larger than his brother's barn and had several places where windows might be placed. The trusses allowed today's sunshine to warm the building.

"Next week, if God is willing and the creek don't rise, we'll have that roof on. All the men are asked to be here tomorrow morning at sunup. Our fine lady folk will provide the noon meal. Elder McCraven has offered the use of his home for preparations."

The town folk whispered amongst themselves as the man continued with announcements.

Hans stared at the fine building. He'd enjoy working with the men and wondered if he and the reverend would stay another day. His own tools sat covered in the cart. Shuffling brought him back to the present.

"Let us pray."

Hans stood and bowed his head but climbed a ladder and nailed shingles into place in his mind. It was the silence that caught his attention this time, and he wedged himself between two older men. A young man who didn't look old enough to shave cleared his throat. With shaking hands, he turned the pages of his worn Bible back and forth until he closed the book and his eyes. When he opened his eyes, he spoke.

"Thank you for asking me to share today since Reverend Jenkins is not well. I appreciate your praying for me over the years, and I need those prayers still. Reverend Jenkins's illness is different from mine, but we share an upset stomach." The congregation offered a laugh.

He does look a bit green, but better him than me.

"I believe God will give me the strength needed to bring you His word."

The boy was quiet long enough to capture Hans's full attention.

"I felt a call to preach when I was ten. Mrs. McCraven was my Sunday School teacher."

Hans followed the direction of the comment to Mr. McCraven, who was wiping at his eyes.

"When I told her I thought God was telling me I was to be a preacher, she beamed. I let her know I didn't want to be a preacher."

The congregation laughed and offered a few 'amens.'

"She made one simple statement. 'If you think you can get to heaven any other way than by obeying God, I'd like to hear how.'" The young man wiped at his face and neck, which had become bright red. "I didn't want to disappoint Mrs. McCraven or God, but I wanted to be a farmer like my daddy, and my daddy's daddy. The land is in my blood."

Hans looked the boy over. He was wiry but tanned and strong. He looked like a farmhand.

"Giving up my dreams near broke my heart." At this, he wiped his eyes. "When Mrs. McCraven was dying, she asked for me. As I held her hand, she reminded me that obeying God's calling on my life was the most important thing I would ever do."

Hans could hear nothing but the boy's breathing, or was that his own? His heart raced, and sweat slicked his palms. Visions of sitting in the chair beside his mother's deathbed, the translucent skin of her hand resting in his, filled his mind as did her voice.

"Hans, my dear son. Whatever you do, obey God first. You, my child, are made for a great purpose. Seek it, and do it with all your heart—but not in your own strength. Let God use His power through you.

Hans felt wetness on his face. His shoulders shook. If he did this, if he asked God to be his Lord and decided to follow His will, no matter what that might be, there would be no turning back. He would be truthful to God and to himself, regardless of the cost. A hand touched his shoulder, then another. Murmured prayers blanketed him in a warmth he had never before felt.

Prayers covered Hans as he wept. He poured out his heart. When he felt completely drained, the prayers of those around him rallied his spirit. His resistance was gone. He raised his hands toward heaven and said the three words he had never voiced before.

"I am Yours."

Chapter 35

Huntsville, Missouri

"**O**w!" Hans clenched his jaw, working it back and forth. He looked at his thumb where the nail was already beginning to turn dark.

"You need a break?" Luke, the preacher boy from yesterday smirked.

Hans glared.

"I'll take that as a no. Seems to me, you'd be ready for one about now. Between that new thumb of yours, tearing your britches, dropping your hammer on your foot, and breaking a rung on the ladder, you've had quite the day. How's that shin doing?"

"Fine. Just fine."

Hans wanted to rub the knot he expected was also turning a dark color but resisted the urge. He needed to change the subject. "Fine sermon yesterday."

"Ha! Now I know you need a break."

"You did all right." He meant it and felt a bit of comradery when Luke hit his own thumb and shoved it in his mouth. "I had to preach once. The reverend was too ill. Finished with the words, 'the end.'"

Luke's thumb popped out of his mouth, and a string of drool edged close to his shirtsleeve. He wiped his sleeve over his mouth. "No foolin'?"

"No fooling. I felt like an idiot." Luke was quiet, and Hans looked over to see the boy staring. "You know, I think I am ready for that break. Let's get some tea."

Both men climbed down. Hans checked each rung for strength before he put his full weight on it, then joined several men in the shade.

Essie strode with purpose, a tray of drinks in her arms. "Here you go." She bent and allowed each man to take a cup.

"I ain't drinking anything that darkie poured. It's possible she spit in it," one man said.

Hans felt the hair on the back of his neck rise. Not even the flies dared make a sound. He looked up and watched a smile form on the girl's face.

"Sir, thank you for givin' me my first opportunity to put my new faith into practice. Them ladies in there is the kindest women I ever met. Not but a moment ago, they done reminded me that being a Christian ain't a feelin' but a decision. Now, my feelin's toward you right now ain't too kind, but my decision is to not throw this here tea in your face." She smiled like she'd won a prize, then turned and skipped back to the house, throwing the liquid into the rose bush.

The men howled. They directed all their comments at the only man without a mug. "That's some girl." "She told you." "That kind of pluck will get her far."

Hans waited for someone to comment about her needing to be put in her place, but no one did. They changed the subject to the roof and estimated how much longer it would take to finish.

"Think you'll be preaching under it next week, Luke?" one of the men asked.

"Me?" the boy asked.

"Yeah, you. You done just fine yesterday. Why can't you be our preacher regular like?" another man added.

Luke stared. Hans couldn't decide if he was in shock or so scared he couldn't answer. Probably both.

Essie came to gather the empty cups, avoiding the man from earlier. "Mr. Hans, sir? The missus need some help with the laundry pot. She's using it to wash things up."

"I'm happy to help," Hans said. "Luke, can you give me a hand?" Both men followed the girl and made quick work of setting the wash cauldron on the crossarms, filling it, and starting the fire underneath.

"They're right, you know," Hans said as they worked.

"About what?"

"About being the preacher. Reverend Jenkins isn't well, and these people need a preacher. Besides, you've already had your first conversion." Hans winked and watched Luke's questioning eyes grow with understanding. "And by the sound of it, the ladies of this congregation helped Essie see the light as well. I'd say that's a better start than most preachers get."

Luke nodded. "Would you let the others know I'm going for a walk? I believe I need some time to talk to the Lord."

Hans placed his hand on Luke's shoulder like Johann had his many times. "Take all the time you need."

Hans watched Essie flit here and there, lifting her skirts to run when able. Her sass, smile, and spunk made him think of the red-haired pixie back home.

"Mr. Hans, sir?"

"You really can just call me Hans."

"Yes, sir, Mr. Hans." She stood before him as he stoked the fire. "The ladies here—they done offer for me to stay. They say I'd be a real nice addition to their sewing circle. One gots a shed she says I can stay in."

"That's wonderful." He paused when her light tone didn't match the turmoil in her eyes. "Is that what you want?"

"Well, Mr. Hans, I don't rightly know. I ain't never had a choice before. Problem is, Reverend Jenkins is mighty sick. He still has that fever. I won't leave him. Iffen he's still ailin' when you leave, I'd like to go with you." Her eyes implored him to let her.

"We'll be here one more day to finish the roof on the church. Let's see how the reverend is feeling by that time. Does that work for you?" Hans tilted his head to capture her gaze, which was on her bare feet.

"Yes, sir. The women folk brewed some kinda nasty smellin' drink. They says it will bring his fever down, but he wrinkle his nose up so much he hardly gettin' any down. He gonna be all right?"

"I'm sure he'll be fine in a day or two."

Essie seemed convinced of his words, but he wasn't so sure.

Chapter 36

On the way to Shumard Oak Bend

"How are you doing back there?" Hans turned in the saddle to see the reverend's head on Essie's lap. She used a damp cloth to wipe the perspiration from the man's forehead.

"He's still powerful sick."

"Should we stop?"

"How much farther?"

"If we keep pressing on, we should be to Shumard Oak Bend just after sunset. Aunt Aideen should know what to do."

"You get us home. I'll care for the reverend."

Home. He didn't feel like he had a true home. The home he wanted included Katie. Essie began to sing, and Rauti matched the cadence of her song. The tune was haunting and tugged deep at Hans's soul.

Worry sapped him of the joy he'd experienced while he'd been at the Huntsville church. They'd be pulling into Shumard

Oak Bend late, and he had no idea how, or if, Katie would receive his return. His heart ached at knowing he'd probably lost the chance to be more than friends. He'd likely lost more than that. He reminded himself that Katie was already spoken for by Paul.

Darkness covered the town when they rode in. Even the saloon was quiet. Dust choked Hans as the wind blew across the dirt road toward Grammie's Boarding House. *Help me, Lord.* His heart quickened, as did Rauti's step, all the way to the front stoop. The horse called to Dorcas, but there was no response from within the closed barn doors.

Hans dismounted and knocked on the front door. He returned to the cart, where two figures huddled. The reverend nestled in Essie's skirts while she lay sprawled over their belongings, a gentle snore escaping her open mouth.

"Essie?"

"Yes, sir?" She rubbed her sleepy eyes.

"We're here." He opened the gate, and her legs spilled out, along with a sigh.

"Oh, that do feel better. My legs were a mite cramped." She wiggled her bare feet and rolled her neck.

"That you, Hans?" Aideen called from the front door, where a single candle illuminated the entrance.

"Yes, ma'am. The reverend is quite ill with fever. I'm sorry to bother you so late."

"Don't you mind that. You and your friend bring him in. We'll get him settled." Aideen held the door as the two did their best to carry the man. "Take him to the parlor. We'll get him upstairs when he's more awake."

Hans wasn't sure if being awake would help. The reverend didn't have the strength needed to assist. "Aideen, I'd like to introduce you to Essie. Essie, this is Aunt Aideen."

Essie curtsied but never took her eyes off the woman. "You look like an angel with your gold hair comin' out your cap."

Aideen snickered. "Oh, you dear girl. Now, let's get you washed up before I start some broth and tea. Come right this way." Aideen led her to the hall bath.

Hans settled Reverend Jenkins on the settee, removed his shoes, and unbuttoned his collar. "Here you go." He placed another pillow behind his head. "This will make you more comfortable." Kneeling before the man, he placed his forehead on the settee.

"Son." The word was a whisper but felt like a prayer. Hans felt a shaky hand atop his head. "You must share your newfound faith with these people." Labored breathing made it hard for Hans to hear, but he understood each word. "Take my place. Be their pastor and their preacher."

"I can't." Emotion overwhelmed him. "I don't think I can." Hans shook his head and wept.

"Looks like you're alone tonight, Rauti. I don't believe Dorcas has been here for a few days." Hans wondered if Katie had gone to the Shankel Farm again. He wouldn't blame her. She would have known this was the Sunday they would return.

Sunday. In two days, people would gather to hear God's Word. Reverend Jenkins expected Hans to give it. Confusion, anxiety, and Joe's voice filled his mind. He stopped the curry comb mid-stroke. He could leave.

Hans cleaned the tack, unpacked, and swept out the cart, then checked the wheels in the faint light of the lantern. On his knees, his hand caressed the wheels. Moses may not want to help him now. Would his friend ever forgive him? Could Hans even call him a friend? He touched his healing scar and looked to the door. He wrapped his arm around his still-sore ribs as visions of men, their fists and boots pummeling him, brought on a new feeling. Fear. Leaving and not facing these people was the easy way out.

He had faced many things in his life, but he had always seemed to find a way or be given a way out. He had not had to say goodbye to his mother. She'd done that for him by leaving this earth before he'd left Finland. The decisions on their journey across the ocean and land as they'd traveled west had all been made by his brothers. The military had automatically placed him in a hospital unit during the war. Even Edna had made the decision for him to leave Johann's home—well, not the decision, but she'd made it easier. The reverend had given him an out when he'd provided time to heal physically and emotionally. He'd asked Hans to take him on the circuit, then tricked him into preaching but not before providing him with a sermon and scripture. Now he was giving him the perfect opportunity to share his good news.

The thought petrified him. These people wouldn't believe

him. He had done nothing to prove himself worthy of that pulpit. Only Aideen knew he had come home. He could leave now. Essie would help Aideen, and Aideen would provide for the girl. As would Katie. Katie. How could he leave her?

"Mr. Hans, sir?" Essie asked.

"Yes?" Hans cleared his throat and brushed the straw from his trousers to keep his head downward. No need for the girl to see his tears.

"Aunt Aideen wants me to sleep in a bed."

"Excuse me?"

"You know, in one of her fancy rooms? I ain't never slept in a bed like that. She even made me wash up in her washroom. I told her that weren't right, but she wouldn't listen."

Hans sighed. Sleeping in a bed and sharing a bathroom stressed this plucky girl. His worries seemed lessened, somewhat. "Is that not what you want? That bed is pretty comfortable."

"Well, sir, want is a confusin' word. I want to, but I also want to make sure the reverend ain't alone. I told Aunt Aideen I'd sleep on the floor by that fancy settee, but she said she was gonna care for him."

"That she will. If you get a few hours of good sleep, you can help her in the morning so she can rest."

"It's morning already."

Hans looked out the doors to see a sliver of light shining through.

"You're the one ought not to be making decisions without a good night's sleep first, Mr. Hans."

"Excuse me?"

"The reverend's right. You do say that a bunch." Essie laughed. "Come get somethin' to eat, then get some rest. Whatever's botherin' you will still be here when you wake. Only after restin' will you be able to figure out a solution to whatever's got you so bothered."

"Wise words." He turned down the lamp and headed into the house.

Chapter 37

Shumard Oak Bend

The sound of the chirping birds grated on his nerves, and the stream of light aggravated him. But it was the murmur of voices downstairs that had Hans on his feet. This was ridiculous. He could have been hours from town by now. Hans rubbed his eyes. What day was it anyway? Saturday. He glanced out the window. He could still leave and get in a full day's ride.

Hans felt for his stowed items under the bed. He pulled out the crate. There on top was his mother's Bible, the worn leather dry under his touch. He took more care with Rauti's tack than with this treasure. "Lord, what am I to do?" He flopped back onto the bed, the Bible on his chest. "What am I to do?"

A knocking sound jarred him from the sleep that had previously not come. "Yes?"

"Lunch is ready, Mr. Hans, and the reverend is askin' for you."

"Be there in a moment." Great. He'd missed his window of

opportunity. He ran his fingers through his hair. Something felt different. He sat up and looked around. When he stood, he saw his reflection in the mirror. No dark circles or puffy eyes. Those eyes widened. He had slept. Not in fits and spurts but a deep, healing sleep. And with no nightmares. He thought back to the last time he'd experienced one. He'd awakened a few times each night, but this time, he'd not woken at all.

He washed his face. There was no time to shave today. Dr. Sheffield's dental crème removed the grime on his teeth, and he spit into the bowl. Everything felt different. He sat on the chair and slipped into his boots.

"You comin'?" Essie asked.

"On my way." He laid the Bible on the chair, made his bed, kicked the crate back underneath, and headed downstairs.

"You be looking fresh as a daisy. Slept well, I gather?" Aideen pointed to the chair and placed a heaping plate of food before him. "Eat up now. I've a coach coming in an hour or so and need the kitchen. Thanks be to God for Essie here. What a blessing you be, dearie."

The smile the girl gave in response to the praise assured him that Essie would do just fine here. Maybe what he was feeling was the freedom to leave. He could go, and she'd find her place in this home. Aideen would care for her. He'd had enough sleep and could ride well into the night.

"Hurry up now," Aideen said. "I need you to help get the reverend cleaned up and to his room. He can't be in the parlor when the coach arrives, and one more night on the settee won't do him any favors."

He'd forgotten about the reverend. "Yes, ma'am. I'll be happy to help." He barely tasted the food as he ate with haste before heading to the parlor.

"Nice to see you awake, Reverend." Hans felt enormous compared to the withered man before him. A bony hand lifted far enough off the cushions for Hans to grasp it in his.

"Might you help me to the privy?" No blush spread over the man's cheeks. They were pallid, the wrinkles of age magnified.

"Of course." Hans released the hand, and it sagged back to the cushion with a slight bounce before resting near the floor. Sizing up the situation, Hans scooped his friend into his arms. "Hold tight, Reverend. I'm not as smooth a ride as Dorcas." A slight movement of the man's chest against his own encouraged Hans. He wanted to believe the reverend laughed, but the heaviness of the head on his shoulder told him the man was no longer conscious.

"Take him to my room," Aideen said.

Hans stopped.

"I'll stay in his room until he can get up and down the stairs on his own."

Aideen's disapproving look at what Hans had been thinking made him swallow his words.

"I'll bring the bedpan." Aideen wiped her eyes with her apron, her hand hovering over her mouth. "Oh, me dear friend." A sob escaped.

Hans turned page after page of his Bible, reading aloud as his friend moved in and out of sleep. His knees ached from kneeling beside the bed after settling the reverend. A knock broke his monologue.

"Mr. Hans? Sir?"

"Come in."

Essie's eyes roamed over the room until they landed on the pile of clothing on the chair. "I'll take this and bring a cushion for yo' knees." She inclined her head.

"Thank you. What time do you expect the coach?"

"The coach? It done come and gone. No boarders—just a kitchen full of dirty dishes. Good thing you brung me. Aunt Aideen's plum wore out."

"Has she rested?" Hans worried the woman was doing too much.

"Oh, yes, sir. I sent her straight away once the coach left. I done more work than this before. Cleanin' a kitchen and doing laundry ain't nothin', especially with that nice breeze comin' through the house. She lets me sing too. Says it's music to her ears." A broad smile graced her face.

Her face. Hans noticed it was clean and quite lovely. Her features were fine. A kerchief covered her head. She must have observed his perusal, for she reached up and touched the fabric.

"Aunt Aideen gave me this here dress and matching kerchief. Still ain't got no shoes but not sure I want any." She lifted her skirts to show clean feet. Gone was the dirty girl, but those scars around her ankles would never be erased.

"You look very nice." He stood and moved the chair closer to the bed before sitting. "I could use a cup of coffee if you don't mind."

"I can do that."

He was sure she could.

"That girl is something, isn't she?" A deep cough accompanied Reverend Jenkins's quiet words.

"Here, let's sit you up a bit and get some of this water in you." Hans placed a quilt and another pillow behind the man, raising him up enough so his friend could take the fluid without choking.

"Thank you." The raspy sound remained, but his words came out stronger. Another cough racked his body.

"You rest, Reverend."

"I's heard the coughin', so I brung this as well." Essie placed a tray on the side table. "Honey and lemon with thyme. It'll soothe your cough."

Hans watched the tender ministrations. Essie spooned the mixture into the reverend's mouth, wiping his chin with a napkin when it dripped. Hans stood with his back to the large window in the room, sipped his coffee, and marveled at the girl. "Where'd you learn that?"

"Feeding? I've been doin' this since before I can remember. There were always a baby needin' somethin' where I come from."

Where did she come from? Hans knew little about this girl.

"I meant caring for those in need."

"Same, I guess. You learn all kind of things in a big family. Not kin, mind you, but family. Since I been knee high to a grasshopper, I been cookin', cleanin', washin', takin' care of babies, workin' fields—you name it. But babies is my favorite. They can cry all they want; I don't mind. This ain't much different."

Hans held back a laugh. He was sure the reverend didn't appreciate being compared to a baby. Footsteps came from the hall, and Aideen popped her head in the doorway.

"Everybody decent?"

"Oh, yes, ma'am." Essie placed the spoon and cup on the tray. "Mr. Hans, you give him more of that in a few minutes and keep at it 'til it's gone. I'll bring up toast in a bit when I bring some tea." She smoothed her skirts like a young lady.

"Thank you, Essie," the reverend whispered.

"You're most welcome, sir." She curtsied though the man didn't see through his still-closed eyes.

"Hans, do you need anything?" Aideen grasped the doorframe as Essie slid through.

"I've got what I need. You focus on keeping up your strength. I can't play nursemaid to two."

Aideen tsked her tongue. "Nursemaid . . ."

Hans didn't hear the rest of her murmuring. He turned to Reverend Jenkins. "How are you feeling, my friend?" Hans touched the reverend's forehead with the back of his hand. "No fever."

"I could ask the same of you."

"Excuse me?"

A slight smile curved on the man's lips. "Feeling. How are you feeling?"

Hans knew what was being asked. "Afraid."

"Mmm. Afraid of?"

Hans delayed his response but knew the answer. "Afraid of failing, of not measuring up . . ."

"Measuring up to . . ."

"God, you, Aideen, the town, Katie." There, he'd said it.

"When you rely on your own strength, it's fear. When you rely on God's strength, it's reverence." Eyes still closed, breathing labored, Reverend Jenkins tapped his fingers on the bed, and Hans pulled the chair closer to hear the whispered words. "The fear of the LORD is the beginning of wisdom."

His labored breathing made Hans's chest hurt. Hans held the man upright as he coughed, then wiped his face with a damp cloth.

"You rest. Talking doesn't seem to agree with you—for once." The chuckle that followed didn't feel as lighthearted as he'd hoped.

"Fear can be a good thing, Hans." A high-pitched wheezing sound came and went as the man toiled to catch his breath before falling into a fitful sleep.

Chapter 38

Sunday morning

The voices in his head were gone, but those around him intensified. The verse about clanging symbols came to mind. His knees bounced as if ready to take flight. He held them down with sweaty palms. The announcements, the music, the children leaving for Sunday School—all moved in slow motion. He should go with them—run away. What was he doing? This was all wrong.

Clint bumped his arm, handing something to him. The offering basket. He had nothing to give—financial or otherwise. Fear gripped him, and he fumbled the basket. Clint's strong hand grasped his wrist, steadying the shaking but not calming the quake underneath. Hans felt the basket being peeled from his fingers, and he turned his focus to Clint.

"All you've been asked to do is share what has happened in your heart. Your testimony is the only sermon you need to preach today, Hans."

Bile rose in his throat. Clint released his wrist moments before Hans would have jerked it away. He felt trapped enough and didn't need physical bonds. Then again, he might. Clint's hand touched his elbow and pushed him upward. His legs shook as he walked the few paces to the front of the church. With his back to the congregation, he looked at the window where the roof and walls met. He followed the stream of light that landed at the very spot his feet were planted. Someone cleared his throat. Hans turned.

With nothing in his hands to keep them occupied, he put them in his pockets, then removed them, then placed them back in confinement to help hide their shaking. He tried to speak. A squeak came out, and he flushed with embarrassment. No one laughed. He heard a deep rumble and focused his attention on Clint.

"You can do this," Clint whispered.

Hans swallowed the lump in his throat and tried again. "Reverend Jenkins is sick." Stupid. They all knew that. "He asked me to tell my story." The magistrate sat a few rows back in the sanctuary. Arms crossed over his broad form, the man gave every indication he was waiting to cast judgment. Yellow caught his eye, and he saw Katie lower her head, her bonnet obscuring her face. His heart sank. He wanted her to understand, to see this new side of him. He wanted to prove to her he was a changed man. Whether or not anyone believed him, he would tell the truth.

"When I first arrived in Shumard Oak Bend, I was running." Hans saw a small smile form on the magistrate's lips. "I've been running all my life. I just didn't know it. My mother called me amenable. The problem with being an easy-going rule follower is you do just that—you follow. I allowed others to dictate what I did, where I went, and how I acted. I thought getting away and starting over would help me change. Only, it didn't because I didn't."

His hands moved in and out of his pockets, and he fought the urge to cross his arms to match the magistrate's stance. He sought out Katie's face, hoping she would give him support with a smile, but her head was still bowed. He faltered. Was she so ashamed of him that she could not look him in the eye? He clenched his tight fingers. If he did not speak the truth now, it would only prove he hadn't changed. Steeling himself for what may come, he continued.

"I was at the lowest point in my life a few weeks back. I found myself battered, bruised, and broken in more than body." He touched the scar on his forehead, lowering the shaky hand in case someone saw the trembling. "The reverend offered to give me time to heal by asking me to escort him on his circuit." Hans watched one eyebrow raise on the magistrate's face. The man didn't believe him.

"Something happened on that trip. I endured hours of sermons." Murmurs and chuckles went through the crowd. The simple sound fortified Hans. "One thing about Reverend Jenkins, beyond the fact that he is a man of God, is that he loves to talk about Jesus. Underneath all those words is a heart that desires for each of us to have a personal relationship with Christ Jesus." He heard a few "amens," which bolstered his confidence to continue.

"I realized that being good, following rules, and conforming to what was expected of me was not enough. I needed a heart change. A young girl on that trip showed me that becoming a new creation in Christ doesn't change us on the outside. No, our skin color and heritage are still the same, but when we follow Christ, our internal desires shift, and there is transformation inside us. I asked the reverend how I could know I was saved. His short response shocked me." More murmurs and chuckles from the crowd made Hans realize his joke. He cleared his throat before continuing.

"The reverend told me that if someone as powerful as the Holy Spirit is in your life, it will show." Silence. "I figured all my old habits would leave and be in the past when I laid them before Christ." This time, he was the one to chuckle. "Apparently, that isn't so. I've learned it's easier to act like a Christian than react like one." Once again, the congregation shored up his strength with their "amens."

"Another thing I learned about is the power of God's Word. Reverend Jenkins can spout off scriptures until the cows come home . . ." Someone in the back snorted, causing another ripple of laughter from some and a few stern looks from others. "But, scriptures are just phrases until we know God on a deeper level and on more than just paper. I learned God's Word doesn't become powerful until it becomes personal."

Hans hoped Katie would lift her gaze and give him some kind of confirmation that she was listening, but her face remained covered by the yellow brim.

"I asked God to forgive me of my wrongdoings. I still have a few people I need to ask the same." He willed Katie to lift her head. He needed to see if she might at least be open to him asking for her forgiveness. She remained unmoved by his speech. Exhausted, he resigned himself to the fact that no one had to accept his apology, but he still needed to offer it. That would have to be enough.

"Today I stand before you a new creation."

He wasn't certain how long he stood there before Clint joined him. The man's arm felt comforting around his shaking shoulders.

"Hans has shared how Christ changed his life. I believe it is the only sermon we require today. Let us pray."

Clint's booming voice echoed in the rafters. Hans felt, as well as heard, the prayer, and his shaking lessened. At the final "amen," Clint led Hans back to his seat.

Thomas pushed a shoulder into him, and Hans responded with an embarrassed grin before shoving back. Clint cleared his throat. The congregation stood and sang the doxology. It was a song of praise, one to the God he now called Friend.

"So, young man, are you telling the truth, or were those just words?"

"Sir?" Hans answered the magistrate, but his eyes followed the fleeing girl in the yellow bonnet. His heart sank.

"Fine sermon, young man," said a man Hans didn't recognize as he wiggled his way in front of the magistrate, who took a step back in surprise.

"Welcome to the family of God." Sheriff Adkins wedged in, moving the magistrate farther back. His hearty handshake and smile eased Hans's nerves.

"What a beautiful testimony of the transforming work of

our Lord," one of the Gray sisters added as she patted his arm.

One by one, the congregation spoke to him. Familiar words rang out, mimicking that first Sunday he had stood before a congregation. Only this time, he didn't have feelings of pride but humbleness. These people were accepting him, based on his new life with Christ. They were willing to see him as he was now, not who he had been.

The magistrate remained off to the side until the final parishioner was gone. "I'd like a word with you, young man."

Clint clapped his hand on Hans's shoulder. "Magistrate, I'm sure whatever business you need to conduct can wait until tomorrow. Aideen's feeding a crowd today, and we're already late."

Hans saw the silent exchange between the two men before witnessing a slight nod from the magistrate.

"We'll speak later then, Hans. Clint." The man donned his hat as he left.

"Any idea what that's about?" Hans asked.

"Nothing that can't wait until tomorrow. Let's go eat. I'm starving."

Chapter 39

Sunday

Shumard Oak Bend

Katie watched Magistrate Marley bully his way to the front of the church almost before the congregation had finished singing. She couldn't face Hans. Not now, possibly never. She was a fool for pushing him away with her harsh words and hurtful accusations. How would he ever forgive her? He'd taken an enormous step in changing who he was by choosing God's way while she had remained the same by choosing her own.

"Aideen, I'm back." Katie swung open the kitchen door to the smells of roast, potatoes, carrots, fresh bread, and greens. Something sweet hung in the air, but she couldn't distinguish the scent. It calmed her.

"Miss Katie, Aunt Aideen is out back feedin' the preacher. He had enough energy to sit on the porch this morning." Essie stirred the gravy.

Katie grabbed an apron. "Wonderful. The fresh air will do

him good. Now, what can I do to help you?"

"Nothin', Miss Katie. Me and Clara—we already done it all. She's nappin', so I's just waitin' for everybody to come in and sit. Is church over?"

Katie looked around. Everything was tidy, with platters full and ready to be placed on the table. "Yes. I left as soon as the doors opened. The others may be late. A line was forming to see Hans."

"Aunt Aideen might like a minute to freshen up. Here, you take this cup of tea, and sit with the reverend for a bit. I'll come getcha when dinner's on the table."

"Thank you, Essie. You're a godsend." Katie took the cup of steaming liquid and padded to the back porch. It was quiet, except for the creaking of the rocking chair. "Aunt Aideen?" Katie whispered. Her aunt jumped at the sound. Katie responded with a jerk, and hot liquid sloshed over her hand.

"Oh, me Katie, I didn't hear you."

She rubbed the red spot with her apron. "I was trying to be quiet in case the reverend was sleeping."

"He is that, and I'm guessing I might have been as well." Aideen brushed wisps of hair from her face.

"I'll sit with him while you go freshen up. Essie has everything under control in the kitchen. The others will probably be late coming from church. It was quite the day."

"Did Hans share?"

"Yes, ma'am." Katie could say no more. She kicked a leaf

from the porch with the tip of her shoe and watched it float to the ground.

Aideen stood. "I'll take you up on your offer. He hasn't eaten much, but I've been able to get a few sips in him when he wakes." Aideen patted the reverend's arm. "I'll be back, my friend," she said to the reverend.

Katie took her post in the rocker Aideen had vacated. She leaned her head against the back and lifted her heel to make a gentle motion. The creak of the wood soothed her troubled soul, as did the hot tea.

"Tell me."

Katie stopped her motion at the reverend's question. "Of the service?"

"Of Hans."

"He did a fine job." Katie smoothed her skirts and continued her rocking. What could she add? She had heard all Hans had said as she'd prayed for him. The moment she'd recognized fear on his face, it had been clear that the best way to support him was by lifting him to her, or rather their, heavenly Father. The last thing he'd needed to see was her eyes on him. How could she have been so wrong about him?

"Ka—" Reverend Jenkins coughed. His body jerked with the repeated action, then slumped as if he did not have the energy needed to remain upright.

"Essie? Essie!" Katie could hear the panic she felt coming out in her voice.

"Yes, ma'am, Miss Katie?"

"Is Clint here yet?"

"No, ma'am. No one's arrived yet. They be eatin' cold food iffen they don't hurry. Oh." Essie came around to see the slumped form of the reverend.

"He needs to lie down. Would you help me move him?"

Essie turned down the bed. Katie placed the man's arms over her shoulders, her head next to his, and leveraged her weight under his flopping arms. "Hold on, Reverend, if you can. One, two, three, lift." Both ladies helped him stand, then each took an arm and dragged him to the bed, damp with perspiration and breathing hard by the time they'd settled him.

"He doesn't weigh but a mite," Essie whispered.

The front door opened, bringing with it the blessed cross-breeze and a chorus of voices. Katie watched Essie straighten the covers, then move toward the kitchen, only to return to refill the full water glass beside the bed.

"Essie, would you like to stay with the reverend while I take your place in the kitchen?"

"Would you mind?" Essie hesitated before she focused her attention on Katie.

Katie watched as tears formed in the girl's eyes and threatened to spill over. She nodded, but the girl did not see. Essie's attention was on the withering body in the bed. Katie shut the door behind her as she moved toward the kitchen. "Lord, help us all."

"Katie, grab the gravy," Aideen said. "I left it on the counter."

The pronounced circles under Aideen's eyes increased the flush on her face. Had she lost weight as well? Katie complied. Anything to avoid Hans.

"Clint, please say the blessing." Aideen's words came out as a harsh order, and her voice cracked.

"How is he?" Clint looked at Katie as he took her hand.

She shook her head and lowered her eyes, trying to avoid the man with whom she desperately needed to speak.

"Lord, we thank You for this food and those who have prepared it," Clint said. "We ask You to allow it to nourish our bodies so we might better serve You by helping those in need. We pray for Your healing touch on Reverend Jenkins and Your comfort and care for those less fortunate. Amen."

Volume increased as plates and bowls passed from left to right before words became muffled with eating. Katie wondered who Clint had been thinking of when he'd mentioned those in need. Could it be he believed in her and her desire to open an orphanage? In her nervousness, she stood without thinking, then scanned the table to justify her action. "Water. We've forgotten the water pitcher." She grabbed it from the side table, then refilled glasses as she continued her controlled pacing.

Aideen's plate looked like she had fixed it for a child. Small portions dotted the cornflower blue bone china, allowing the pattern to show through around the outside edges. She had eaten little while the others at the table were serving themselves second helpings.

"Thank you, Katie girl," Aideen said as Katie topped off her already-full glass.

"My pleasure." Katie touched her aunt's shoulder as she moved to the next person. *Rap, rap.* Water splashed on the tablecloth when Katie jumped at the sound. The front door swung open, the slight creaking of its worn hinges loud in the new stillness around the table.

"Mrs. O'Sullivan." Sheriff Adkins entered the room and removed his hat. "I apologize for interrupting your Sunday meal."

"We have plenty, Sheriff. Would you care to join us?" Aideen moved to stand, but the sheriff held up his hand.

"Wish that I could." He looked at Clint, then continued. "We've received word of some trouble."

Katie watched Clint wipe his mouth before placing the napkin on the table and pushing back his chair. He did not stand but looked the informant full in the face, his actions asking the unneeded questions.

"There have been several recent home robberies in the area. Word is, Joe's gang is responsible."

"Do you know where they are now?" Clint asked.

"A rider delivered a message that they were a few hours northeast and looked to be heading east. The last homeowner they burned out was a decent shot and hit two of Joe's men before one of them got him. Joe and his men will be looking for shelter."

"Is the man all right?" Aideen's voice was full of concern and emotion.

"I don't know." Henry turned his hat in his hands.

"Lord, help us," Aideen whispered.

"We do need the Lord's help—and yours." Henry directed his statement to Clint.

Katie's eyes burned. She understood the meaning behind the words. Motion caught her attention as Rachel reached over and placed her hand in Clint's. Katie ached to look at Hans, and her body strained to reach for his hand, but she couldn't handle the rejection.

"Can I go?" Thomas asked.

"No, son, but I'd be much obliged if you'd see your mother home."

"Dad." Thomas drew out the one-syllable word.

Clint raised one eyebrow.

"You can trust me, Dad. I'll get her home."

"Thank you, Thomas. And thank you, Aideen, for this lovely meal. Men, let's move to the parlor to finish our discussion, so these ladies can enjoy the rest of their dinner."

All the men stood, including Thomas and Gabe. Katie no longer had an appetite.

"I believe I'll check on the reverend and relieve Essie." Aideen stood.

"Would you like me to save this for you?" Katie looked at the plate of untouched food. Half a piece of buttered bread was all the woman had eaten.

"Thank you." Aideen nodded, then grasped the table as if she needed the support.

"Are you well?" Katie rushed to her side.

"Ach, just me old bones. You two take your time."

Katie sat sipping her now-tepid tea and watched as Rachel twirled her fork in her greens, her gaze following the circular motion.

"Are you all right, Rachel?" Katie heard the scraping of silver on china.

"You can turn in your badge, but you'll always be a lawman."

Katie wondered at Rachel's glassy-eyed response and tried to think of something to say when Essie came through the door.

"Aideen said the men are formin' a posse. Are both Mr. Shankel and Mr. Hans goin'?"

When Rachel didn't respond, Katie nodded for her. Words would not come. She lifted her hand and rested it on her chest, doing her best to hold back the emotion clawing its way to the surface.

"Excuse me." Rachel stood, hand shooting up to cover her mouth, before racing out the door.

"Looks like she'll be growing her family again." Essie wiped the counters.

"How would you know that?"

"I done birthed enough babies to know the signs."

Katie's heart ached. Would she ever have children of her own?

"Miss Katie?"

"Yes?"

"Is Hans your man?"

She had not expected that. The reality that he was not hit her with a force she had never experienced. Tears fell on the back of her hand and dampened her sleeve. She shook her head. "No."

"You sure 'bout that?"

Katie took a deep breath. "I once rejected him—hurt him deeply. We went our separate ways, and now he's changed while I've remained the same. I'm not worthy of him, Essie." Katie pulled the hanky from her sleeve and dabbed at her eyes.

"Sounds like a bunch of malarkey to me."

Essie's words caught Katie off-guard, and she snorted. "Oh, dear. Am I being foolish?"

"Yes." Rachel rejoined them at the table. Her face was ashen. She cleared her throat and took a sip of tea. "Don't let that boy go off without saying your piece, Katie. Life is too uncertain. Trust me on that."

Chapter 40

Shumard Oak Bend

"**A**re you certain Joe won't try to head back to town?" Hans felt his voice shake. He hoped he did not expose his nervousness while his knee bounced on the settee as the men discussed scenarios and devised a plan.

"Deputy Leupp will care for the town, but I don't expect Joe will come crawling back. There's not much forgiveness waiting for him here," Sheriff Adkins said.

Forgiveness. Hans had settled his affairs with God. He needed to settle with Katie. Asking for her forgiveness and seeking reconciliation for how he'd wronged her and done nothing to prove he was a man of worth seemed of utmost importance. Taking down Joe and his gang carried risk. His heart yearned to have her forgive him, accept him, give him another chance. He wasn't even sure there would be another chance. Joe had proved he was armed and dangerous.

"Come now, boys." Aideen popped her head into the parlor, motioning for them to return to the table. "You can have a moment with your loved ones after we've spoken to the Lord." The men followed. "Now, sit." She pointed Hans to the chair beside Katie's slumped form.

He smiled, remembering the first time they'd met. She had slouched in that chair and given him the stink eye. He'd like to see that fire again.

"Essie, leave that coffee, and come sit." Aideen pulled out a chair. Hans watched the girl's eyes go wide.

"Oh, no, ma'am."

"Essie, I said sit." Aideen pointed to the chair. "Reverend Jenkins is sleeping."

"It's not that."

"You are a part of this family now, not some hired hand. We need all the prayers we can get, and yours count as much as anyone else's."

Hans smiled. He'd known Aideen would accept the girl. His heart felt lighter at the thought.

"Where two or three are gathered . . ." Aideen lifted her hands to the tabletop, and each took the one hand to the left and right.

Hans could not breathe. Katie's hand intertwined with his. Her tight grip made his fingers ache, but he did not care. Without thinking, he lifted them to his lips and kissed a knuckle, then blushed at his boldness. He was thankful Clint had already started praying, beseeching God for their safety. She held tight, and he lowered their hands to quell the constant moving of his knee. Glancing up, he chanced a look at

Katie to find her gaze on him. He couldn't read what was going on behind those tortured eyes. Flecks of gold seemed to fall from them with each tear that traipsed down her cheeks. Had he hurt her that deeply?

"We commit ourselves to You and Your service, Lord. We want to follow You in all things and bring justice to those who have lost their lives at the hands of Joe and his gang." Clint's voice continued to increase in volume.

Is that what Hans was doing? Was he choosing to follow God, or had he allowed men to conscript him once again to do their bidding? He felt a prick in his spirit. Would God ask him to choose between Katie and Joe? Was catching Joe God's way of giving him an opportunity to show Katie he cared for "the least of these"? Would this be how he could win Katie's trust and show he was a man of worth and of his word? Hans did not feel strong enough in his newfound faith to answer those questions.

Hans listened as everyone joined their voices in a chorus of prayers. The battle in his heart and mind caused a familiar squeeze in his chest. Joe's words slipped through the crevices, filling him with doubts and fears. He was being pulled deeper, further, back into the prison he had escaped, but then a light shone in the darkness. Essie's sweet voice rang clear, breaking the chains threatening to bind him.

> "Nobody knows the trouble I've been through
> Nobody knows my sorrow
> Nobody knows the trouble I've seen
> Glory hallelujah!"

"Glory, hallelujah," Aideen echoed.

Choosing joy in difficult times was what Christ had done. He would as well. Hans heard the hissing of demons as they scattered, not finding a place to settle. One by one, those at the table stood, except for Katie. Her hand remained intertwined with his under the table, away from prying eyes. She lifted her apron to her face with her other hand, and he followed the motion. She was the most beautiful thing he had ever seen, even with one eyebrow arched over puffy eyes.

They were alone now. He'd not even seen the others leave. With his free hand, he wiped Katie's cheek, and she leaned into his touch. Was it possible? Did she have feelings for him as well?

"Do you remember the time I said I'd do anything as long as I didn't have to do the dishes?" Hans asked.

"I do."

"I hadn't quite planned on this."

"This?"

"Joining a posse and chasing down a bandit."

"Then let's do dishes."

"Excuse me?"

Hand still in his, she pulled him to his feet. She took the connection with her when she let go. She gathered the cups and saucers on the table and motioned for him to open the kitchen door. Hans watched her fill the sink from the kettle on the stove, shave soap into the hot water, then plunge her arms deep, churning to make small bubbles. He handed her a few dishes at a time, then moved to the other side to rinse and dry.

They worked in silence.

"We make a good team." Her voice was soft.

"Yes, we do." He paused but only long enough to gather his wits. It was now or never.

"I'm sorry." They spoke the words in unison.

"You are?" Katie whispered.

"What for?" Hans spoke overtop her words. They laughed, and he gave Katie the other end of the cloth he was holding, so she could dry her hands. "Ladies first."

"I'm sorry for speaking out of turn, for not believing you, for making a judgment without first hearing your side of the story, for—"

Hans put his finger to her lips. The touch sent fire through his veins, and his eyes landed on the source of heat. "No, Katie. You were right in all you said, and had you asked me what had happened with Moses, I would not have been able to give you a satisfactory answer. It has taken me this long to realize the wretch I was—still am."

She shook her head, but he did not give her a chance to speak. His hand moved to cup her cheek. She leaned into him and placed her hand on his chest. *What am I doing? She's already spoken for—by Paul. I have no right—no claim.* He took a step back and felt a chasm extend between them. The deep green of her eyes held shock, then anger. He had made a mistake in touching her.

"Katie, I . . ." Hans hesitated and continued to retreat. Her hands rested on those swaying hips. He forced his gaze to return to her eyes.

"Mr. Korhonen, you are the most exasperating man I have ever met." She stomped her foot and crossed the kitchen to the outside door, the fierce swishing of her skirts screaming their frustration. "And quit looking at my ankles."

He blinked and lifted his gaze.

The horses alerted the three men to the pungent odor of wood smoke before the smell enveloped Hans's senses. A pile of rubble smoldered. There was nothing they could do here. Except bury the dead. They dismounted and walked the perimeter.

"Looks like they left the land untouched. I'm not sure how that fire didn't spread," Clint said to the wind.

"The good Lord. No other explanation." Henry patted his horse and checked the saddle.

Hans rubbed water over his face and neck, then used his canteen to do the same to Rauti before stowing the item. It was ridiculous and dangerous for the three of them to confront Joe and his group. The miscreant had upgraded from bullying and name-calling to arson and killing.

"You two able to keep going?" Sheriff Adkins checked for lesions at the places where his tack connected with his horse. When all seemed well, he focused his attention on Clint and Hans. "We need to go as far as we can. We'll stop when the horses do. No need to push them. They're used to the terrain and distance, so I think they have a few more hours in them."

They traveled through the night at a working trot, taking care that the horses did not become overly taxed. They took breaks when needed, checked their mounts, and refreshed themselves when they came upon water. Hans listened to the two men tell stories of war, got caught up on news of newcomers to town, and gained insight into the growth of Thomas and Gabe. No matter the subject, he spent most of his time thinking about hazel-flecked green eyes and remembering the softness of freckle-covered cheeks.

"Smoke ahead." Clint's words pulled Hans from his musings. "I'm guessing a hearth fire."

"Let's go in quietly. If it isn't Joe, we don't want to get ourselves shot by a trigger-happy homesteader." Sheriff Adkins lowered his voice. "Clint, you go around left. Hans, you head around right. I'll go straight in."

Even in the twilight, blue light created familiar shadows. A row of fruit trees in the distance stood like sentries who had not done their job guarding the home. The earth beneath Hans's horse lay in clumps, the mounds of dirt and rock fresh. He struggled to breathe as the air became heavy. Lowering himself from Rauti, he picked his way around the new grave. Memories of standing in this spot weighed on him, pushing him to his knees before a cross on an older grave. He did not need to read the inscription to know the intricate detail carved on its form. Wildflowers had grown over the mound. Rauti's reins were the only offering he had to give, and he placed them on the marker.

"Keep an eye on my horse, will you, Otto?"

Creeping through the tall grass, he made his way to the barn wall and hid behind it. His pulse quickened. He'd not wanted to come back, especially under these conditions.

"Lord, please." He wiped at his eyes. He needed to focus. Edna's scowl, Johann's disappointment, and Franc's weariness at having to take on more of the load all kept him from seeing straight.

Listening for any sounds, he crept around the side wall of the barn farthest from the house and settled into the lean-to, wedging himself between the familiar equipment. This was as close as he could get to the house and stay concealed. He worked to slow his breathing. In the dark, he focused on the dancing flame of a lantern in one of the windows across the clearing. Even as the oncoming of morning brought with it a fresh breeze, sweat trickled down his back. With clammy hands, he wiped his brow. Squinting, he blinked back the stinging sweat. He needed to walk, release this pent-up energy, and keep his mind from succumbing to the thoughts that threatened to invade it.

Hans heard the call of a nightjar from the tree line. With the sun nearly over the horizon, that bird should have been quiet. He searched the brush at the base of the trees. Barely discernible, Clint hunkered down between scrub bushes and fallen limbs. A reply came from the outhouse. The sheriff had managed to get close without notice. Hans turned his attention back to the front of the house. The door jerked open, and a man pushed a woman through the opening. He kept a firm grasp on her hair. With her head tilted back, she could not see where she was walking, and she missed the step and fell to the ground, taking the man with her.

"Edna." It was no more than a whispered prayer.

Chapter 41

Korhonen Homestead

Hans felt his stomach clench harder than his hands. There was no way he could make a clean shot from this distance. He may not like Edna, but he was not about to put her in harm's way just to bring this man down.

Strands of hair spilled loose from her bun. Gone was her fierce gaze and stern mouth. Instead, Hans watched a frightened woman struggle to regain her footing and dignity. She grasped at the front of her dress before standing and stretched her other arm out to keep herself from running into anything in their path. The collar of her dress flapped with the motion.

Filth spilled from the man's mouth as he pushed her across the yard. "Time to do the only thing you're good at, woman."

Edna's hand retreated and wrapped around her thin midsection. Edna may be a thorn in the flesh, but she was family, and Hans would not see harm come to her. Hans caught movement near the outhouse to the left and tracked the sheriff's form as he hid himself in the bushes, farther from the atrocities Hans did not want to witness. Where was Clint? Hans searched the area but did not locate him.

The creak and groan of the barn door, along with Edna's scream, echoed in the night. The cow lowed a mournful sound, repeating Hans's feelings that he needed to help Edna. *God, help me.*

"Listen."

There was no mistaking the voice. The wind stopped, and every sound vanished. Hans closed his eyes and imagined the interior of the barn. He heard another shriek, more muffled this time. Edna was now in the cow stall. He followed her movements in his mind. The scrape of the three-legged stool as she pulled it from its shelf, the swishing of skirts, and the clop-clop of cow hooves as the animal backed into the stall, helped him follow her position.

"I have no bucket." Edna's voice was frantic, not her usual clipped and arrogant tone.

Hans heard the bucket hit the ground, then soft sounds as streams of milk hit the bottom of the pail. No other noises made it to his ears until humming started. Edna's? It was a hymn. It wasn't likely the man. Hans listened for any signs of where he might be, but it was too quiet, making Hans's pulse increase and his breathing shallow.

"Hey, Ed." A call from the house drew Hans's attention.

"What?" the man called Ed spat out. Hans heard footfalls, then a squeal from Edna. "Them doors is open, and I can see you, woman. Try anything, and I'll slit your throat." More insults followed. "What?" Ed yelled with more agitation.

Ed stood outside the barn now, and Hans could see dried blood on his shirtsleeves. He did not need to be any closer to recognize the splotches were likely not his own. Hans recognized the man on the porch as the one who had been glued to Joe's side in town. His scraggly clumps of hair stuck out like poorly laid barbed wire.

"Hey, Ed, I'm sending the boy to get the eggs. Says he's gotta, you know."

"No. Know what?"

"The outhouse." The man pointed to where the sheriff hid.

At the top of the steps, Michael stood shaking.

"Looks to me like he already took care of that." Ed pointed to the stain running down the front of Michael's pants as the other man shook his head and slipped back into the house.

Hans felt something new building inside him. This boy did not deserve such cruel treatment.

"The least of these."

Hans stilled. "The least of these." He needed to do this for the Lord, not for anyone else.

"Hurry up, boy." Ed spat on the ground.

Hans knew the moment the boy saw him. Hans lifted a single finger to his lips, then used two fingers to mimic walking on his other palm. He pointed to the outhouse, then flopped his fingers on his open hand. He cocked his head and let his tongue hang out of his mouth for effect. The boy didn't move. Great, he'd given away his location to a statue who, if he spoke, would alert Ed to his position.

"Hurry it up, boy," Ed growled.

Edna's humming became louder, the sound rousing the boy from his stony slumber, yet he didn't move.

"I said hurry it up, boy."

Hans heard the click of the hammer of a gun at the same time he saw Michael blanch. Whereas Joe was mean, this man was evil.

"That's more like it.," Ed said.

Michael began to move, and Ed put the gun away. Ten paces later, the boy tripped, his arms flailing but catching his fall. Hans heard a low groan. Either the boy was a talented actor or in worse shape than Hans had thought.

Hans heard Ed yell God's name, but not in a manner the Lord would consider pleasing, before heading straight for the boy. As soon as Ed passed where Hans hid, Hans took advantage of the moment and slipped into the barn. He glanced out the door to see Michael pick himself up and utter a "sorry" before running into the outhouse and shutting the door.

"Edna," Hans whispered. She jumped, eyes wide with fear before they changed to recognition. "Shh. Keep doing what you're doing. We will get you out of this."

"'We?'" Her familiar, haughty tone matched the features he remembered. Returned was the condescending glare in her eyes and the thin line of her lips.

Hans nodded. Everything in him wanted to remind her he was here to help. Instead, he put his finger to his mouth to show the need for silence—both his and hers. He took the ladder's rungs two at a time and slid to a halt, flattening himself near the edge. He prayed that anything floating down would land before Ed returned. From this vantage point, he could see out the window at the back, where the sun's rays would soon enter. Hans could also see the open barn doors at the front facing the house, as well as the stalls on the opposite side of Edna. Below him, if he squinted through the narrow crack, he could see Edna's back. He watched the slight movements between her shoulders, and he heard the milk spray hit the filling bucket. Edna resumed her humming.

"You done yet?"

Edna must have said "no" if Ed's oaths were any sign of his frustration. Ed walked back and forth between Edna and the barn door, peering out and yelling for Michael to finish his business and get the eggs. All was silent, then a scraping sound pulled Hans's attention to the floor below.

"Done now?" Ed asked.

"I'll be done by the time the sun comes up."

The sun. When the sun peeked above the horizon, the glare blinded those looking from the house toward the barn. Could Edna have it in her to help? Likely, she thought he wouldn't have remembered that detail, and he hadn't, but she didn't need to know that.

"Onward Christian soldiers . . ." Edna's voice lifted in song.

"Why, you crazy woman, you'll wake the dead." In a rage, Ed

flew back into the barn.

Hans dropped from the loft. Something cracked as he landed on the man's back. He heard another thud and snap, then silence. He turned to find a now-two-legged stool over the man's head.

"I guess you'll need to carve another leg," Edna said as if it were an everyday occurrence that she had struck down a man. "That is, if you live long enough."

He clenched his jaw. "We'll see." There was no time for pleasantries, even if he could think of any. "Tie him up, and gag him. I'll get to Michael." Hans watched her face pale. He touched her shoulder. "We are family, Edna. Trust me."

"Trust you? Ha." She jerked her shoulder out from under his touch.

Like a switch to his backside, her sting hurt deeply. He would not allow this woman to gain control over him once again. His sides swelled as his legs spread into a stance customarily used only for fighting. He would fight, if necessary.

"You spilled the milk." She pointed to the overturned bucket before placing her hands on her hips.

"I saved your hide." Hans's nostrils flared, and he squelched a guttural sound from deep within.

"The light." Edna's simple words held disdain. The lift of her chin toward the open doors added to her pretentious air, as did the flick of her hand ushering him out. "I'll finish your work, as usual." She bent and gagged the still-unconscious form with her apron, then used the strings to tie his hands behind his back.

Hans slipped out before he said anything he would regret or missed his window of opportunity. With the sun's bright light at his back, he rushed to the chicken coop.

"Michael," Edna called from the barn. "Son, get the eggs, please."

Please. Hans shook his head. She had never used that word with him. The outhouse door opened slowly. The chickens squawked, and Michael hurried over.

"Hans, what are you doing here? Is Mom all right? There's someone behind the outhouse."

"Your mom is fine. She's tying up Ed as we speak. Get in here, and take your time gathering the eggs. Don't look my way. The man you heard is Sheriff Adkins. Now, focus, Michael. I need information."

Michael did as he was told. Hans watched through the cracks of the coop as the boy pulled the basket from the hook, opened the door, and entered the wooden structure.

"Can you hear me?" Michael asked much too loudly.

"Keep your voice down. I hear you just fine. Use a singsong voice like you're talking to the chickens. Tell me who is in the house."

"Like I told the sheriff, there are two injured men. Aunt Betsie is caring for them. They tied up Uncle Franc and Dad." The boy's voice quivered, but Hans almost laughed as the boy's deepening voice changed into a child's.

"Are my brothers injured?"

"Bruises and a split lip for Franc. Dad put up quite a fight, but he'll mend."

"Anyone else?"

"No, just Ed and Larry."

"Now there's just Larry." Hans tried to keep the chuckle from his voice.

"Larry's about as smart as a nailhead. I—"

"Wait, what about Joe?"

"He's one of the two Aunt Betsie is caring for. I don't expect he'll live through the night. You need to watch out for the other one they call Slim. He keeps a gun at the ready. His horse got shot out from under him, and the weight crushed his leg. But he shot off the top of Mom's medicinal whiskey while it was still in her hand. She gave it to him after that."

"What room are they in?"

"Yours."

"Does the sheriff know this as well?"

"I didn't think to tell him."

"All right. You did just fine, Michael. Head on in with those eggs, and let Johann know I'm here if you can without warning the others of our presence. If shooting starts, you and your mother get to the floor, you understand?"

"Yes, sir. And, Hans?"

"Yes?"

"Thanks for coming back."

Hans heard the creak of the coop door, the rusted hinges sounding much like his joints felt. The sound of Michael's heavy footsteps as they trudged to the house reminded him they were all weary. *And afraid.* He took a deep breath, praying the boy would use some common sense when he got inside. The smells of chicken feces and stagnant water caused him to gag, and he slid his back down the rough wooden frame of the coop to bury his face in his knees. Dry grass cracked under his palms as he steadied himself.

He checked his gun, not wanting to use it, but knowing he would if needed. A fly buzzed near his head, but he ignored the pest. Hans shook his head to clear his thoughts, but the fly remained nearby, its buzz a reminder of his past. Dozens of flies buzzed in his mind, creating black clouds each time he placed a body on the decaying corpses in the wagon. That was the trouble with the past—bad memories overshadowed the good ones, at least in his experience.

He closed his eyes and willed himself to remember the first years on this farm—the good years—before Edna had come. He smelled the sweet blossoms of the fruit trees he and Otto planted, watered, and tended. He felt the clods of dirt under his feet as Franc taught him how to till the soil while singing made-up songs about worms chewing and excreting dirt. Hans held in a laugh. Franc had known what it took to get a teenage boy to work. That song would probably be in his mind all day now.

A large form loomed before his closed eyes, and Johann

came into focus. His oldest brother may not have been exactly fun, but he'd imparted wisdom, shared their family history, and told of God's love, much like his father would have. Johann had invested his life in him. He'd taught Hans valuable skills, even when he hadn't wanted to learn. The deep bass of Johann's voice enveloped him in a hug. *"This may not be fun now, but you'll appreciate our stores when winter hits."* Cool dampness relaxed him as he remembered hours spent digging a hole, shoring up its sides, and building shelves for the root cellar.

The root cellar. His memories evaporated like the morning dew surrounding him. He needed to get the sheriff's attention. He picked up a rock and threw it at the outhouse but came up short. He repeated the action. A muzzle poked out before the rest of Henry's face emerged. Without a sound, Hans waved. The gun lowered. Sign language would have to do. He mimicked eating an apple, then pointed to the side of the house. With one hand flat, he used his other to show going under, then up the other side. He finished with his hand in front of his mouth as he used his other to pantomime eating with a fork.

He sure hoped the sheriff played charades. Otherwise, he did not know what the man might have taken from that craziness. The sheriff gave him a single nod. Good, he'd understood, or, at least, Hans guessed that was what the sheriff's nod had meant. It wouldn't be easy, but they could do it with God's help.

God's help. Hans raised his heart and his gaze. "Lord, I sure hope You're in this. I desire only to do Your will. Give me the strength of Samson and the fearlessness of David." He lowered his head. A ladybug crawled across his arm. Those spots reminded him of the freckles on Katie's nose. Today may be his last day on earth. He may never know if a chance with Katie would be possible, but if he didn't survive the day, at least he was secure in the knowledge he was going to heaven.

Chapter 42

Shumard Oak Bend

"**M**armalade, you silly cat." Katie shooed the animal curled up on Dorcas's back. Dorcas whinnied. "Was she keeping you company, girl? Hmm?" Katie saddled the old mare. "Time for your daily exercise. How does that sound?"

Katie ducked as they left the barn, leaving the doors open. A little fresh air might help clear out the stale smell. She took in the town. There was little color on the street, save for the newly painted mercantile sign. She did not know where Mr. Taylor had found blue paint to match the inside of an ocean swell, but it took her back to her travels to America. She tasted the salt air, felt the sea spray on her face, heard the jingle of the ship's rigging, and smelled . . . Ugh, what was that smell?

Katie looked between the buildings, then returned her focus forward. Whatever it was, she didn't want to know. She pushed her heels into Dorcas. "Let's get over the hill, and leave all this behind, eh, girl?" Dorcas seemed to understand and picked up speed.

The breeze begged her to let down her hair. Her red waves tossed behind her as she lifted her face to the sun. Freeing her curls was nothing compared to the freedom she felt from being out in the open. Near the edge of the tree line, she spotted a deer and slowed. Where there was one, there were usually others. Such lovely creatures. She had once felt one's hide, expecting it to be wiry and coarse like Mr. Finch's goats, but the ears had been soft. She leaned forward and stroked Dorcas's neck.

"We'll give you a good brushing when we return, girl. I know my company isn't as good as the reverend's, but it will have to do."

The reverend. He had stopped eating, and it was almost like he'd forgotten how to swallow. Even spooned liquids spilled out of his mouth. He had rare moments of clarity when he would request his Bible or paper and pencil, but deep coughing and exhaustion followed any spoken words. He became agitated, especially when Katie was near, so she did her part in his convalescing by caring for Dorcas while Aideen and Essie tended to the man's needs.

"Lord?" Katie focused on the low, puffy clouds forming rows in the sky, willing God to speak to her in the same way He shared knowledge through his creation. Those gray clouds overhead suggested dry weather, and the slight temperature difference from last night to this morning confirmed it. Just once, she would like God to give her a sign of what to do next. But even if He wasn't going to talk with her, it didn't mean she shouldn't speak to Him.

"Lord, it looks like Clara and Mr. Finch are getting along

nicely, and her son seems pleased with the situation. I expect wedding bells will be in their future. I'm guessing Sam is enjoying his new family and having a dog. That rascal took advantage of the moment in asking for one." She laughed, then sobered. "It appears Reverend Jenkins will join You soon." Her words caught in her throat, and she wiped at the moisture on her cheeks. "Even Essie has found a home with Aideen. Lord, what about me?" Katie wiped her nose on her sleeve. "Is there nothing for me?" Blue eyes swam before her like the waves of the ocean.

"Katie?"

"God?"

"Katie."

Through blurred vision, Katie searched around her. There, coming toward her from her right, were five riders, one waving his hat. She shielded her eyes. Clint Shankel placed his hat back on his head. The sheriff lifted a single hand in greeting. Three other men sat astride horses. But none of them held the familiar face of the one man she yearned to see.

"Essie? Aunt Aideen?" Katie worked to get the words out with her spent breath.

"Whatever be the matter, me Katie girl?" Aideen came from the kitchen, her eyes wide.

Katie followed the woman's gaze and touched her wild hair. "Dear me."

"'Dear me' is right. You'll be up half the night getting those tangles out. Now, what's got you all riled?"

"Mr. Shankel and Sheriff Adkins have returned with three bound men. Clint asked if you would prepare meals for the five of them."

"And Hans?" Aideen worried the lace of her apron.

"He wasn't with them." Katie burst into tears and ran into Aideen's open arms.

"All right, child. It's all right. I'm sure they'll explain. Now, dry those tears, and come help me fix a basket."

Katie stood and wiped her nose on her sleeve.

"How about you wash up first?" Aideen held her at arm's length.

"Yes, ma'am."

Katie did her best to manage her hair before placing her mob cap on top. It looked like an upended bread bowl on her head, with her hair now twice its normal volume. She splashed water on her face, her shaking hands leaving droplets on her blouse. She patted herself dry as best she could before taking a cleansing breath and heading to the kitchen.

"There you are and looking much better. I've got the basket almost ready. Sit, and drink this tea before you go. I would send Essie, but I know you want to ask about your man."

"My man?" The cup made it halfway to her mouth, then stalled.

"Oh, dearie. He is all that and more if you'd pay a wee bit of attention." Aideen placed another cloth-wrapped sandwich in the basket. "Now 'tisn't much, but Martha will have a meal for Henry this evening, and you tell Clint he's staying with us tonight. I'll have a fine meal prepared for him."

Katie's hands shook, and she was grateful Aideen had only filled her cup partway. *My man. Oh, Lord, please give me a chance to make things right with Hans.*

"Off with you now." Aideen placed her hand over Katie's. "I've been praying and will continue."

"Thank you, Aunt Aideen. I believe I'll walk over to the jail. Would you mind asking Essie to take care of Dorcas for me?"

"Of course. You go on."

Katie felt as if she were walking to her judgment. Why hadn't Hans returned? The three men she'd seen tied to their horses had been filthy and bloody. One had had his arm wrapped in a splint and sported a bandage around his head. He'd looked familiar, but she couldn't be sure with all the bruising, blood, and dirt. Her heart raced. Neither of the other men had looked like the picture she had seen of Joe or her memory of the man from the day she'd seen him in town. That had been at a distance, but she remembered him as a small-framed man, and these other men had both sat tall in the saddle—well, as tall as they could with their injuries. Before opening the door to the sheriff's office and jail, Katie released her worry on a breath and gulped, knowing that God was with her, no matter the outcome.

"Deputy Leupp, I'm here with the food Sheriff Adkins

requested." Katie flinched as the man's chair scraped the floor, startling her at the quick motion when he stood.

"Thank you, Miss Murphy. He surely will appreciate that. It's been a long few days." The man shifted from one foot to the other and struggled to keep eye contact.

"Might I speak with him?"

"Him?"

"The sheriff?"

"Oh, right. Well, um, it might not be proper at the moment." The man's gaze darted back and forth between a spot on the floor near her feet and the hallway to the cells.

Loud cursing, a sharp cry, and then silence filled the room. Her heart skipped a beat.

"Miss Murphy, it might be best if you leave that for now." He walked around the desk, took the basket, then escorted her to the door.

"But ..."

"Thank you for this." He lifted the basket as he closed the door behind them.

"All right, Deputy. Please let Mr. Shankel know Aideen will have a hot bath and dinner for him this evening." Her eyes pleaded for him to give her news of Hans, but he refused to look at them long enough to understand her request.

"Good day, Miss Murphy."

If walking to the jail had felt like receiving judgment,

walking home felt like stepping up to the gallows. Her heart ached with the not knowing.

"Mrs. O'Sullivan?" A man's voice echoed in the front hall.

Katie ran to the door, skirts lifted. She slid to a halt in front of a startled deputy.

"Hello again, Miss Murphy." He presented the basket with an outstretched hand.

Katie composed herself and took the empty offering. "Won't you come in and have some coffee and a cookie, Deputy?" Katie worked to keep the pleading from her voice.

"Oh, no, ma'am. I'm just returning the basket with our thanks for the fine meal and bringing news that Clint won't be in tonight."

"He won't?" Katie prayed he would offer more information.

"Now, Miss Murphy, you know I can't go sharing official business with you. Clint said he'd be back in a few days. He headed to—" The man stopped abruptly and put up his hand. "No, ma'am, I won't say another word. Now, you just let Mrs. O'Sullivan know—"

"But, Deputy Leupp, please, can you give me word of Hans?" Katie interrupted.

Like a child, the man reached up and used his fingers to mimic turning a key over his lips.

Exasperating man.

"I bid you good night, Miss Murphy."

Katie held the door in one hand and the basket in the other. It would be another fitful night of sleep.

"He's asked me to marry him." Widow Easton's words were quiet, a sheen covering her dark lashes.

"What did you answer?" Aideen poured more hot water into the woman's cup as they finished their dessert.

Aideen sat, and Katie placed her hand over her aunt's.

"I didn't." Clara Easton lifted a dainty hanky and dabbed at the tears. "I didn't know if it was proper."

"Proper, my heinie. Who cares if it be proper?" Aideen sat back in her chair as if the matter were settled.

"I hardly know the man. William is kind to Danny, and my boy likes him. But marriage? I've only been widowed a short time, and—"

"From the sounds of it, widowhood was part of your life long before your husband's death," Aideen interrupted.

"Yes. I suppose you are right. But it's only been—"

Aideen flattened her hands on the table. "The only consideration you need to ruminate on is if you feel God would have you marry the man. We gave up on etiquette and proper mourning attire long ago. We might as well give up the customary two-year mourning period as well. Life is short, Clara. You, more than many others, know the reality of that. You have a son to care for, and William Finch appears to be the best solution. If, and I mean only if, you feel it is what God would have you do."

Katie watched the woman work her jaw as gentle tears continued to fall. Clara moved the floating tea leaf around her cup, the spoon never touching its edges.

"Do you have family, Clara?" Katie asked.

The woman shook her head, then lifted her right shoulder slightly before placing both hands in her lap. "I suppose I have my husband's family, though they made it clear they wanted nothing to do with the boy or me. But, no, I do not have a family of my own."

"Well, you have us." Aideen leaned forward, touching Clara's arm. "We only want what is best. Who are we to judge what is right? Ain't no law that says you can't remarry, only the standard of some high and mighty society. We're in the wilds of Missouri, Clara, and sustaining life is more important than some made-up rule."

"Have you asked Danny for his thoughts?" Katie asked.

"What? Oh, no. I hadn't considered it. He didn't know his father. I learned I was pregnant with Danny after my husband left for war. But . . ."

"No buts. Doesn't the boy deserve a man like William Finch to raise him?" Katie offered.

"I suppose he does. Do you think he's old enough to

understand?"

"I think he is old enough to be given the opportunity to try to understand."

Clara's head bobbed up and down in slight movements. Her breathing steadied. "But there is something bigger that I'm not sure the boy will understand."

"Whatever it is, dearie, it will work out," Aideen said.

Clara lifted her gaze to the woman. "I haven't told William, and he may not want to marry me after he finds out."

"What could possibly keep that googly-eyed, starstruck man from marrying you?" Aideen lifted her cup and sipped.

"I'm pregnant. It was the last gift my husband gave me."

In a small town where gossip reached the far side before the wind did, Katie could not get a single detail out of Deputy Leupp or Sheriff Adkins. She'd even taken cookies to Martha who'd held up her hand and said, "I know no more than you. My husband is being as tight-lipped as a horse, and he's refusing to share details of what happened." The two women enjoyed the cookies, but Katie walked home with no more information than when she'd arrived.

Spirits low, she continued past the boarding house to the fresh air and quiet hills beyond. Sitting under the swaying branches of a stately Shumard oak tree, she leaned against the sturdy trunk, soaking in its strength. This tree had seen many seasons and storms, yet still it stood. It had withstood drought and heavy rain. Her fingers traced the grooves of the rough bark from the trunk to the ground where the roots burrowed deep.

Katie bent forward and released a long, low sigh. She pulled her knees in, making herself as small as possible under the massive tree overhead. Her chin trembled, and she clamped her mouth tight, willing the tears to remain in their hold, but they did not obey. Dropping her head to her knees, she wept until there were no more tears. She wiped her face on her skirts and stared at the dust-covered boots peeking out from beneath her rumpled skirts.

"Lord?" Thick emotion choked her voice. She cleared her throat and tried again, this time lifting her head high. "Lord?" Tears started falling again. "Please, Lord. Please let Hans be safe and unharmed." She felt the pulse in her throat move to her temple, and she rubbed the spot, remembering Hans's touch on her face and how she had leaned in. A feeling of emptiness encompassed her in his absence. She ached for him. When she next saw him, she would waste no time in letting him know she loved him.

I love him. The thought caught her unaware yet felt comfortable. She did love him. She loved his playfulness, his creativity, and his heart. His testimony had been raw and his conversion experience transparent. She even liked how he annoyed her and didn't let her sass impede their delightful bantering. They shared their secret about Sam and their stolen glances during prayers. His hand fit perfectly into hers, and she loved his willingness to take her good-natured teasing about him looking at her ankles. Heat filled her still-damp cheeks, and she raised her hands to cool them.

"Oh, Hans." Urgency filled her, and she scrambled to her feet. "I'm no namby-pamby. I'll give that sheriff the 'what for' and get my answers. He won't know what hit him." The ground shook under her steps as she marched back into town. She took deep, fortifying breaths until one caught in her throat, causing her to choke.

There, in front of the boarding house, was Rauti.

Chapter 43

One week prior

Korhonen Farm

Hans ran his fingers over the grooves of the two crosses he had crafted before staking them deep into the earth at the heads of the graves. Clods of earth had broken down and filled the small vacant holes with the recent rains, and he felt much the same. He had tried but failed. No matter how much of himself he poured out, there would always be places in his mind he could not reach—could not heal. He removed his hat, ran his fingers through his hair, then dropped to his knees, burying his head in his hands.

"Are you well, brother?" Johann's deep voice carried on the wind.

Hans did not look up and gave a half-hearted shrug.

"You did your best."

"Did I?" Hans picked a rock out of the dirt and flung it.

"My heart aches too." Johann kneeled beside him and

touched the cross on Otto's grave.

"I miss him." Hans's voice was but a whisper.

"I do as well, but that is not why my heart is aching."

Hans rocked back and sat on the damp earth, resting his forearms over his knees. Johann joined him as the sounds of God's creation filled the space between them.

"Why?" Hans asked.

"Why am I not sad over Otto's death? Or why did God allow this to happen?"

Johann always seemed to understand the deeper meaning of things. "Both, I guess."

"I miss Otto, and my heart yearns for the day we reunite in heaven. He's with God now. In that, there is rejoicing."

A huff came out of Hans's nose. Rejoicing was not something he felt at the moment.

"As for the other graves, my heart aches for a different reason." Johann picked a blade of grass beside him and rolled it between his fingers, taking his time before speaking. "The life of the man we buried before you arrived was snuffed out before you could share the gospel message. But you did a difficult and brave thing when you forgave Joe and offered him the gift of God's forgiveness. A lesser man would not have done so."

Hans lifted his head and saw only truth in Johann's eyes. He stared into their light blue depths and knew what his brother said was true, but believing it was a challenge.

"It was Joe's choice to turn that gift away. My sadness is that I know that the torment he endured on earth is now increased."

"What about Edna?"

Johann dropped his gaze. He threw the blade of grass, but the wind blew it back into his lap. He brushed it off his pant leg. "You did your best to reconcile with Edna, but she has chosen to ignore your offering in the same manner. I pray she will come around in time and not allow past grievances to eat at her until she becomes bitter."

"She's still angry with me." Hans snorted, and Johann shot him a look he knew meant to mind his thoughts.

"What are your plans now?" Johann changed the subject.

"Michael and I thought we would finish the repairs on the house. Obviously, the root cellar needs some work." Both men laughed.

"How did the sheriff know the root cellar came up into the kitchen?"

"Apparently, I told a few too many tales of my youth to Thomas and Gabe, and they shared that detail with Henry at some point. That, and my amazing pantomime skills." He made crazy gestures with his hands and laughed.

"Could be, or it could be a God incidence."

Hans stared at his brother. Katie had used those words.

"Looks like you and Michael have reconciled," Johann continued.

"I believe so. Speaking of Michael, I wanted to ask you something. I know the boy enjoys learning . . ."

Now it was Johann's turn to snort. Hans had to smile.

"Thomas and Gabe come once a month for a week of schooling in town. The teacher, who is the sheriff's wife, works with them during and after school. The boys are the same age as Michael, and I wondered if he'd like to stay with me and go to school?"

"So, you're settling in Shumard Oak Bend?"

He hadn't considered it until now, but the thought gave him peace. "Yes, I believe it's as good a town as any." He stared off into the distance, seeing red hair bouncing in the wind.

"You are still welcome to build here."

Hans shook his head. "Thank you, but I think I have a future in Shumard Oak Bend."

"Might there be a lady there?"

He jerked his gaze to his brother, and the muscle in his neck ached at the quick movement. He rubbed the spot.

Deep, throaty laughter filled the air as Johann's hand came to rest on Hans's shoulder. The familiar touch crumpled his resolve.

"Yes," Hans said.

"Does she have a name?"

"Katie. Kathleen Orla Murphy."

MATTERS OF THE HEART

"I see. And what color are her eyes?"

"Green with little golden flecks." Hans stopped, and his eyes went wide. He slapped his brother in the chest. "That wasn't fair."

"Oh, that was fair and telling." Johann's voice and eyes held laughter, then turned serious. "What are your intentions?"

"I'd marry that girl in a heartbeat, but I think she has another beau."

"Think?"

"Paul. She mentioned him once."

"Once?"

Hans swiveled and leaned back, his wrist supporting his weight. Doubt filled his mind.

"Hans, if a girl has a beau, you will know it. Women have a way of dropping a man's name and referring to him in unique ways. Has she done this?"

"Well, no, not that I can think of."

"Mm-hmm. You might want to clear up that one minor detail." Birds chirped their agreement. "How much longer will you stay?" Sadness tinged his words.

"I have an order I need to finish up back in town, but a few more days won't hurt."

"Fine. We're happy to have you for as long as you'd like."

Hans looked at his brother. "And Edna? You know she

blames me for all of this." His arm swept over the sparse fields, then the house with shingles lying on the ground that left behind openings for rain and weather to enter, and finally returned to the graves of Otto, Joe, and another of Joe's crew beside him.

"Do not concern yourself with her whims. You can ask for forgiveness, but whether someone gives it is their choice." Johann's touch soothed Hans's soul. "I am proud of you, little brother. I remember you once told me you were running toward something, not from it. I believe you now and give you my full blessing. Whatever it is you are seeking, I know God is with you wherever you go. My heart soars with the knowledge of your newfound faith."

Emotion crawled up Hans's throat, keeping him from giving a proper response. He nodded and wiped at a tear. Johann slapped his shoulder and stood, offering a hand up.

"Now, how about we stay out of Edna's way and get busy with those repairs?"

Chapter 44

Shumard Oak Bend

Katie slowed her pace to catch her breath, then ran, jumping the steps to the open front door and into the foyer before slamming into a muscled chest.

"Oomph."

Two powerful hands steadied her as she wobbled. "In a hurry?"

Why, of all the . . . She'd wipe that smirk right off his face. She watched as his gaze took in her cheeks, then moved to settle on her eyes—ones that felt like sand from so much crying. His arms moved from her shoulders down to her hands, which he turned over in his. Glancing down, she noticed dirt caked under her nails. She must look a fright. She lifted her gaze to find concern etched in his brow. Without thinking, she wrenched her hands from his and tore up the stairs to her room.

"How embarrassing." She flopped on her bed. "Of all the nerve." She stood and stomped her foot. The clip, tap, clip of her shoes hitting the floor as she paced matched the increasing beat of her heart. "Does the man not have the decency to let me clean up first before barreling into me?" Her footsteps slowed, as did her racing heart. Her arms wrapped around her shoulders where his hands had been only moments before.

"Pull yourself together, Kathleen Orla Murphy. He's a man and likely didn't notice the dirt. Make yourself presentable, and then hold your head high and act as if nothing happened." She talked to herself in the mirror as she changed clothing and replaced the loose pins in her hair after washing her face. Eyes still puffy, cheeks now flushed a soft pink, she dabbed rosewater on her neck. "I might look a fright, but I can at least smell nice."

Grit covered the bottom of her stockings as she turned. Dirt clods covered the floor where she'd paced before removing her shoes. Aunt Aideen would have a fit that she had made such a mess and be even more upset if she tracked it downstairs. Katie went to the hall closet and pulled out the broom and dustpan. She swept the landing, down the hall, and finally, into her room. Holding one shoe in each hand, she pushed the offenders out the window as if ready to send them to their deaths, then clapped them together. The remaining dirt flew in all directions. She did it once more for good measure before putting them on her feet.

"There. Let's see what you have to say now, Mr. Korhonen."

Halfway down the steps, she saw him. His blue eyes followed her every move. She stumbled, and he ran up two steps, reaching for her hand, which joined his without thinking. She stopped before the last step, meeting his gaze with her own. Everything inside pulled her toward him, but this was one impulse she would not give in to. She would not run headlong into a broken heart. She longed—no, needed—to hear him speak words of love or at least indicate his feelings before she gave in to her own.

"You look a mite better than you did when you came in. But, for as long as you were up there, I guess it took a lot of fixing."

"Oh!" With both hands, she shoved him hard enough that he stumbled. The open front door crashed into the wall, stopping his motion but creating a bang loud enough to echo in the foyer. "Of all the . . . If you had a single . . . Hans Korhonen, you are the most exasperating man I have ever met." Her last words came out high-pitched and louder than expected.

"Everything all right?" Aunt Aideen poked her head around the corner as if staying out of the path of a duel.

"No," Katie yelled. At the same time, Hans said, "Yes."

"Well, now. Which is it?" Aideen looked back and forth between the two. "I see. Well, might I suggest the two of you take this out to the barn? Reverend Jenkins doesn't care for the noise, and Rauti needs tending." She raised her eyebrow when Katie did not move.

Katie spied a ridiculous grin on Hans's face. He bowed, his arm gesturing to the fresh air and light outside. She had no desire to go, but one look at Aideen's glower and the finger pointing to the open door, and Katie gave in. A deep *humph* punctuated her feelings.

Hans took down a chair and placed it where he could see Katie's face when she sat. He held in a laugh when she picked it up and moved it to the other side. Dust clouds billowed as she plopped herself most unceremoniously into the chair, her skirts upsetting the dry straw. He wasn't sure what to say or do, so he removed Rauti's tack and began the steady motion of brushing down the horse. One of them had to say something.

"Did you miss me?" Hans asked.

"Oh! You are infuriating."

"Katie. Katie. I'm sorry." Hans ran around his horse and grabbed her arm as she made her way to the barn doors. "What I meant to say was, I missed you."

He felt her still before she turned, her skirts taking up more space between them than he liked.

"You did?" Her tone was light until fire lit her eyes like flint to stone. "Then why in tarnation didn't you come back with the sheriff and Mr. Shankel or send word or—"

He reached up and cupped her cheek in his hand. Her mouth stilled, and his thumb caressed her lips.

"I was worried," she whispered.

The softness of her voice returned, and he willed his gaze to leave the redness of her lips and travel back up to drown in the emerald green pools of her eyes.

"You were?"

"Of course, you ninny. I'm beginning to think that bump on your noggin affected your brain."

He winced inwardly at the comment. The blow to the head from Joe had knocked sense into him, as far as he was concerned.

"Sorry, that wasn't a pleasant memory. What I'm trying to say is—"

"Who's Paul?" Hans interrupted.

"Pardon me?" Katie's eyes were full of questions, and Hans wondered if she was trying to figure out how he'd found out about her beau.

"Paul. Who is he?" he repeated.

"I have no earthly idea what you are talking about." She took a step back and moved her hands to her hips. Her tone became harsh.

"Katie, when I arrived that first day, we ate dinner, and you said, 'I'm sorry, Paul.' You were distraught and struggled to eat your meal."

Hans watched as a flurry of scenes passed through her mind, showing in her eyes until she landed on the one she'd been seeking. Light laughter turned into cackling, followed by several snorts rivaling Rauti's. He joined her even though he did not know what she was laughing at. It could be him, for all he knew. Tears streamed down her face.

"Paul, is—was . . ." Another snort and she bent over, her arms wrapping around her midsection as if holding something in. "Paul . . ." She snorted, causing herself to laugh louder.

Hans led her back to the chair and assisted her as she dropped into the seat. Leaning forward, she gathered her skirts and used them like a giant handkerchief to wipe her face and eyes. He stood, waiting for her to regain her composure.

"Paul . . ." She lifted one finger before taking a deep breath and continuing. "Paul was a goat."

Hans wasn't sure if this unfamiliar word was a new one he'd missed while away at war, but he didn't suppose any man would appreciate being called a goat.

"We ate him." She pulled her lips between her teeth as tears flowed fresh before she burst out again in hysterics.

"Excuse me?"

"Oh, Hans. Paul was Mr. Finch's goat. We were low on meat, and he gave us a fair price." She dropped her rumpled skirts from her hands, which bunched up on her knees.

"We ate goat?"

"Mm-hmm. That nutty flavor you couldn't quite distinguish wasn't ground chestnuts. Technically, Aideen used ground chestnut flour for the coating, but more than likely, it was because that goat had ingested an entire barrel before Mr. Finch decided he'd had enough of the varmint and sold him to Aideen. It took her an hour of pounding to get that meat tender enough to chew."

Hans felt green.

"Do you need to sit?" Katie asked.

She jumped from the chair and twirled him around like they were in a dance before he felt the back of the chair on his knees. He grabbed her elbows.

"You mean to tell me Paul is not your beau?"

"Well, I certainly hope not, especially since I ate him. Although I felt sorry for the old goat." She laughed at the reference.

"Do you have any other beaus?"

Hans watched the flecks of gold shimmer in her green eyes as her lashes came down to cover their intensity.

"No, Hans. I do not have a beau."

"Then I'd like to apply for the job."

He was an idiot. Apply for the job. Maybe Joe truly had done damage to his brain. He took a step back, forgetting the chair behind him, and fell into the seat, pulling Katie with him. The chair toppled, and the force of Katie's motion propelled them both to the floor. He felt her warmth and weight. Panic seized him, and he lifted her from his chest and held her aloft. He could not speak. The impact and the realization of how he longed for more of her closeness knocked the breath out of him. Her skirts flew every which way, and Katie scrambled to stand.

"Oh!" In her haste to stand, she tripped on her skirts and sprawled next to him, laughter emanating from deep within.

"Are you hurt?" He asked in a breathy tone and watched her shake her head.

She was beautiful. Her hair spilled over the straw-covered floor, and her hands were at her trim waist. Her skirts gathered above her knees, showing white pantaloons with dainty lace on the edges where her slim ankles peeked out. Everything stilled and quieted.

"Quit looking at my ankles." Her words were soft as she edged her dress down.

Heat washed over him. He cleared his throat before standing and offering her a hand. He pulled her to her feet, and she continued toward him, her free hand resting on his chest.

"Hans Korhonen, what is your intent?"

"To see those ankles every night for the rest of my life." He blushed. He had not meant to say that out loud.

"Well, we'll have to see about that," she said as she leaned in and erased every memory he'd ever had in a single kiss.

Chapter 45

Hans stood before the large crowd gathered in the churchyard. The borrowed suit fit loose through the waist but felt constrictive across the chest. Or were those just nerves? He ran his finger around the inside of his collar where his skin felt irritated by the fabric. With his palms sweaty even with the breeze blowing atop the hill, he wiped them on his pant legs one at a time as he shifted his weight. Nausea rose from the pit of his stomach, and he swallowed, wiggling his neck to release the stranglehold of his collar.

People arrived in their finery, some alone, others with friends or family, but all with reverent steps. The Gray sisters alighted from Clint's cart, which Hans had taken up to the family only a few days prior when he'd delivered the news. He'd begged Clint to do the honor of leading the service.

"I'll be there to support you, my friend. You can count on that. Let Aideen know the children will bring their bedrolls, so she doesn't have extra sheets to wash." Clint's words reverberated in his mind.

How had he gotten to this point? Standing here in front

of these people, some of whom he didn't even recognize, he wondered if he should have eaten such a large breakfast. Clint walked his way, thrusting his hand forward. Hans grasped it, needing the support.

"You ready?" Clint whispered.

"As ready as I'll ever be." Hans cleared his throat when the words stuck there.

Clint raised his arms, and the crowd quieted. "Before we pray, I want to thank you for taking the time to come to this most unusual occasion. Distance keeps us from gathering regularly. Your Town Council of Magistrate Marley, John Sneed, William Finch, George Taylor, Sheriff Adkins, and I agreed that today would be an excellent time to take care of several things at once. Unfortunately, to make those things happen, they won't go in the most appropriate order, if there is such a thing, but in order of necessity. Thank you for being so understanding. Let us pray."

Hans clutched the small book in his hands and did his best to listen as Clint prayed, but his mind was on the task before him. "Help me, Father. I am not worthy," he breathed silently.

"In Your precious name, amen." Clint nodded, then moved to stand beside Rachel.

Hans cleared his throat, once again looking over the crowd. He spied Katie, and his heart leaped inside him. He could do this.

"Dearly beloved, we are gathered today to pay our final tribute of respect to that which was mortal . . ." Hans began.

Katie heard the sniffles around her as tears flowed freely from those mourning the loss of Reverend Jenkins. She was so proud of Hans for preaching the burial service. He had openly wept when Essie had entered the kitchen with the news, her grief pouring from the depths of her soul. The words now flowed from his mouth as if spoken hundreds of times before, and he barely referred to the manual in his shaking hands.

Katie's heart grieved with everyone else's. She would miss the reverend at their table—his dry humor, insatiable appetite, banter with her aunt, and wisdom he'd imparted both from behind the pulpit and in his everyday walk with his Lord.

"1 Corinthians 15:58 says, 'Therefore, my beloved brethren, be ye stedfast, unmoveable, always abounding in the work of the LORD, forasmuch as ye know that your labour is not in vain in the LORD.' Reverend Jenkins was a true servant of the Lord, and he labored for the Lord every moment of every day. His joyous, often boisterous laughter"—he paused as many people laughed—"reminded me that God is good even in the tough times."

Katie stifled her giggle. Boisterous was one way to describe the reverend and his laugh.

"The man introduced me to the personal, relational, compassionate, forgiving Christ. He did not labor in vain, seeing as my life—and many of yours—is a testimony to the investment he made. Because of his efforts, my heart opened to receive the work of the Holy Spirit."

Katie watched Hans bend down and reach for a clump of dirt. Small pieces dropped onto the wooden casket.

"Forasmuch as the spirit of our departed loved one has returned to God, who gave it, we therefore tenderly commit the body of Scott Earl Jenkins to the grave in sure trust and certain hope of the resurrection of the dead and the life of the world to come." Hans released the last of the dirt.

Katie's heart could take no more. She buried her head in her hands and wept, not caring if her outburst disturbed those around her. She'd loved this man, and he was gone.

"Well done, young man," Mr. Sneed said as he placed his hand over the one he clasped. "You did just fine."

"Mighty fine, Preacher." The magistrate offered much in those few words.

"Thank you both," Hans said. "I don't know if I'll ever be much of a preacher, but I'd be honored to be your pastor."

"The job is yours, son." The Magistrate placed his hand on Hans's shoulder.

One after the other, people greeted Hans, Aideen, Katie, and Essie. Essie had done a fine job lifting to the heavens an offering of song and bringing more tears to those in attendance.

"Are you ready?" Clint stepped up beside Hans.

"I am."

"Ladies and gentlemen." Clint raised his hands, quieting the crowd. Some resumed standing at the back, while others settled themselves on quilts. "We will continue to grieve the loss of our brother in Christ, but we also want to honor that man's wishes. I had the privilege of writing his last requests. One of those was that he be present for Hans's baptism. This is about as close as we will get to fulfilling that desire."

Hans handed the manual to Clint and removed his jacket, shoes, and stockings. He climbed into the horse trough.

"I cleaned it real good, Hans," Mr. Finch whispered.

Hans nodded and kneeled in the tight space as Clint found the page in the manual.

"Dearly beloved . . ."

Hans marveled at how burial, baptism, and marriage ceremonies began the same way. He did not want to miss a moment and focused all his attention on Clint.

"Christian baptism is a means of grace, proclaiming Jesus Christ as Lord and Savior," Clint continued.

Clint handed the manual to Mr. Finch. Hans looked at the mound of dirt only a short distance away. Reverend Jenkins may not be here in person, but his influence would forever live on in Hans's mind.

"Hans Korhonen, do you acknowledge Jesus Christ as your Lord and Savior, and do you believe He saves you now?"

"I do by faith."

"Then it is my honor and privilege to baptize you, Hans

Korhonen, in the name of the Father, and of the Son, and of the Holy Spirit. Buried with Christ in baptism . . ."

Cold water covered him, sucking out any last remnants of doubt. Emotion welled inside his soul. He was clean, ready to start fresh as a child of God.

". . . raised to walk in newness of life."

A subtle feeling of peace filled him. A reverence covered him like the water flowing over his face. He was new, dead to his old identity as a sinner without God, and now risen to a new identity as a child of God. He thrust his fist heavenward and let out an impressive "Whoop!"

Katie helped the other women set food on the makeshift tables. The day was not yet over. She watched as Hans returned from Aideen's, his hair slicked back, one rogue lock falling over his broad forehead. He'd never looked so handsome. His eyes shone with each handshake and pat on the back, welcoming him not only to the community of believers but also as the new pastor of their town. She was so proud of him. He had found his way and established himself. Unlike her. She would not allow the disappointment and frustration she harbored at not reaching her goal of starting an orphanage to ruin this day. A piercing whistle drew her attention to the church. Connor stood waving, then cupped his hands over his mouth.

"We're ready," he yelled before popping back inside.

Katie followed the crowd up the hill and into the building.

Her breath caught when she entered. Candles and greenery filled the windows and graced the front of the church. The townsfolk filed in and filled the pews. Reverend Jenkins would have been surprised at a few of the people who graced the doors for this occasion but hadn't been to service in a month of Sundays. A few mothers stood at the back, jostling their tired and hungry children, while fathers held little ones on their laps to make room for the crowd. Hans took his place at the front, the familiar book once more in his hands. Only this time, Katie noticed it did not shake.

Down the middle aisle came two children. Katie immediately recognized Danny, Clara's boy, and Delphina's girl, Mary Ellen. Chuckles and murmurs filled the room as Mary Ellen reached for the basket of petals, only to have Danny lift it above her head.

"Hey, that's not nice." The girl's lower lip quivered.

Danny lowered the basket, allowing the girl to grab a handful, which she promptly threw at him. Essie rushed up, grabbing the basket before Danny could upend it on Mary Ellen's head. Somehow, Essie got the two children down the aisle before there were tears or tumbles.

The piano played, and Rachel and Aideen rose from the first row on the left side of the church. Hans lifted his hands, and the congregation followed. A quiet hush filled the far corners of the building as light footsteps padded up the aisle. Moses and Delphina walked, resplendent in their finest. Loose braids encircled Delphina's head, framing her face. The yellow of her dress made her slender frame look like a willow tree blowing in the breeze.

Behind them came William Finch and Clara Easton. Mr. Finch walked like a proud peacock displaying his tail, but Clara had no color in her face, save for a tinge of red creeping out from under her high collar. The bride looked lovely in Katie's borrowed floral blue, the empire waist covering the growing life underneath. Their gazes connected, and Clara offered Katie a sweet smile and gentle nod.

They would make a lovely family, and Mr. Finch's excitement at knowing he would be a father again, even though the child to come would not be his own blood, made him act like a giddy youth. He had seen it as a blessing, losing one son to war and gaining two children by marriage in his place.

Katie dreamed of the day she might someday have children to call her own and a husband with which to share the joy. Hans hadn't exactly asked her to marry him, but he'd given her hope that he had feelings for her. At least she thought so. But the kiss they'd shared in the barn had changed him. She knew she'd initiated it, but he certainly had responded. So why, then, would he no longer be alone with her, not even with the barn doors open? Did he not want a repeat of the tenderness they'd shared? He'd avoided her since then at all costs. Even this morning, when she had been in the kitchen alone, he had stood outside the open doorway until Essie had entered. When she'd found him later in the barn, he had given an excuse to move Rauti outside into the open.

Shame on me, Katie berated herself. *I should be happy for my friends and share in their joy, not wallow in my own self-pity.* But her heart was heavy and focusing on the shared vows was a difficult task.

"Have you seen Katie? I mean, Miss Murphy?" Hans asked one lady as she cleared the tables of used plates and emptied containers.

"No, sir, Reverend. But I'll let her know you're looking for her if I do."

He didn't miss the smirk the woman tried to cover at his slip of using Katie's Christian name. The sun was not yet down, but the moon was already beginning its lazy entrance, making it difficult to see. Strains of fiddles and guitars carried across the field beside the church. It was the perfect place for dancing, and he planned to enjoy the evening if he could ever find the girl with whom he wanted to share it.

"Let me help with that." Hans lifted one edge of a board, then hefted a sawhorse in his other hand.

"Right nice of you, Reverend," Connor said.

"Don't know if I'll ever get used to that name."

"Oh, it'll grow on you."

The two walked down the gentle slope to Aideen's barn.

Hans heard soft weeping and slowed. "Let's leave these here. You head on back for the next load."

"Will do." Connor must have heard the crying—if his blanched face and quick retreat were any indication.

Hans stepped into the darkness. Two bare feet stuck out

from the far corner. He would know those feet anywhere.

"You all right, Essie?" He heard shuffling, and the feet disappeared under her pale green dress.

"Yes, sir, Mr. Hans." She sniffed. "Or should I call you Reverend Korhonen now? That sure is a mouthful."

"Just Hans is fine, Essie. Would you like me to sit with you?"

Motion in the corner suggested she would. Hans took down the two chairs, placing them near the barn entrance. He waited for her to sit before taking a load off his own feet.

"Do you have something on your mind?" Hans tilted his head, trying to make eye contact.

"Mr. Hans?"

"Yes?"

Essie sniffed, and Hans wished he had a hankie to offer.

"Do you know what Reverend Jenkins said right before he died?" she asked.

Hans knew Essie had been with the man in his last moments, but he'd not heard her share what had transpired.

"No, Essie. Would you like to tell me?"

The whites of her dark eyes shone in the dim light. "He hadn't spoken for days, not knowing nobody or where he was. He'd just get all agitated-like and tap his hand on the quilt until I'd put his Bible in his grasp. That book meant more to him than anythin' else he owned. That last day, he clutched that Bible like usual, then let go. It slid to the floor, and I thought he was gone, only he lifted his arm like he was reachin' for somethin'. He said, 'Essie, I see Jesus.'"

The deep, heart-wrenching sobs from her slight frame broke Hans's soul. He let her cry it out, and when she'd quieted, tears covering her face, she spoke in a whisper.

"He said my name." A small gasp escaped her lips. "For days on end he done forgot every livin' soul, but he knew me—and he knew the face of Jesus."

Hans joined Essie, their harmony of tears a song he would never forget.

"Mr. Hans?"

He dried his tears. "Yes?"

"You're going to be a mighty fine preacher." She wiped her final tears.

He watched her go and heard the kitchen door open and close. That girl was a wonder.

Chapter 46

Shumard Oak Bend

"Y ou go on up to the dance, Miss Katie. I'll finish these dishes," Essie said, her hands deep in soapy water.

"I'm not much of a dancer," Katie lied. She loved to dance.

"Mm-hmm. I don't believe you for a skinny minute. That man of yours is—"

"He's not my man," Katie interrupted.

"Mm-hmm. You go on tellin' yerself that, and you might just believe it."

Katie moved a stack of dry dishes to the shelf, then picked up several cups. One slipped from her grasp. Before Katie could utter a sound, Essie's wet hand caught the falling object.

"You must have eyes in the back of your head," Katie said.

"Have to, with dishes this fine. Where did Aunt Aideen get such fancy plates and all? Don't seem like her kind of thing." Essie rewashed the cup.

"This boarding house was once the home of Serafina Brooks and her husband. Aunt Aideen said they'd come from money back east. They helped establish Shumard Oak Bend and built this home."

"Where're all the children that filled them rooms?"

"God never saw fit to give them any." Katie watched Essie shake her head and understood the sentiment deep inside. "When she died, she gave her home to Aunt Aideen and Uncle Paddy to use as a boarding house and restaurant for the stagecoach and weary travelers. Aunt Aideen told me God answered the prayers of Widow Brooks in a way she hadn't even considered and, in doing so, fulfilled the dreams Aideen didn't realize she herself had."

"God has a way of doin' that."

"When Uncle Paddy died, she considered selling, and then I showed up. Providence—she called it, all in God's perfect timing. And now, she has you." Katie smiled as she dried.

"Mores like I have the two of you. I don't know what to do with all my free time. When there's no boarders, I'm not of much use. Besides, my mammy always told me idle hands is the devil's workshop, and I'm not payin' him no mind."

"But you bless others. Aideen and I love the company, and I understand you've worked for a few people in town."

"Them Gray sisters is teachin' me to knit, and they're helpin' me learn to read for doin' their laundry and such. I made potholders for Delphina and Miss Clara as weddin' gifts." Essie beamed.

"How thoughtful. I don't have the skills required to make a gift, so my gift is to keep the children tonight. Thank you for agreeing to help." Katie chuckled. "You saved the day at the wedding."

"I saw that happenin' afore it even started. Those two are somethin' else. I'll be sleepin' with one eye open for sure and for certain."

"Speaking of children." Rachel walked into the kitchen, holding a sleeping Serafina. "Poor girl could not make it. She lasted long enough to eat the cake."

Traces of icing outlined the girl's cupid mouth, and her long lashes lay on the toddler's chubby pink cheeks. Katie pushed down the resentment creeping up and wrapping its way around her tightening bodice. She reached for the girl, the desire to hold the sleeping child almost unbearable. "Here, let me take her."

"Oh, no, you don't. I'm bushed, and I plan on resting my feet. You need to get up to the dance. Where can I put her?" Rachel asked.

Essie dried her hands. "You come right back to Reverend's— I mean, Aunt Aideen's room. We have all the bedrolls ready for the little ones."

Katie forced a smile. "She'll settle in, knowing you are near." She schooled her features, praying her longing did not show.

"Go on now. You head on up to the dance. Once I've rested a moment, I'll help Essie finish the dishes." Rachel turned before leaving the room.

Katie protested, but Essie took a stance beside Rachel. Two against one. The odds were not in her favor.

"I heard you shot the gun clean out of Joe's hand," Connor added to the conversation the men were having around the refreshment table.

"That's not quite how that happened," Hans responded.

"Seems a mite odd for the reverend to be a sharpshooter and all," a man as short as he was round added.

"Now, men." Sheriff Adkins drew out the words, taking the attention off Hans. "Let's not start tall tales." He sent a knowing glance to Hans.

"Then tell us what did happen. You've been tight-lipped about the whole thing," a tall, lanky man interjected.

"And for good reason," the sheriff said. "This was bigger than any of us knew. Thank the good Lord, none of our townsfolk were hurt, but several families lost their lives or their farms."

"Ain't ya gonna tell us anything?" A man missing most of his teeth spoke, all while keeping a piece of straw bobbing with each word.

"Let me say this. We're blessed to have a former US marshal in our town who transported the prisoners to the county seat for trial."

"That Clint Shankel is a good man," Connor offered.

"Did I hear my name?" Clint joined the group, pouring himself a cup of punch and swiping a cookie from the table.

"We want to hear all about the shootout and killing Joe and capturing his gang," Snaggletooth said.

Clint's forehead wrinkled, and he looked first at the sheriff, then Hans. Hans lifted his shoulders in a shrug.

"Well, not much to tell. All I did was ensure those horses were not in a position to ride should anyone try to escape. I didn't even unholster my weapon until it was all over." Clint shoved the entire cookie in his mouth and chewed slowly.

"So that means you took 'em down, Hans? I mean, Reverend?" Mr. Tall-and-Lanky asked.

"To tell the honest truth, it was Sheriff Adkins—" Hans started.

"What he's trying to say is that no weapons were necessary in taking down the three remaining outlaws," the sheriff interrupted. "Let's leave it at that."

"Ah, come on, Sheriff," Short Man whined.

"Boys, we've come here to celebrate. Find yourselves each a girl and dance." The look on the sheriff's face was enough for the men to disperse.

"A sharpshootin' preacher man. Who'd a thunk it," Snaggletooth said under his breath.

"Well, there will be some interesting stories out of this one." Clint wiped his mouth of crumbs.

"Thanks for not sharing all the details. Mortification does not look good on me." Hans blushed.

Henry slapped his back and laughed. "That secret is safe between us." He lifted his chin to Clint, who shoved another cookie in his mouth.

"And I thought Pete Manning was the only man I knew who screamed like a girl," Clint said, his mouthful only partially hiding his smile.

"I don't know about you, but I believe it's time for a dance with my beautiful wife." The sheriff's brightened tone pulled Hans from his musings. "Where's that girl of yours, Hans?"

"Mine?"

"Best find her before someone else does."

Hans watched the sheriff pull his wife into the sway of the music as if it were a practiced step. Clint asked one of the Gray sisters to dance. Hans searched the crowd but did not see Katie until the moonlight glinted off someone coming up the slope. Her red hair pinned atop her head looked like an angel's halo. She pushed a wayward curl behind her ear, then lifted her skirts as she climbed. His eyes went directly to her hem.

"Already? The night hasn't even begun."

His head popped up at her teasing. The strum, pluck, and screech of the fiddle and banjo faded into the distance, yet his heart kept beat with the frantic rhythm. The ground moved under his feet. He wasn't sure if it was the jumping and twirling of the townspeople as they danced or God trying to get his attention.

"Would you care to take a turn?" Words finally moved from his brain to his mouth.

"Will you be stepping on my toes?"

"Highly likely," he replied with a smirk. He offered his hand, and she took it. They stood at the edge of the crowd, watching wide, smiling faces, swishing skirts, and stomping feet, but they did not join in. Several women waved as they turned in their direction. Hans felt his stoic heritage wrap itself around his neck, and he used his fingers to ease around the inside of his damp collar. He ran his hand through his hair, trying to release the rising tension.

"Everyone seems to be enjoying the festivities." Katie released his hand when the music stopped.

Hans felt the air rush out of him like a depressed bellow, and he labored to pull fresh air back in. He turned to her and opened his mouth to speak, but nothing came out. How would she understand how uncomfortable he was? He felt on display in front of all these people, each watching and scrutinizing his every move to see if he was indeed the man he claimed to be. What would these people think if he joined in on the merriment?

"You're wrinkling your forehead."

"Excuse me?"

"You do that when you are uncertain."

Head down, he watched the swish of her skirts.

"You owe me nothing, Hans. You've made no commitment, and I have taken care of myself for most of my life. Do not feel obligated to drag me along. We can still be friends."

His head jerked in her direction. "Excuse me?"

"What I'm trying to say is, if you need the church to be your bride, I do not want to get in God's way."

"Katie."

"Young lady, might I have this dance?" Magistrate Marley bowed as far as his protruding girth would allow.

"It would be my honor, sir."

She didn't look back, and he heard a light giggle come from her beautiful lips at something the magistrate said. What had just happened?

"Looks like you got bested. Of all the people to offer her the first dance, I hadn't expected you to let it be him." Clint breathed heavily. "This leg of mine can do no more. How about you walk me back to Aideen's?"

Hans nodded, and the man placed a hand on his shoulder. Hans wasn't sure whom it supported.

"You know, the reverend was quite the dancer in his day," Clint said.

"He was?"

"That he was. Every woman in town got a turn. That's how they knew when it was time to end the evening." Clint stumbled, then stood tall, inhaling deeply. "Hans, I'm not sure what's going on in that thick head of yours, but there are no second chances for making a first impression. These people will remember you for who you are today. Some you may not see again until you head out to their farm to bury their dead. You've proven yourself a capable preacher with a tender and compassionate heart. You've established you don't see color, have what it takes when the going gets tough, and are a man who abides by and upholds the law. Now they need to see the everyday side of you. The one they'll run into at the mercantile, toting loads in your carts, and raising a passel of children." Clint turned at the steps to the house.

"Children?"

"Hans, a dozen men are itching to ask Miss Katie for a dance."

Clint's hearty laughter caught Hans by surprise.

"Katie only wants to dance with you. I suggest you stake your claim and let those other fellas and Katie know your intentions."

A slow smile started on Hans's face, then faltered. "But what will people think?"

"You may be the new reverend, but you're still human. And if that girl up there doesn't light your fire, well, then, your wood's wet."

From the expression on Clint's face, Hans knew his eyes must be as round as Aideen's saucers.

"Go on, now."

He didn't have to be told twice.

Chapter 47

Katie wasn't sure what had changed, but she knew something had. Gone was the meekness and confused look of moments before. Hans barreled toward her as she worked to keep her feet out from underneath Mr. Sneed's. The man might manage money, but he did not know how to count steps.

"Excuse me."

It wasn't a question this time. Hans stood firm in their path, and Katie halted before Mr. Sneed ran her into Hans's broad chest.

"I'd like to dance with my Katie girl."

Katie's knees went weak at the endearment Aideen used. The words felt different coming from Hans. She released Mr. Sneed's grip.

"Thank you, Mr. Sneed." She stepped back.

"My pleasure, Miss Murphy. Reverend." Katie gasped at the wink Mr. Sneed gave her. "I'm thankful to have gotten in one dance. I doubt there will be another."

Fingers entwined with hers as the music changed to a waltz; Hans lifted her hand to his lips and kissed her knuckles, taking every scrap of resolve she had with them when he pulled away. She melted into him when his fingers gently touched the small of her back.

"It's been a memorable day," Katie said as they moved in sync.

"That it has."

His eyes were dark, and his hand around her tightened. She opened her mouth to speak, but he shook his head and pulled her closer. She heard only the rhythmic beating of his heart. He smelled of sandalwood and man. She felt him stop, but she didn't want to. His finger swept up her neck, the motion tugging on her heart and chin.

"Let's get some punch."

No music played, and Katie stepped back and wondered how long they'd been standing there in each other's arms. She blushed.

"Our turn around the dance floor may be over, but those freckles are still at it."

She swatted at his arm as his finger tapped the tip of her nose.

"They have a mind of their own." She tried to sound good-natured, but her voice felt pinched, as did her insides. "I think punch might be a good idea."

Hans held Katie's hand, never letting go as they mingled with the townspeople and made their way to the refreshments. Her heart soared as the congratulations and well-wishes flowed. She listened with growing admiration as parishioners offered words of support and acceptance of Hans as their new pastor. She marveled at how he thanked each person while turning the conversation back to them and how he might serve them.

Oh, how she loved this man. He turned as if hearing the words she hoped had passed only through her mind and not her lips. A lively tune started, and people dispersed from the refreshments and returned to dancing.

"Care to walk?" he asked. "I do my best thinking when in motion, and not the type requiring me to count as I go."

"Yes, I'd like that."

How should he start? What words could he say to explain the feelings exploding in his heart?

"Do we need to turn back?" Katie asked.

He followed the tilt of her head to those in the distance.

"You haven't wanted to be alone with me since . . ."

"It isn't that." *Lord, help me.* "Katie, that is the farthest thing from the truth. I've wanted to be with you so badly I didn't trust myself. I put distance between us because I care more about your honor than my desires." He rolled his shoulders, then turned around to walk back the way they'd come.

A sigh escaped her mouth and was nearly his undoing.

He rammed his free hand into his pocket. The music volume increased as they got closer, and he didn't want to raise his voice over the noise, so he pulled her to a stop. Tears glistened in her eyes. Had he hurt her feelings? He'd never know her feelings if he didn't ask.

"Katie." He took her other hand, leaving plenty of space between them. She looked at him, expectation in her eyes. "Katie, would you honor me by letting me court you?" There, he'd said it. Only, she wasn't responding. A knot formed in his stomach, and it took all his willpower not to pull away from her intense gaze.

"What does that mean, exactly?"

"Excuse me?"

"We live under the same roof, Hans. Don't you think people will talk?"

He hadn't thought about that. He'd thought he'd considered every angle, but that one detail had slipped past him.

"And what does courting mean? How long?" She'd released his hands and moved hers to her hips.

"Well, I . . ." He didn't know how to respond. "I don't rightly know."

Katie dropped her gaze and shook her head. "Infuriating. Absolutely, positively exasperating. Comical, really. Maddening. Definitely annoying and downright . . . Hans Korhonen, do you have anything between those two ears?" Her skirts swished as she headed toward the dancing.

Hans tried to keep up with her pace and the one-sided

conversation. How in the world had it come to this?

He watched her retreating form even as Sheriff Adkins came his way.

"What was that all about?" the sheriff asked.

"I don't have the foggiest idea what I did or said to upset her." Hans wiped his hand over his brow and rubbed his temples. "I think she's upset that we live in the same house. All I did was ask if I could court her proper-like."

"Well, she has a point about staying at Aideen's. I've got an idea if you're willing to rough it. Moses has a cot in the back of his blacksmith shop. It won't be comfortable, but you can take your meals at Aideen's."

"I can do that if you don't think he'd mind."

"He won't mind. I see him over there. Let's go ask him."

The men maneuvered through the crowd.

"Moses, we've an opportunity to discuss," the sheriff said. "Can we steal you from your lovely wife for a moment?"

"You go on now. I'll take Mary Ellen to get punch and be right back," Delphina said to her husband.

"What can I do for you?" Cheerful eyes and a brighter smile graced the man's face.

Hans desired to experience the joy he saw in Moses's face. He yearned to make Katie his wife.

Moses's laugh filled the air, pulling Hans back to the conversation.

"You may have to stay in the jail when I come to town, Hans. There's not room for the two of us in my shop."

"Wouldn't that have tongues wagging?" The sheriff joined in the laughter.

"Thank you, Moses. I appreciate your hospitality." Hans stuck out his hand.

"When do you plan on moving in?" Moses asked.

"No time like the present. Let's not give her or the church folk fuel for a fire. We'll get your stuff and settle you in your new home right now." The sheriff slapped Hans on the shoulder.

"You said what?" Essie hissed over the sleeping children rather than whispering. "What did you expect? A marriage proposal?"

"I don't know," Katie said. "It felt like Hans was only doing it to save face with the congregation."

"But you said he explained why he'd kept his distance. He's a man, Miss Katie. Iffen I was in your shoes, I'd be mighty thankful for a man willin' to treat me that way."

"Shh, we'll wake the children. I had one cup too many of that punch. I'll be right back."

Katie tiptoed down the hall to the washroom under the stairs. She heard the front door open and two sets of boots cross the floor.

"You head on up and gather your things. I'm going to see if Clint is in the kitchen."

Katie recognized the sheriff's voice. There was no way she was coming out in her nightshirt and embarrassing them both, so she remained inside. Soon, she heard him return and call up the stairwell.

"Hans, are you about ready?"

Boots crossed the floor above her and continued down the stairs.

"Got everything?" Henry asked.

"I believe so. Aideen washed my bedroll, and it took me a moment to locate it. Should I wake her?"

"No. In the morning, I'll let Aideen know you've gone. Here, I grabbed a few things for you from the kitchen."

"Thank you. I'll appreciate this come morning. I heard Clint snoring away upstairs."

Katie heard the front door open and close. He was leaving? She'd made a mess of everything. Katie rushed down the hall, flung herself on the bed, and stifled her sobs to keep from waking the children and Essie.

Chapter 48

"**E**ssie, thank you for getting up with the children last night." Katie yawned.

"Sounded like you had a rough night. I was happy to do it. I'll get them up and ready while you start breakfast."

Katie mouthed a "thank you" when she saw Danny stir. Rachel and Delphina were already up, filling their baskets with leftovers for their journey back to the Shankel ranch.

"Did I oversleep?" Katie looked out the kitchen window into the darkness.

"No, we knew we'd need to have everything ready to go before the children woke," Rachel said.

"Oh. Let me help. Essie will dress the children. Since you are packing, I can start the breakfast."

"Biscuits are already in the oven. If you gather the eggs and head to Mr. Finch's for the goat's milk, I'll start the bacon in a moment." Rachel never stopped moving as she spoke.

"Where's Aideen?"

"She isn't up yet. We brought down our sheets, and Moses is out back, heating the pot for laundry now. I'd hate to leave you with all that work," Delphina responded.

"Essie and I don't mind. We'll need something to keep our minds occupied today." Katie sighed.

Both ladies stopped and looked at her. She didn't have to look in a mirror to know the ladies recognized her puffy eyes and raw nose. Thankfully, they shouldn't be able to tell her hair, which was bunched up under her mob cap, remained uncombed from the night before. She lifted the egg basket, then swept out the door before the questioning could begin.

The chickens squawked and preened, ruffling their feathers and causing a cloud of dust to rise as she lifted the latch on the narrow coop door.

"Good morning, you pesky little creatures," Katie crooned, using as soothing a voice as possible. "I do not care for you filthy beings, but I need your eggs." Even with her singsong words, one hen pecked at her ankle. "Ow. Why, you mean little —"

"Need rescuing in there, Miss Katie?" Moses came from the back. "Boo," he yelled into the cage. Chickens went flying, getting as far from the offender as possible. His booming laugh kept them in a flurry. "Best grab those quick, or they'll be back and madder than hornets."

Katie picked up the eggs, placing them in the basket with care before slipping back out. "Whew. Foul creatures."

"F-o-u-l or f-o-w-l?" Moses laughed at his own joke.

"Both. I dislike that chore."

"Most do. A necessary evil if you want to eat, though. You want me to get the milk from Mr. Finch?"

"Would you? That's my second-least favorite chore. I don't expect he'll be up yet, so you'll likely have to milk the goat."

"Don't mind at all. I need to stop in at my shop, anyway. I'll be back as soon as I can."

"Thank you, Moses."

Hans heard the whistling before the rattle of the door opening pulled him from his slumber. He jumped from the cot, feeling every aching muscle this morning.

"You in here, Hans?"

"Back here, Moses. Be out in a moment." He pulled his shirt over his head and buttoned his trousers but didn't bother with his shoes.

"How did you sleep?"

"Not well, but it had nothing to do with the accommodations."

"You stay here as long as you like. I won't likely make it back for a month since we've lost so much time at the farm, so you make yourself at home. Not much here, but you're welcome to whatever. And, if you've got a mind to help someone, you know how to use the forge."

"I can do that."

"Not much space, but you can work from here on your carts. Just clean up good. Sparks and wood shavin's don't mix."

"Yes, sir."

"Sir. You're right funny. You know that?" Moses used his thumb to point next door. "I'm headed over to get milk. You joinin' us for breakfast?"

"I think I need to spend some time in prayer this morning. I'll let Aideen know when I'll be in for a meal but let her know it may be a few days. I have enough to keep me and need some time with just me and God."

Moses's reply came in the form of an offered hand and a firm shake before leaving.

Chapter 49

Several days later

Katie woke in a horrible mood, as she had on most mornings this week, and it continued throughout the day. Being angry was exhausting. She would not be responsible for her actions if someone crossed her. Her nerves were raw and her emotions fragile.

"Katie, me darling girl, we be having a guest for dinner." Aideen popped her head in the kitchen.

"Lovely," she huffed. "Shall I break out the fine china?"

Aideen frowned. "Child, I suggest you change that attitude of yours. If you were a mite younger, I'd change it for you."

Katie's breath came out in a shudder, somewhere between suppressed anger and uncontrollable sobs.

"Dearie, it will all work out. Trust in the Lord."

Trust in the Lord. Humph. Everyone around her seemed to be getting the desire of their hearts, except her.

What is the desire of my heart? A verse from Philippians ran through her mind. "In every thing by prayer and supplication with thanksgiving let your requests be made known unto God. And the peace of God, which passeth all understanding, shall keep your hearts and minds through Christ Jesus."

She hadn't thought to unburden her heart before the Lord recently. Perhaps in doing so, the peace mentioned would come. She craved peace. Fixing herself a cup of tea, she sat.

"Lord, I'm a miserable failure." She laid her forehead on top of her hands, resting on the table. "Am I wrong to feel this way?"

"How do you feel?"

Katie lifted her head. How did God do that? At times, He remained silent, and at other times, it was like having a conversation with a friend. "For starters, I feel alone. I want to feel loved."

"You are."

It wasn't as if she heard God's voice, yet it was clear in her mind that He was communing with her spirit. She took a sip of tea, determined to lay it all before Him.

"I want to help others. I believe You put the desire in me to start an orphanage, yet I can't seem to convince others of the same." Shame filled her as she listened to her words. "There were a few too many I's and me's in that statement, weren't there, God?" Silence. "Let me try that again." She took a sip of tea and sat up straight. "Lord, if it be Your desire, I would gladly, wholeheartedly, work to provide for the widows and orphans as You say in Your word."

No peace came. "And, if it is in accordance with Your plans for me to raise children of my own flesh, it would please me greatly. And, just as a friendly reminder, that will require a husband. If You haven't yet picked one out for me, I happen to know a nice young man who would do just fine."

"Who you talking to, Miss Katie?" Essie took a tentative step into the room as if judging Katie's mental state or checking to see if she was holding something that might be thrown in her direction.

"God. Myself. I don't know. No one seems to be listening these days."

"We's all listenin'. Don't always want to, but when you get riled, you get loud." Essie slapped her hand over her mouth. "I didn't mean that, Miss Katie."

Katie laughed for the first time that day. "Essie, you are a joy. Did you need something?"

"Aunt Aideen said we're having a guest for dinner, so I thought I'd help."

"I sure hope it isn't the magistrate. With his wife out of town, it would be just like Aideen to invite him."

"He could stand to skip a few meals." Essie repeated the gesture from earlier.

"Essie, you do beat all."

"What are we going to have for dinner?"

"Chicken, and I know just the one."

Chapter 50

"I'm glad you could come for dinner, Hans. How is it, staying at Moses's place?" Aideen asked.

"I've never been on my own, so it's a little bit of adventure and a whole lot of lonesome." Hans heard a crash from the direction of the kitchen. His eyes widened, but Aideen didn't seem to be bothered.

"I'll let the girls know you're here. Make yourself comfortable at the table." He watched as Aideen went through her usual evening meal routine of checking to ensure everything needed was on the table, before heading into the kitchen.

Hushed words went back and forth behind the closed door, and he began to feel uncomfortable. Maybe this wasn't such a good idea. Essie entered, carrying one bowl of roasted vegetables and another of fried apples. Aideen followed with a pitcher of water and a plate of her famous golden-crusted bread. His mouth watered as the ladies sat.

The kitchen door swung open and out came Katie's backside. She turned with a platter of roast chicken and, in a most unladylike manner, plopped it onto the table. Had he not seen the crispy skin and darkened rosemary leaves, he may have thought the bird was making a run for it. Katie plopped into her seat, slouched against the chairback, arms flopping as if the last bit of escaping air had left them limp. Wisps of fiery red hair stuck out beneath her slightly askew mob cap. Red tinged her cheeks. She remained relaxed in her chair, a vivid portrayal of how tired she must be, until her penetrating green eyes met his. Her direct eye contact made him squirm in his seat like a schoolboy.

She gave him a smug look, and the memory of their first meal together surfaced—the day he had fallen in love with her.

"Essie, I need your help." Aideen stood from the table when they'd finished their meal.

"Yes, ma'am. Sorry to leave you with the dishes, Katie." The girl looked from her to Hans. "I'm sure Hans will help you."

The two were gone before dessert had even been served. Katie rolled her eyes. They had planned this. Hans stood and gathered the dishes nearest his. Without a word, he moved to the kitchen. She remained and listened as he pumped water into the wash basin.

"Oh, bother." Her hands hit the table and made the dishes rattle. She gathered them with care, determined to have this discussion, once and for all. Her step faltered when she saw him, towel over one shoulder, hands deep in the sudsy water. His body moved as he scrubbed the pan. He was doing it all wrong.

"Never start with the pans." She huffed and pulled it from his dripping hands, causing water to spill down his front and onto the floor. With more force than necessary, she clunked it onto the counter. "Cups and silver first." The plop, plop of silverware splashed, and Hans took a step back. "When doing dishes properly, Mr. Korhonen, you start with those items that touch your mouth first, then move on to the plates and bowls. Serving dishes are next, and pots and pans always come last." She knew her tone was haughty, but she didn't care. Hadn't his mother taught him anything?

Each time she returned from the dining room, he turned and smiled at her, never once stopping or saying anything. *How infuriating.* She put the remaining carcass into the stock pot and pushed him aside with her hip. She filled the pot with enough water to cover the bird and placed it on the stove, then filling the teakettle with water and placing it on a separate burner.

Moving to his side, she sighed. Soap remained on the back of the plate on the drying rack. She rinsed it and replaced it. She nearly fell when Hans bumped her with his hip. She gasped and stared at him. A small smile curved on those lips of his. She made to return the gesture, but the devil himself must have snuck up behind her, for she scooped dirty, soapy water in her hand and flung it into his face. Hans sputtered but didn't move. Guilt and regret fell on her like the drops of water off his strong nose and chin.

He took the towel and dried his face, hands, and arms, then ran the cloth down his still-wet neck. Everything he did fascinated her. As if in slow motion, she watched him twirl the cloth in his hands, the motion mesmerizing.

Snap!

One end of the towel left his hand and caught the edge of the counter. She jumped.

"Be careful, Kathleen. Starting a fight with me might be more than you bargained for," he teased.

He began twirling the cloth again. Realization dawned on her, and she squealed, putting the butcher block between them.

Snap!

He hit the top of the wood directly in front of where she stood. He began to move, and she glanced to the kitchen door. Could she get there in time?

"I don't think so. We are having this conversation, and we're having it now." His teasing tone and the glint in his eyes did not match the words he used.

Snap!

Katie backed into the corner. She would not let him bully her. Her chin jutted forward, and she crossed her arms. She would show no fear. In one swift movement, his lips were on hers, soft yet urgent in their exploration. She was ever so thankful for the wall behind her.

Breathing hard, he lifted his head but did not pull away. He tucked her under his chin, and she heard the rush of his beating heart that matched her own.

366

"Just making sure you haven't killed each other." Aideen poked her head in. "Looks like all is well. Carry on."

Katie felt her cheeks flush and heard the deep rumble of laughter bubbling up in—and eventually out of—Hans.

She leaned her head back and looked him in the eyes. "You could have hurt me with that towel. That thing is a deadly weapon in your hands. I have proof since I've swept the fly carcasses you've left in your wake in the past."

"Kathleen, it has never been, nor will it ever be my intention to hurt you—ever." The back of his finger trailed down her cheek, causing more heat. "Only, I know I have, and I'm sorry." He kissed her forehead. "Please forgive me."

"No." She watched confusion, then hurt surface in his eyes and felt bad for her teasing response. "Because I forgave you long ago. It is I who needs to ask for forgiveness. We seem to have some difficulty communicating at times."

He placed his finger on her lips. "How about we spend the rest of our lives figuring out how to fix that problem?" He dropped to one knee.

Katie's breath caught, and her hand moved to her throat.

"Kathleen Orla Murphy, would you do me the honor of becoming my wife? Soon. Real soon."

"Yes," she squealed.

"Glory be! It's about time." Aideen barreled through the door, Essie right behind her. "Now, let's eat dessert and discuss the particulars."

Epilogue

Christmas

K atie watched Essie struggle down the aisle in her new shoes. Pine boughs filled the windowsills, and their fragrance filled Katie's senses. Hans's friend Luke stood resplendent in a black suit, Bible in hand, while Johann stood like a bulwark at the outside. But only one man mattered —the one to the preacher's left. Hans squirmed like a boy at his first dance. She watched his shoulders rise and fall before he bowed his head. She watched his lips move as if in prayer.

Katie was overcome with emotion at the sight. She would not cry. Lifting her bouquet of holly and greenery, she inhaled, then released everything as an offering to God. Before moving her flowers away from the exquisite overlay of tatted lace that covered the bodice of her gown, she smoothed the full skirt of her white dress trimmed in the same style. Her eyes misted, and she lifted a linen hankie and marveled at the matching dainty pattern on the flowing cuff of her sleeve. Aideen had spent countless hours making this—the most beautiful wedding dress she had ever seen.

Cold air blew from behind her as Magistrate Marley entered and took his place beside her.

"You look lovely, my dear. Thank you for giving me this honor. With no children of my own, it is a blessing to walk you down the aisle."

Katie took his offered arm. "I'm glad we came to an understanding."

"My dear girl, there was no understanding. You railroaded your way into my heart with your stubbornness. That lecture you gave at the town council meeting rivaled a few political speeches I've heard." He patted the tips of her gloved fingers. "We'll start building your orphanage come spring after the ground thaws. Until then, I'm pleased Aideen has offered the boarding house as your temporary facility."

She reached up and kissed his cheek. "Thank you."

"No, young lady, thank you. You opened my eyes to a world I did not see." He cleared his throat. "Now, let's attend to matters of the heart. That man of yours up there looks like he might fall over at any moment."

Her man. Her heart. God had done everything in His time.

Healing of the Heart

Thomas's story is next!

BOOK 4

Available on Amazon

https://www.amazon.com/dp/B0CW34Q3VR

Afterword

Writing Historical fiction in a world where political correctness often means staying silent can be challenging. I work to remain faithful to the day's vernacular and word usage in all of my books, even if that means using a term not currently in vogue. Hearing the character's voice through shortened words, halted speaking, use of slang, or incorrect grammar breathes life into them.

Genesis 1:27 tells us "we are all created in the image of God," and Acts 17:26 tells us "God made from one man every nation of humankind to live on all the face of the earth."

Please, dear Reader, know that my heart is to edify Christ in all things.

Sincerely,
Heidi Gray McGill

Thank You

Thank you for reading *Matters of the Heart*. If you would like to read about Melvin's and Mary's journey in the Prequel, *Deep in My Heart*, it is available only to those who sign up for my newsletter at heidigraymcgill.com under the FREE BOOK tab.

Desire of My Heart, the first book of the Discerning God's Best series, is available on Amazon and in Kindle Unlimited.

I would be honored if you would follow me on Amazon, BookBub, Goodreads, Facebook and YouTube under Author Heidi Gray McGill and on Instagram under @AuthorHeidiGrayMcGill.

DO YOU LIKE AUDIOBOOKS? Consider purchasing my audiobooks straight from my store at Store.HeidiGrayMcGill.com.

However you choose to connect (hopefully all the ways), I thank you. I value your support and look forward to getting to know you as we journey together.

Heidi

Acknowledgement

Thank you, Reader, for choosing to read my book. Readers are instrumental in the writing process, and a precious friend ignited a spark for this book because of an email I received. Thank you, Regina Bassett, for reminding me of the importance of baptism—Acts 22:16.

Patrick Lee, thank you for providing insight into the life of Moses and his profession as a blacksmith. I saw heat, heavy tools, loud noises, and lots more heat, but you helped me recognize the craftsmanship and fun. Thank you for keeping the art of blacksmithing alive today. I have the Armadillo you made, and he winks at me whenever I look out my kitchen window.

Dave Thomas, I'm so thankful you invested in my girls as their teacher. Thank you also for your willingness to share a morsel of your vast knowledge of the Civil War with me. If there is any inaccuracy in my story, it is my doing, not yours. Thank you, Dave, for answering my out-of-the-blue phone call.

When I have a horse question, Nancy Manning is my go-to cowgirl. Nancy, you are a regular Dr. Doolittle when it comes to talking to and understanding what a horse is saying with sounds and body language. Both Rowdy and Dorcas have fun and whimsical personalities because of your stories and animal awareness. I look forward to our monthly Girls' Game Nights and the laughter we share with Michelle and Nancy F. Now, to finish that puzzle...

Dee Manning introduced me to Maria Soukka, Linguist, SIL Senegal-Guinea Bissau Branch, who provided colloquialisms for my Finnish phrases.

The "I am learning Irish" (Tá mé ag foghlaim na Gaeilge) Facebook group assisted me with Irish sayings. What a fantastic group of people with huge hearts for helping others and keeping the language alive. I had no idea there were so many dialects.

I reached out to Chaplain (LTC) David B. Crary, USA Retired, to ensure I was clearly sharing the Gospel of Jesus Christ. Thank you, Dave, for marrying my sister, Robin, and being a man after God's heart. I appreciate your guidance and the time you give to help me understand the bigger picture. Your story of Dad's response to your call to preach moved me profoundly. The character of Luke is a small representation of your account. Reader, this book's final wording and thoughts are all mine and do not necessarily reflect Dave's views.

For those who adored Reverend Jenkins and appreciated his wisdom, you have my home pastors, Reverends Jeff Bedwell and Shannon Ford, to thank. These men speak the Truth from the pulpit and practice what they preach, but neither is as long-winded as Reverend Jenkins! You do not labor in vain—1 Corinthians 15:58.

This book, nor anything I do author related, would happen without my amazing friend, Danica Lohmeyer. Danica, you so get my limited ability for technology. Thank you for walking me through the steps multiple times, creating cheat sheets, and answering my texts that start with "Are you available?" We both know that is never good. I can honestly say you've gone to the far ends of the earth and back for me…because I've lost multiple documents, and you've traveled to cyberspace and beyond to retrieve them. I cherish our Danica Days, car rides of non-stop talking, and even the rare moment of silence that is amazingly comfortable. Thank you for being my friend.

I may write the words, but my sister Davida Gray Sabine makes sure they are in the correct order and flow. Thank you, Sis, for doing the most difficult job of telling me something "needs a little work." I appreciate the way you challenge me to do my best. It is easy to love you even when you squash my grand ideas because I know you have my best interest at heart. I love you fully, deeply, and unconditionally.

Stephanie Brank Leupp, Sheri Sweatman, and Amy Bovaird, you three precious friends are a treasure. You beta read this book under an intense time crunch and did it joyfully. Reading the crazy comments you leave in the margins is always fun, and I especially enjoy the ones when you share why something is meaningful to you. Thank you, ladies. I love walking this journey of ministry with you.

A special thank you to Kathy McKinsey, my editor. Kathy, you must stop your world to focus on my books because your response time and attention to detail astonish me. Thank you for using your giftedness to help me.

Thank you, ARC team! This group of select individuals doesn't just read and review; they encourage me with emails and messages, comment and share on my posts, and promote my books with their friends and on their social media. I appreciate each one of my Insiders. You all are the best—always showing up with enthusiasm and support. Thank you.

Tina Grayson, Susan Bedwell, and Faye McCraven, you've not only prayed that God would be glorified through this book, but you have prayed for me—the person. You see the non-author "me" and know my struggles. Thank you for your support, consistency, and friendship over the years. I cherish our prayer group.

Writing is my ministry, and I thank the Lord daily for the love He lavishes on me. I never dreamed I would reach so many across multiple continents with my books...yet...God, in His perfect timing, has allowed it. Thank you, Lord.

> *"When our identity comes from anything or anyone*
> *other than God, we will fail. It's in the time between*
> *when we ask, and God answers that He brings to light*
> *what we value or what has become an idol."*
> *Delphina, <u>Matters of the Heart</u>*

More From This Author

Discerning God's Best series

Sometimes, it's the unexpected twists that make life an exciting adventure. At other times, fear, trouble, and deep heartache make it feel perilous. But at all times, accepting God's will, even if it means losing the one you love, makes it worthwhile.

Embark on a journey from South Carolina to Missouri with characters who quickly become family, adventures that become real, and hope that becomes a promise.

Prequel: Deep in My Heart – FREE *with newsletter signup. Search Heidi Gray McGill to locate her website.*
Book One: Desire of My Heart
Book Two: With All My Heart
Companion Christmas Novella: Stitched On My Heart
Book Three: Matters of the Heart
Book Four: Healing of the Heart
Book Five: Written on My Heart – *Preorder now*

You Are On The Air Series

Finding love, repairing relationships, and healing broken hearts happen when you are on the air with your favorite radio station. Unique, clean, A-to-Z romance stories from fifteen authors make this a can't-put-down RomCom series.

Dial E for Endearment
Dial P for Perfect

The Proxy Bride series

A Bride for Harley
Available in Audiobook format at Store.HeidiGrayMcGill.com
La Elegida para Harley - *Coming soon*

About The Author

Heidi Gray Mcgill

Heidi infuses God's love into her award-winning Christian fiction works.

Everything Heidi writes is purposeful. She believes in bringing a reader into the awareness of who God is to them and how He interacts with them on a personal level. She does this by crafting characters so relatable you feel part of who they are.

Heidi's masterfully written words reach deep into the reader's heart and offer healing through God's Word.

Heidi is an optimist who chooses to find the silver lining in life's clouds of doubt. She lives with her husband of thirty years near Charlotte, NC. When she isn't writing, you will find her outside playing with her two grandsons, walking, scrapbooking, reading, cooking, traveling, or finding an excuse to have an outing with a girlfriend.

Made in United States
Troutdale, OR
08/17/2024

22100146R00216